Roscoe Ann

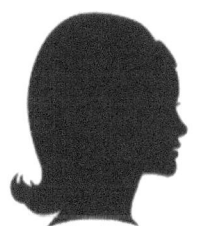

By

Irene Ebel Ertell

Irene Ebel Ertell

Ertell Publishing

Richland WA 99352

ISBN 978-0-9962157-0-1

To

My husband, Charles

Our children,

Robyn, Karen, Keith

Preface

Roscoe Ann began as short stories about a girl growing up during the Great Depression into World War II. There was no chronology. I wrote as different ideas occurred to me. After a while, Roscoe Ann began to tell her stories. Now that they are in a book, it's like saying goodbye to someone you don't expect to see again. I admit I have left the door ajar, in case she reappears with more to tell me.

The story of Roscoe Ann is not autobiographical, though I was born in Texas about a hundred miles from fictional Duddley. I grew up in Louisiana after my father's job transferred him in 1933. Every summer, before the war began, my parents and I visited relatives and friends who lived in the area of Texas I write about. As a young woman, I lived in Washington D.C. from January 1951 until November 1953 and again from summer 1960 until summer 1964.

A few names and characters are from my past. Miss Ethel McGhee models Miss Ethel Magee, my sixth grade teacher who read to us and managed to have a record player made so we could listen to classical music. Miss Magee was strict, but she cared about us and we learned. She worked her way through college, selling a one-volume encyclopedia door to door. My mother bought one.

Roscoe Ann and I took piano lessons rather than blow a horn in the band. We loved to read, but I didn't buckle down to writing until late in life. I wish I had been like her in that respect.

The Roscoe Ann stories were written for a group I belonged to while living on the North Oregon Coast. Six women with varied writing goals met every other Thursday at someone's home. Coffee and tea with a simple pastry was the rule. Fortunately for me, store-bought was welcome. We read our work aloud, giving and receiving comments and suggestions with equanimity. The group encouraged me to put my Roscoe Ann stories into a book.

Just as I decided to organize and revise the stories I'd written, I moved to Washington State. Fortunately, Vera Haddan, friend, editor and online publisher, guided me through putting the stories in the pages that follow. This has been an amazing and exhilarating experience. Vera's patience and sense of humor smoothed many potential potholes.

I want to thank each of the friends from my writing group for their sincere wish to see Roscoe Ann in print and for their help in making it possible: Gail Balden, Mary Barthelemy, Vera Haddan, Deena Lindstedt, Jean Peterson and Phyllis Sanderson.

A special thank-you goes to Deena Lindstedt's late husband, Don. Over dinner at their home, Don related his life as a young naval enlistee out of high school in 1944. His war experience in the Pacific gave me background for Buddy's story.

Sandra Fouchée and Michael Burgess taught the classes I attended at Clatsop Community College and Tillamook Bay Community College, Oregon. They critiqued my work with care and encouraged me to write.

Prologue

September 1939

She seemed to float about the classroom, reading to us after the day's lessons were finished. I always looked to be sure her shoes touched the floor. Tall and slender with a cap of unruly brown curls, her skin reminded me of the cameo pin my grandma wore to church every Sunday. Pale freckles dappled her longish nose. Her southern voice was the softest I'd ever heard, not twangy Texas like the rest of us. I felt happy and safe in Miss Ethel McGhee's sixth grade classroom.

Duddley's elementary school library was limited. Miss McGhee read from her own collection, and from books she checked out of the Duddley Public Library.

Mr. Manning, the janitor, made a cabinet with a hinged lid for a turntable and sound box Miss McGhee had taken from a large console. He sanded the rough wood and varnished it to a high gloss. *Aida* was the first opera she played, telling the story as we listened.

If, during a reading or music session, one of us caused a "small disruption," Miss McGhee pinned you to your seat with a piercing, questioning look. My cousin, Travis, tried to get away with all kinds of stuff.

"Is something wrong, Travis?" She always sounded concerned, as though she didn't know what he was up to.

"No, ma'am."

"Remember, this is a special time, a time that enriches and gives pleasure. You don't want to miss it or deprive your classmates. Don't you agree?"

"Yes, ma'am."

Without fail, my cousin, or anyone else who misbehaved, was assigned to write a one-page report, due the following morning on how that day's session enriched and gave pleasure.

Nearly every day, Miss McGhee exhorted us. "Read. Read. Read. Listen to the radio, so you'll know about our world." The war in Europe seemed far away until Miss McGhee suggested we listen to the radio news with our folks. We felt a little better when President Roosevelt told us he would never send our boys to war. *Little Orphan Annie, Tom Mix Ralston Straight Shooters* and *Jack Armstrong, the All-American Boy* were some of our favorite programs. We kept up with the popular songs of the day on Saturday night's Lucky Strike *Your Hit Parade.* Many times Miss McGhee told us about a movie she thought we should see. Mama always managed to let me go.

"There's a different world out there," Miss McGhee said, "and you need to know how others live." Different countries and different people found their way into our English, arithmetic, spelling, geography and civics lessons. Her personal subscription to the National Geographic enthralled us.

Whenever someone expressed a new idea or asked a searching question, she said, "Let's write that down," and printed the topic on the blackboard in large letters. "Let's really think about that."

Sometimes we discussed or debated into the next period. She assigned topics to be researched and reported on the next day, and the next, until she was satisfied we had "mastered the material." Miss McGhee rejoiced at every small intellectual step we took. Though she seemed to float about the room when reading to us or playing her records, she never let us forget we were there to learn what she taught.

One day after classes, I decided to show Miss McGhee some of my stories. I'd never shown them to anyone, not even Mama. She was writing, unaware that I stood in front of her desk. I cleared my throat.

"Oh, excuse me, Roscoe Ann. I didn't know you were here." She smiled. "Can I help you with something?"

I wondered if I really wanted to do this. I wasn't afraid, but wondered if it was worth bothering her? I took a deep breath.

"I like to write."

"Yes, I've noticed. You write very well."

I placed a mottled black and white composition book on her desk.

"Would you read one of my stories? Please?"

"Thank you," she said, reaching for the book.

"If it's not too much trouble." I took another deep breath.

"Oh no. Not at all. I'm glad you want me to read your work." *Work*! I couldn't believe my ears. She turned a few pages and began to read. After a few minutes, she looked up.

"May I take this home?"

"Yes, ma'am." I could hardly breathe.

"Shall I make corrections? Suggestions?"

Miss McGhee could have done anything to my *work*.

When she returned my book the next day, there were many red marks from which I began to learn.

"Don't ever give up writing your stories. You have a special gift, Roscoe Ann. You must learn to use it." She opened a drawer in her desk and handed me a ledger covered with embossed wallpaper. Big pink roses bloomed over a background of green stems and leaves. Miss McGhee had made an everyday business ledger beautiful. I clasped it to my chest and tried not to cry.

"Oh, Miss McGhee," I gasped. "I've never had anything so beautiful."

"This is your journal, Roscoe Ann. Write something every day, if you can. Write about the things you see, think and feel. Write your dreams. Write your stories." She smiled.

We talked about keeping a journal and she suggested that I include some stories about my family and me, like when I helped Mama with her laundry business and the day I started school.

"Roscoe Ann, you're a born storyteller. Put it on paper."

Chapter 1

Early Memories

When I asked about my daddy, Mama said, "He's with God's army of angels."

I wasn't sure who God was, but I'd seen angels in the windows of Grandma Dickey's church.

"When can we go see him?" I asked.

"Not for a long time, Annie." She hugged and kissed me, and then went outside to get the laundry. She didn't answer when I asked, "Why?" I figured she didn't hear me.

We have no pictures of Daddy. "Lost in the move," Mama said. I'd seen photographs of Uncle Riley when he served in the army during The Great War, and I formed a mental picture of my daddy in a khaki uniform, puttees and three rows of medals across the left side of his jacket. A halo hovered above his shallow, rounded helmet, and large white, feathery wings loomed over his wide shoulders. I imagined a young, handsome, determined face, eyes looking off to a distant forever.

One day Grandma Dickey said she thought it strange that Mama never talked about her husband. Tears filled Mama's eyes. Grandma put her arms around Mama and patted her, "Oh, my poor darlin' girl." I didn't ask about my daddy for a long time because I didn't want to make Mama cry.

The move Mama talked about was coming to live in Duddley, Texas soon after I was born. Our small house is about two miles out of town on the county road. It is part of Uncle Riley's farm. We can see his house, but it's too far to hear anything. Mesquite trees and prickly pears grow in the pasture between. Grandma, my aunts—Fritzie, Geraldine and Judy—and their families, live in Duddley. Grandma's house is big. It sits on a quarter of a block surrounded by trees and a beautiful garden. Grandpa Dickey died shortly after Mama and I moved to Duddley. He was a lawyer and a judge.

Mama says we are poor. I know we don't have as much as some people, but I don't feel poor. We have everything we need. Our furniture is what different ones in the family weren't using. Mama bought a treadle sewing machine from Mrs. Stacey who bought a new electric Singer. Mama makes our dresses from flour sacks that come in florals, stripes and solids. Sometimes it takes a while to get enough of the same pattern, but we trade with my aunts and Grandma.

I love our little house that sits in the middle of a big yard. There's a front room where Mama has her sewing machine. A big horsehair sofa and matching chair make it kind of crowded. Mama's bedroom, big enough for a bed and dresser, is off the front room. Our kitchen and my small bedroom make up the back of the house.

A white picket fence surrounds the yard. Mama painted the house white, inside and outside. "You can tell when it's dirty," she says. Uncle Riley buys the paint. Mama taught me how to paint as soon as I got big enough. It's one of our favorite things to do.

There is an open porch across the front of the house. Another porch, across the back, is screened to keep out bugs and mosquitoes because we spend a lot of time there. The house sits on cement blocks about twenty inches off the ground. Mama planted privet around three sides so you can't see underneath. She left it open across most of the back. We store potatoes and onions on a suspended shelf that Uncle Riley built under the back porch. He surrounded the shelf with open lath and a two way sliding door across the front to keep out critters. It's my job to go under the porch when Mama needs onions and potatoes. I'm careful of spiders, especially black widows.

Three tall, spreading live oak trees shade the house and keep us cool in the hottest part of summer. The one off the back porch is my favorite with its crotched limb, perfect for reading.

Mama didn't put in flower beds. "There's enough weeding to do in the vegetable garden." She's right about that because it takes both of us to keep it weeded and watered. The garden feeds us year round because Mama cans and preserves enough to carry us through the winter. During the growing season she trades our surplus for staples at Mr. McGinty's grocery store.

Between the garden and the house are six clotheslines strung between two T-shaped poles. Uncle Riley made them from pipe he found. Sometimes I think he "finds" stuff by paying for it because he doesn't want Mama to feel beholden. Mama painted the poles green to blend in with the green outhouse and privacy fence that sits in the far corner of the yard.

Uncle Riley keeps us in eggs, milk and cream, some of which Mama churns into butter. Whenever Mama wants to cook a chicken, Uncle Riley brings us one—plucked and ready. He butchers a couple of hogs in the winter, and we enjoy ham, bacon and sausage. Sometimes he brings a steak and Mama fixes it for the three of us.

My uncle has never married and lives alone. Mama washes and irons his clothes as well as his house linens. She bakes bread for him every week and shares our butter. Grandma keeps him supplied with cakes, pies and cookies. He always has someone's jelly. Four times a year, Mama, Grandma and I go over and clean his house top to bottom. Sometimes the aunts help and it turns into a party.

—

Mama makes our money by washing and ironing house linens for some of the rich people in Duddley. There are double wash tubs on the back porch, a wash board for each and an old manual washing machine which Mama uses to rinse and wring. Everything dries on the clotheslines. "Nothing smells as clean as sheets and towels dried in fresh air and sunshine." When I was little, I handed her the clothespins as the wash went up and made sure nothing touched the ground when she took it down. Now that I'm tall enough, she lets me do some of the hanging and bringing in.

Mama's customers leave their dirty laundry and pick it up clean, ironed and folded. By the time I was five, I could count money. When Mama was busy, my job was to sit on the front porch with the baskets of clean linen and collect the money. Mama made sure I had a good supply of one dollar bills and coins. The ladies would keep their five dollar bills if we couldn't make change, promising to pay next time. Problem was, we needed the money and they usually didn't remember. It embarrassed Mama to remind them.

One day, Mrs. Hooper looked in her purse and realized she'd left her money at home. I was quick to say, "That's all right, Mrs. Hooper. I'll sit right here and watch your basket 'til you get back." When she reached for the basket, I tightened my grip on the handle and smiled from ear to ear. I heard her muttering as she strode down the walk to her shiny black Packard. Before long, she returned with the correct amount. In fact, she never forgot her money again.

Chapter 2

Mama and Me

I realized at an early age that some people in Duddley thought unkindly of my mother. One day, I overheard Mrs. Hooper talking to Mrs. Gorsham as they waited for Mama to bring their clean laundry to the front porch. I was just inside the open door behind the screen.

"She says her husband was killed serving his country." Mrs. Hooper spoke in a loud whisper. "Maybe so. Maybe no. Humph."

"And that name she gave the child. Roscoe Ann," spat Mrs. Gorsham.

"I wouldn't call my dog that."

It made me mad and I wanted to smack those old biddies right across their gossipy old mouths. I never told Mama because I knew it would hurt her feelings. Besides I wasn't supposed to eavesdrop, but sometimes I couldn't help it.

—

One Sunday, after we came home from taking Grandma to church, we decided to take a picnic lunch to our favorite spot on the Grandland River that winds through Uncle Riley's back acreage. It's more like a big creek except when it rains too much north of us, then it's all over the place. Flash floods are scary. There are stories of houses washed away and babies pulled from their mothers' arms. It has never come up to our houses because we sit high, but we keep an eye on it.

That day, it was running shallow, and we caught a couple of trout for supper. Mama filleted them on a big rock, wrapped them in a damp dish towel and put them in the basket she'd brought our lunch in. We never fish more than we're going to eat.

Afterward, we waded in the clear water. The river bubbled, frothed and splashed around small sand bars and rocks. We found some colorful pebbles but decided to leave them. They are never as pretty when they dry off. We lay down on a grassy spot shaded by a willow. Mama reached for my hand and started humming "Annie Laurie." I love that song, even though my name isn't Laurie. I began singing the words and she sang the alto in her low, silky voice. She taught me lots of songs. We sang to our heart's content that afternoon.

At suppertime, Mama dipped our catch in beaten egg, then cornmeal and fried the fish in hot bacon grease. It was crisp and dry on the outside, moist and flaky on the inside. Home canned green beans and tomatoes completed our supper. Mama let me help in the kitchen as soon as I was big enough, but she made sure I understood about hot handles and heavy pots. We cooked on a wood stove.

Later, we sat in our rocking chairs on the back porch, watching the sun go down behind faraway hills. Deep pink swirls and slender fingers of scarlet splashed among gray shadows and blue patches left over from the afternoon. I never get tired of sunsets.

—

I can't remember when Mama and I started going to the Duddley Public Library. I loved Saturday morning story time. Mama let me take home as many books as Mrs. Wilson would allow. Mama made me a special bag from a piece of canvas. She appliquéd BOOKS on both sides from bright flour sack scraps. Mrs. Wilson always let me fill it up.

One day, I was on the back porch with a book trying to remember the words beneath the pictures. Mama came from the kitchen.

"What did you say, Annie?" She looked surprised and I wondered if something was wrong. I looked down at the page.

"Where have you been?" I read the words.

"May I look at your book?" She turned a page and handed it back.

"What does that say?" Mama smiled and pointed to the words.

"You have been a …" I couldn't read the next word.

"Naughty," Mama read.

"Boy," I finished the sentence.

After that, Mama helped me read. Sometimes, I'd ask her to read because I loved her voice. We didn't tell anyone. Mama said, "People in Duddley think we're strange enough already." She chuckled and smiled. Of course our secret was out soon after I started school.

Chapter 3

A Girl Named Roscoe Ann

"Roscoe Turner." Miss Cora Thomson, the new first grade teacher, called the roll. It was my first day of school.

"Present," I answered.

"Oh?" She looked up. "I thought you were a boy."

"No, ma'am. My middle name is Ann. A-n-n. Mama calls me Annie."

"I see," she said, writing in her pad. "Roscoe Ann Turner."

My smart aleck cousin, Travis, has a big mouth and at recess he started in.

"She's got a boy's name," he snickered to a couple of his friends.

It was bad enough being teased about having a boy's name, but when some older kids realized my initials spelled rat, they thought it was hilarious. I ignored it as best I could because I didn't want to hurt Mama's feelings or embarrass her by getting into a fight over the name she'd given me.

"Act like a lady," she always told me when I left the house without her. Most of the time I didn't have any trouble, but that first day at school was hard, especially Travis and his gang. Walking home, I waited until we were by ourselves.

"Travis Hawkins, if you call me rat one more time, I'm gonna give you what for."

"Aw Rat, you cain't give nobody nothin'." He was taller, but he had a fat belly and walked pigeon-toed. He was about to say something when I punched him in that fat belly and ran like the dickens. He fell and couldn't get up, like a turtle upside down, covered in dirt. His mama would have washed his mouth out with soap if she'd heard the words he yelled at me. I knew he wouldn't tell anyone. It wasn't the first time I'd gotten him good.

That evening I asked Mama why she'd named me Roscoe. I didn't tell her about the kids or Travis.

"You know it's your daddy's name," she said. "It's a good name." She drew me to her for a hug. "Besides I wanted you to have a strong name. Strong people have strong names."

I understood, but right then I wished she'd given me a regular girl's name, like Mary, Helen or Betty. I wondered why she called me Annie, but it's not unusual for children to be named one thing and called something else. I got used to being called Roscoe Ann at school, but the name Rat really got to me. One day on the way home, Emile Corse followed me.

"Rat, Rat, Rat-a-tat-tat." He chanted.

I turned and surprised him. Using my book bag, I shoved him in the belly as hard as I could. He wasn't fat and clumsy like Travis, so even though I'm fast, he caught up with me. I held my book bag over my stomach, hunched my shoulders and got ready. Nothing happened. Instead I heard screams and screeching. When I turned around, Buddy Longmire was astraddle Emile knocking the tar out of him. I kind of felt sorry for Emile when his nose began to bleed.

"Run, Roscoe Ann," Buddy said, grinning. He was about the same height as Emile, skinnier, but stronger. His mop of black hair flew to and fro. I heard him call Emile a bad name as I ran toward home.

The next day, Emile apologized in front of all the kids while Buddy stood next to him. No one ever called me Rat again.

Buddy became my best friend, though he was in third grade, and I asked him to call me Annie.

—

First grade wasn't as great as I'd expected, but I didn't tell Mama. She would have told me to make a better effort. One day Miss Thomson asked me to stay after class.

"Roscoe Ann, I've noticed that you don't pay attention, yet you do good work. Can you read and write? Do you know how to add and subtract?"

I hung my head, remembering Mama had said not to tell anyone.

"Is first grade boring?"

"Yes, ma'am." I had to tell the truth.

She smiled and took my hand.

"I'm going to talk with your mother and Mr. Fields, our principal. Maybe I can help you enjoy school. How would that be?"

In second grade, I learned something new every day and loved doing homework. The kids didn't tease me about my name. Miss Root called me Annie.

Chapter 4

Rodrigo

"Thanks, Laney. That was delicious, as always."

"You're a good listener big brother. It helps to have someone to talk to. She's never asked about it."

"I don't know what I can do, but I'll think on it." I loved Uncle Riley's soft chuckle.

I was up in the oak tree outside the back porch reading and couldn't help hearing. It sounded like they were talking about me, but I decided it was probably Grandma Dickey. Mama makes sure Grandma takes her pills, and sometimes she balks.

A few days later, Mama gave me two loaves of warm baked bread and a dish of butter fresh out of the churn. "Take these over to Riley. If he needs any help, it's okay to stay. I won't need you for the laundry."

She gave me a kiss on the top of my head and held the screen door open. I often took things over to my uncle and stayed to help. I knew how to milk a cow, feed the chickens and collect eggs. Slopping the hogs wasn't my favorite chore. Uncle Riley taught me to drive the team while he piled corn or sorghum into the wagon. I loved that.

When I walked into the yard, Uncle Riley was coming out of his house.

"I'm getting ready to go out and check on the cows," he said. "They're grazing down in the pasture by the river. Want to go for a ride?" He knew the answer and soon we were on our way. When I was little, I rode in the saddle with him, but as soon as Mama said yes, he taught me to ride. Loony was my horse. Uncle Riley bought her at a farm auction. When he got her home, he said she acted like a loon. It turned out she had some kind of stomach problem. When Doc Ford straightened it out, she was a great animal. She was gentle and let me ride the first time without any trouble. I loved Loony.

When we got to the lower pasture, some of the cows were grazing, some were lying in the shade and a few had gone down to the river. This July day was hot and cloudless.

Suddenly there was a commotion down at the river. Uncle Riley's prize bull, Rodrigo, was having his way with one of the cows. I'd never seen that before. It didn't take long, but I had the impression that Rodrigo liked it a lot better than the cow. Uncle Riley was checking on another cow and didn't seem to notice.

We rode back to the barn in silence. I took care of Loony the way Uncle Riley taught me and afterward we drank ice tea on his back porch. I talked about how hot it was, how Mama's tomatoes were coming on, how fussy Grandma Dickey was some days.

"Yep, your grandma can be a pill sometimes, but your mama's a good one to keep her on track."

I didn't tell Mama about Rodrigo because I didn't want to embarrass her.

Thanksgiving and Christmas came and went. It got some cooler and rained a lot in January, but we never saw snow. Mama had

Grandma on a schedule. Uncle Riley ate supper with us most evenings.

One Friday evening in April, my uncle put on his Stetson, ready to go home. "Annie," he said, "how about coming over tomorrow after breakfast? I can use your help most of the day."

The next morning, I was sitting down to eggs and Mama's biscuits, when I heard the triangle clanging at Uncle Riley's. We didn't have a telephone, so this was our signal to come over—not an emergency, just don't fool around. Mama had left for Grandma's a little after six. I gulped my coffee-milk between bites of scrambled eggs and put the biscuits in my jacket pocket. I ran through the field between our houses. Doc Ford's truck was parked at the barn, and all kinds of squalling and moaning was coming from inside.

"You almost missed it," Uncle Riley said. His overalls were bloody and his hair hung down his forehead in wet strings. Doc Ford had his arm inside the cow, Mary Lou, up to his elbow. She was hollering and her eyes rolled around like pinballs in a machine.

"I almost got it turned around," said the vet. Mary Lou hollered louder, and here was this red, slimy creature lying in the straw. Mary Lou breathed deeply a few times and began to look for her baby.

"Well," said Uncle Riley. "What do you think of that?" He looked at me expectantly.

"I think I'm going to throw up." I ran outside and did.

Later, I sat on Uncle Riley's back porch drinking a glass of milk and eating the biscuits from my pocket. My uncle and Doc were having coffee and smoking their hand-rolled Bull Durham cigarettes. I didn't listen to their conversation. I thought about Mary Lou and her beautiful calf. Why did something so wondrous have to hurt so bad?

After Doc Ford left, Uncle Riley and I went back to the barn to check on the mother and baby.

"He's perfect." Uncle Riley beamed.

"Like Rodrigo?" I asked.

"Yep." He looked surprised, and then continued. "You remember last summer when we went down to the lower pasture to check on the cows? That was the day Rodrigo planted this little guy in Mary Lou. He's been growing all this time. It's the miracle of life, Annie." My uncle looked pleased with himself.

Chapter 5

Tarnished Halo

"Oh sinners, come to Jesus. Be washed in the blood of the Lamb. He will take away your sins and make you white as snow." Reverend Ralph Stimp stood in front of the pulpit, his arms upstretched toward the tent top. Mrs. Baker quietly played "Bringing in the Sheaves" on a small pump organ. Throughout the congregation, hands were raised and eyes were closed. I heard murmurs of "Oh, precious Lord. Come sweet Jesus."

Even though there was a good turnout, no one moved up the aisle toward the preacher. It was the last night of the revival and I figured all who wanted to reserve their place in heaven had gone up during the previous four nights. June tent revivals in Texas could put the fear of hell into anybody. Perspiration ran from my hair into my ears and my dress stuck to my back. I hated breathing among all those sweaty bodies, most of which probably hadn't been washed since the Saturday before, if then.

I jumped when the preacher bellowed.

"Brothers and sisters, we've been blessed by Jesus during this revival, He has saved lost souls and reclaimed the fallen away. I want everyone who now rests in the Lord to shout, 'Hallelujah.'" Mrs. Baker played louder. Everyone shouted and the benches emptied as the saved headed outside. I don't think the preacher expected an exodus, but I saw him grin and wipe his face with a big white handkerchief.

Mama and I helped Grandma Dickey to her feet. She got stiff when she sat for a long time on a hard bench.

"I think we should go up and shake the preacher's hand," Grandma said.

Mama made out like she didn't hear, and we took Grandma out through the nearest flap.

"Lord a mercy," Grandma said. "That young preacher is truly one of God's own. Look at all the souls he saved this week." Mama didn't say anything. She wasn't much on church, but we brought Grandma to the revival meetings because everyone else in the family said they had something else to do. We'd been coming to these revivals since I could remember. When I was little, I told Mama I didn't want to be washed in blood. The idea gave me the creeps. I didn't want to be white as snow either.

"You don't need washing." Mama laughed. "Your color is fine."

That was good enough for me.

On Sunday, Grandma, Mama and I sat in the second row at church. Grandma liked to sit where she could see and hear everything better. The preacher looked a little tired. Dark curls fell over his forehead as his clear brown eyes swept over the full pews. He was tall and handsome, with a wide smile and the biggest white teeth I'd ever seen. Waving an open Bible, he shouted for us to confess, repent and sin no more.

After the service, Brother Ralph—that's what he'd asked to be called—stood at the door so everyone could shake his hand and tell him he'd preached a good sermon. I noticed his eyes light up when he saw Mama. He shook Grandma's hand quickly, reached past her, and grabbed Mama's hand. We had to stop because he wouldn't let go. Mama and I usually slip behind Grandma because it isn't Mama's nature to speak to the preacher.

"Mrs. Turner, I believe." He bent toward Mama and his eyes glittered with wanting. I'd read that in a book recently and now I knew what it meant. I didn't like his looking at Mama that way. She pulled her hand free, glaring at him.

"Will you be at tonight's service?" He kept that big smile aimed at Mama.

"No," Mama snapped and grabbed Grandma's arm. I took the other and we were down the steps lickety-split.

"Good grief, Lanelle," Grandma huffed. Mama didn't answer but she slowed down after we got to the street. I was glad it was only three blocks to Grandma's house.

We had Sunday dinner at Grandma's. My aunts and their families plus Uncle Riley made fifteen around the table. Everyone brought something or fixed it in Grandma's kitchen. It was delicious.

"Brother Ralph is going to be the new preacher," Aunt Fritzie announced. "The deacons liked his revival so much that they asked him to take the pulpit."

"Doesn't he have a church now?" Aunt Geraldine asked.

"No, he's been doing revivals for the last year."

"Sure will be nice to have a regular preacher," said Aunt Judy. "Those boys from the school in Houston try, but they don't have the experience."

"And there's a different one every Sunday," said Grandma.

Mama got up and started taking dishes to the kitchen before we'd finished eating.

"What's the matter with Laney?" Aunt Geraldine asked. "She hasn't said two words and looks like a storm coming on."

"Oh, the preacher kind of made over her after church," said Grandma. "You know how she is about church anyway."

"Yes, and I wish I knew why," said Aunt Judy.

"It's none of your business," said Uncle Riley, getting up and going into the kitchen.

Not long after Brother Ralph settled into the manse, Mrs. Hooper paid Mama a visit. I hadn't planned to eavesdrop, but I was under the front porch cooling off when I heard them talking.

"Really, Lanelle. I can't imagine you not making time for Brother Ralph. He asked if you would like to help him. Being single and all, he needs all the help he can get." Mrs. Hooper chuckled. "You know how men are in the house."

"I have as much laundry as I can handle." I knew Mama's back had stiffened.

"You could use the new wringer washing machine we bought for the manse," Mrs. Hooper continued. "It's electric. Brother Ralph said you could do your customer's laundry there too." I figured Mama's hands were clenched by now.

"Thank you, but no." Mama was gritting her teeth.

"I'd think it over if I were you, Lanelle Dickey." I didn't realize until sometime later that calling Mama by her maiden name was the way some Duddley women told her they didn't believe she'd ever been married.

Heavy footsteps crossed the porch and I heard muttering as Mrs. Hooper strode toward her shiny black Packard. The front door slammed before Mrs. Hooper got her car started.

After Brother Ralph became the pastor, Mama and I didn't have to take Grandma to church because my aunts never missed a Sunday. Mama and I worked in the garden and went fishing on Sundays. Brother Ralph slipped from our world.

When school started in September, I came home the first day and was surprised that Mama wasn't in the kitchen ironing or putting up vegetables from the garden.

"Mama," I called.

"In ... here," she answered from her bedroom. I knew something was wrong when I saw her lying on top of the rumpled bedspread. She lay on her side, knees pulled up to her stomach, her brown hair mussed and covering most of her face.

"Oh, Mama." I tried to be calm, though my heart was beating a mile a minute. "What's the matter?" Are you sick?"

"No, honey. I'll be fine. Please get me a wet wash cloth and a glass of water."

When I returned, she was sitting on the edge of the bed. Blood covered her lower lip and her right cheek was turning purple. I cleaned her lip and held the cool cloth to her cheek.

"Thank you darlin'. You have a gentle touch." Mama flinched when she tried to smile.

"What happened, Mama?"

Her cotton print dress was torn at the neck and the skirt was ripped from the bodice in several places. I sat beside her and put my arms around her. We both began to cry. In a little while, she spoke.

"Brother Ralph. 'A pastoral visit,' he said, so I let him in and we went to the kitchen. I poured some ice tea and ... oh, honey." Deep sobs shook Mama's body. We hugged as tears rolled down our cheeks.

Before we went to bed that night, Mama said, "Annie, I'm going to be all right, so don't tell anyone, not anyone, about this. Not

Grandma, Uncle Riley or your aunts. It has to be our secret." I thought we should tell Uncle Riley, but she said that would only make things worse. I didn't sleep good that night, but at least Mama had told me what happened and trusted me not to tell.

One day we were helping Grandma and she started needling Mama about us not going to church anymore.

"You should be thinking about Annie's salvation."

Mama continued straightening the sheets on Grandma's bed without answering.

"Brother Ralph's a fine looking man. I remember how he made sure to talk to you that day after church." Grandma paused and Mama kept on making the bed. "He doesn't seem interested in anyone in particular. He always asks about you and Annie. I think he's the best preacher we've ever had."

"He's a son of a bitch," Mama said.

Chapter 6

Brother Ralph

Mama and I were weeding the vegetable garden. Sweat crawled over my skin and a tingling itch crept up my nose, but I had something else on my mind.

"Mama?"

"Yes?"

"I'd like to go to the Sunshine Club at church."

Mama sat back on her heels and frowned.

Brother Ralph had done something bad to her. Since then, Mama wasn't herself. Noises bothered her at night, and one day I saw her crying when she was taking sheets from the clothesline. I tried to be good and prayed every night that God would send Brother Ralph far, far away.

Mama continued frowning and I knew she was wondering why I wanted to go to anything at the preacher's church. If I'd told her my real reason, she'd have forbidden it.

"What brought this on?" Her voice rose a bit.

"Doris Watson asked me to go with her. It's for fifth and sixth graders. She says it's not like Sunday school or church. It sounds like fun."

When Doris first asked me to go, I had refused, but changed my mind when I heard her and Iris Skinner talking about Brother Ralph teaching them a Bible verse. I can't explain what came over me, but I felt compelled to look that snake in the grass right in the eye. I was sure God would give me a plan to get rid of him.

Mama was trying to guess what was going on in my head.

"Please, Mama?"

"When do they meet?"

"Every Wednesday at three o'clock in the church basement."

"Who's the teacher?"

"Mrs. Terry."

She sighed and searched my face. She didn't like the idea, however, Mama did Mrs. Terry's linens and I knew they were friendly.

"All right, but you stay with Doris while you're in that building. The entire time, you hear me? And come straight home afterward." She shook her head and bent down to pull more weeds. I pulled weeds like it was the most important thing in the world.

The next Wednesday, I went to Sunshine Club. We played a word game and looked up the answers in the Bible. During music time, Mrs. Terry played hymns by Bach and told us how he made his living playing the organ in churches. I was having such a good time, I forgot about Brother Ralph until he came to teach the Bible verse.

"Hi, boys and girls," he boomed, quickly printing the verse in large letters on the blackboard. He smiled and looked at our upturned faces. "Let's say it together: 'Be ye kind, one to another.'"

He didn't see me at first. Sometimes you don't see what you don't expect. When he recognized me, his eyes widened and his smooth cheeks reddened. I stared up at him trying to look inscrutable, a word I learned recently. When I put my hand up and asked him how to be kind to bad people, he turned to Mrs. Terry, whispered something and bounded up the stairs. I thought Mrs. Terry was a little put out with him, but she tried not to show it.

The next week, Brother Ralph was looking for me. There I was, inscrutable as ever. He wrote a line from The Lord's Prayer. "Forgive us our trespasses as we forgive those who trespass against us." As we recited together, he avoided looking at me and wiped perspiration from his forehead with a big white handkerchief. I didn't ask any questions, but he left in a hurry. I was pleased that my being there seemed to bother him, but I wondered why he didn't leave Duddley. I knew better than to tell Mama about it, so I spent a lot of time talking to God.

The next Wednesday, Doris and I walked to Sunshine Club together.

"Doris," I said, "have you noticed something different about Brother Ralph?"

"What do you mean?"

"I don't see it all the time, but every once in a while, especially when he's giving us the Bible verse, I think I see a faint glow above his head."

Doris is as levelheaded as they come, but she went for it hook, line and sinker.

"Oh, Roscoe Ann, I wouldn't be surprised. My mama says Brother Ralph's a saint. He really knows his Bible and he's so kind and thoughtful."

"Well, today," I said, "be sure and watch, especially when he looks at us and explains the verse. I can't be sure, but I know you have a good eye."

"I'll watch every move he makes. Thanks for telling me."

Brother Ralph picked up on Doris right away. She didn't realize she looked inscrutable. In the middle of reciting the verse, he began coughing and choking, finally running up the stairs like something was after him. Mrs. Terry said we should pray for Brother Ralph.

"I didn't see anything," Doris said as we walked away from the church, "but I think that's because he got that coughing fit."

"Didn't see what?" Iris Skinner came up behind us.

I looked at Doris, raised my eyebrows and shrugged my shoulders. Doris jumped right in.

"Roscoe Ann sees a glow over Brother Ralph's head."

"You mean a halo?" Iris caught her breath.

I couldn't believe it was so easy.

"It's not all the time. Just when he's giving us the Bible verse," Doris said, like she'd seen it too.

"Do you think we should tell some of the other kids?" Iris asked.

Oh, happy day, I thought. As we walked, Doris and Iris planned who to tell and decided they definitely would not mention it to parents.

"They'll laugh at us." Iris said.

"Or say we're blaspheming," said Doris. I hoped this wasn't getting out of hand but didn't say anything.

The next Wednesday when Brother Ralph stood before us, I looked around and was amazed at the faces peering up at him. No one realized they looked inscrutable. Brother Ralph looked miserable. He stumbled through the verse and skipped telling us to memorize it. Without a word to Mrs. Terry, he rushed up the stairs, wiping perspiration from his face. Mrs. Terry shook her head.

Doris and Iris were disappointed. The other kids thought we were nuts.

Two days later, I stopped to see Grandma Dickey on my way home from the library.

Instead of asking me what I'd been up to, she said, "Have you heard about Brother Ralph?"

"No, ma'am." My heart skipped a beat.

"He's leaving," Grandma said. "Seems his health is failing." She shook her head. "Such a shame."

"That's too bad." I crossed my fingers behind my back. "What's the matter with him?"

"Seems Brother Ralph just gave out," Grandma said. "He couldn't sleep or eat and was jumpy as a cat on a hot tin roof. Mrs. Hinson told me this morning. Her husband's a deacon, you know? I thought Brother Ralph wasn't preaching as good these last few Sundays, but figured it was just a slump. Everybody gets those."

"What do you suppose caused it?" I hoped he hadn't mentioned us kids.

"Oh ... uh." Grandma's cheeks turned pink. "Bad nerves."

"What are they going to do for a preacher?" I had trouble not jumping for joy.

"Mrs. Hinson says the deacons will be looking for a new preacher right away. A married man with a family this time."

"Why's that?"

"Oh ... uh." Grandma turned pink again. "Better nerves."

Mama was ironing when I got home. I sat at the table with my usual glass of milk and cookies.

"How was school?"

"Good." I wondered how to break the news. "I stopped to see Grandma."

"What's the latest in Duddley?"

"Brother Ralph's leaving town," I said matter-of-factly.

Mama didn't say anything for a moment and I felt one of those "What aren't you telling me?" looks. Finally she spoke.

"Did Grandma say why he decided to leave?"

"Mrs. Hinson told her it was failing health due to bad nerves."

Chapter 7

Mrs. Hooper, February 27, 1941–April 12, 1941

February 27, 1941

"Laney?" Uncle Riley called from the back yard. We'd finished breakfast and I was in my room getting ready for school. It had to be important because my uncle rarely came over this early.

"Something wrong?" Mama opened the screen door.

"Annie can't go to school this morning." My uncle sounded out of breath.

"Why not?"

"Jack Roberts just came by and told me there's been a murder in town. Everybody and everything's in an uproar."

"A murder? What happened?"

"It's Mrs. Hooper. Her husband found her in their back yard this morning. Somebody stabbed her to death."

"Who'd do something like that?" Mama asked.

"They don't know. Jack says it could be a homicidal maniac on the loose." He paused. "I kinda doubt that, but everybody's got their doors locked. Chief Miller called the county sheriff for help."

"What about Mama?" My Grandma Dickey lives alone in Duddley.

"I'm on my way to check on her. I'll bring her to my place until things settle down and look in on the sisters to be sure they're all okay." I heard the screen door slap shut.

"Riley, bring Mama here. You got enough to do. And be careful."

I finished dressing and went to the kitchen.

"I guess you heard your uncle. If everybody's as upset as it sounds, there won't be any school today. We'll just wait until we hear more." She hugged me.

"Mama, I feel terrible about Mrs. Hooper."

"I know, honey. I didn't always feel kindly toward her, but no one deserves to die like that." Mama washed and ironed Mrs. Hooper's house linens every week.

Duddley has a small but self-important high society over which Mrs. Hooper once reigned. It all changed about a year ago when she drove her Packard into Mr. Booth's gasoline pump. I was coming from the library and saw it happen. She wasn't going very fast, but the pump got pushed over and there was a crease in the car's bumper and radiator. Some men were standing around, more interested in watching Mr. Booth yell and curse, so I went over to see if Mrs. Hooper was hurt.

"Get away from there, Roscoe Ann," someone yelled. I ignored them. Mrs. Hooper was slumped over the steering wheel and I thought she might be unconscious.

"Mrs. Hooper?" She raised up, but didn't seem to recognize me. "Are you all right?" She hiccupped right in my face and I smelled something strong. Later, when I told Buddy about it, I said it reminded me of Uncle Jasper when he'd had too much moonshine. He smiled.

"Annie, it probably wasn't moonshine, but she must've had something."

"She didn't seem to be hurt at all."

"Whiskey relaxes people and can keep them from getting too banged up." Unfortunately, Buddy knew about people who drank. His daddy spent a lot of time in the Happy Days saloon.

"Mama made me take Mrs. Hooper's laundry to her house because we figured she wouldn't be over to pick it up any time soon. I didn't tell Mama about smelling moonshine because she'd have said I was imagining things."

"What did you see?" Buddy asked.

"When she opened the door, I could tell she wasn't her usual highfalutin' self. Her face was swollen and bruised. When she went to get the money, she limped like a real old lady. I felt sorry for her."

"Her old man probably beat her up for smashing his car and embarrassing him. After all, he's the town banker and a pillar of the church." I didn't know Mr. Hooper personally, but I couldn't believe someone rich and important would stoop so low.

Uncle Riley came back a little before noon, but Grandma wasn't with him. She refused to leave her house. The aunts were going to take turns looking in on her and spending the night. He stayed for lunch and told us what little he knew.

"They're still looking for the knife. Chief Miller says they think a carving knife was used. They went through Hooper's house and all over the outdoors, but didn't find a thing. Lucy Mae, their maid, always sleeps in a room next to Mrs. Hooper's with the door open, but she didn't hear Mrs. Hooper get up."

"Where was Mr. Hooper?" Mama asked.

"He sleeps down the hall. Didn't see or hear anything. Mrs. Hooper's doctor gave her something to make her sleep, but Lucy Mae forgot to make sure she took it. The back door was unlocked. They found Mrs. Hooper in the side garden, in the gazebo. Doc Bailey says he thinks it happened several hours before Mr. Hooper found her. She probably bled to death."

March 1, 1941

I kept thinking about Mrs. Hooper. After the accident, she was never seen driving. We'd catch glimpses of her when Mr. Hooper drove her somewhere. They went to church, but never stayed to visit. According to him, his wife wasn't up to being in groups of people. Her doctor insisted on quiet and rest.

I heard my aunts talking one day. "Corinne says he takes her to a doctor over in Mechlenberg for her nerves. There's a small hospital

34

for people who've had nervous breakdowns or are just plain off their nut," Aunt Fritzie said.

"Flora Jean told me she heard they gave Mrs. Hooper some kind of shock treatments," Aunt Judy said.

"What's that for?" Aunt Geraldine asked.

"Flora Jean says it's supposed to shock people back to their senses."

"That husband of hers is enough to shock anybody out of their senses." Aunt Fritzie snorts when she laughs. I wondered if she was referring to Mr. Hooper's appearance. He was medium height, with narrow shoulders and a round stomach. Even in his suit and tie, he reminded me of a pear. I'd recently seen a picture of a ferret's face and immediately thought of Mr. Hooper. He never smiled, and when he spoke to Mama, he lifted his chin and peered through his pince-nez glasses.

"Well, he's sure kept her under wraps since the accident. That poor woman." Aunt Judy has a kind heart.

"Wonder if he's keeping her off the bottle." Aunt Fritzie snorted.

After the accident, Mr. Hooper brought the laundry on Monday mornings. He paid Mama extra to have me deliver the bundles to his house. Lucy Mae always opened the door and took the basket. One day I asked how Mrs. Hooper was feeling.

"She doin' just fine, missy." She smiled.

"Tell Mrs. Hooper, Roscoe Ann says, 'Hi.'" Lucy Mae nodded, closed the door and that's the way it was until someone killed Mrs. Hooper.

March 3, 1941

Today Uncle Riley stopped on his way home from town.

"Well, it looks like they've got Mrs. Hooper's murderer."

"I'm glad to hear that," Mama said. I was too—at first.

"They arrested Jim Longmire. Put him in the county jail over in Clavin."

"Where's Buddy?" I asked, feeling sick to my stomach.

"They're looking for him. Seems he ran away when the sheriff came out to their place." Uncle Riley saw my face. He knew Buddy and I were good friends. "They'll find him. He'll be okay." I grabbed Mama and tried not to cry.

"Why did they arrest Mr. Longmire?" Mama asked.

"He's done yard work for Mrs. Hooper for years. Seems that Lucy Mae saw him come into the yard the day before Mrs. Hooper was killed. Said it looked like he'd been drinking. He was weaving and almost fell a couple of times. Mrs. Hooper was in the gazebo. They spoke a few minutes and Mrs. Hooper said something in a loud voice. Lucy Mae couldn't hear, but she thought Mrs. Hooper was angry. Says Mrs. Hooper stretched out her arm and pointed her finger as if telling him to go, which he did. Weaving and wobbling."

"That doesn't sound like enough to put him in jail." Mama was upset.

"I don't understand how all that works, but they arrested him for being drunk and resisting arrest. I think they want to calm folks." Uncle Riley paused. "They're still looking for evidence that will prove he's involved."

"What'll they do with Buddy?" My voice cracked.

"They have to find him first, Annie." My uncle patted me on the shoulder, but I wasn't comforted. I held on to Mama.

Buddy and his daddy lived out by the pens where they put cattle before they ship them to market on the train. Mr. Longmire worked at the pens as well as odd jobs around town, mostly yard work. Their house was one room made from scrap lumber and tar paper. No windows. A stove pipe slanted out of the flat roof, but there was rarely any smoke. Buddy's clothes, always clean, were from different churches. When he came to school barefoot, Mr. Perkins, the principal, always found him shoes. Mr. Jenks, the barber, gave him haircuts and change for sweeping out the shop and cleaning the shelves. Last summer he was strong enough to work for Uncle Riley when they pulled corn and cut sorghum.

Buddy and I have been friends since the day he beat up Emile Corse. I got books for him from the library because he didn't want to fill out the application. Said he didn't think Mrs. Wilson would give him a card. I knew better, but realized Buddy was embarrassed about how he and his daddy lived. Buddy told me one time that his daddy had been a banker on Wall Street, New York before the 1929 crash. His mama died when he was born.

March 4, 1941

School opened today. At recess all the kids talked about was the murder. I was glad Buddy wasn't there.

"Wonder where ole Buddy is these days?" Emile Corse sneered. I bit my tongue and tried not to listen. Betty Lou Lowry, who has a crush on Buddy, surprised me.

"They'll have to put him in an orphanage when they find him," she said, like she thought it was a good idea. I wanted to smack Miss-Know-It-All but controlled myself. I knew where Buddy was and if I let my temper get away, it would ruin everything.

Yesterday late evening, after they'd arrested Mr. Longmire, Uncle Riley was out in the dairy when Buddy showed up.

"I sure was glad to see that boy." Uncle Riley came over before I went to school this morning, so I'd stop worrying. "Now, Annie, don't say anything to anybody until I can talk to some people and we figure out what's best for the boy." I nodded.

"What are you doing about him now?" Mama asked.

"He's in the attic. I got out my old army cot. There's a chair and a small table. He ate breakfast with me, but for now he's staying out of sight."

I feel so sorry for Buddy, but I know my uncle will make sure he doesn't have to go to an orphanage.

March 5, 1941

Uncle Riley came over after supper.

"How's everything?" Mama asked.

"Pretty good, all things considered. I still haven't figured out who to talk to about Buddy. Chief Miller's got his hands full and some people really have it in for Longmire." He paused and turned to me. "Annie, Buddy wondered if you'd get him a few books from the library. Said you know what he likes."

"Sure."

"He's also worried about his schoolwork. Afraid he won't get promoted if he misses too much." My uncle looked at me for a moment. "I don't know what to do about that."

"I can help." I knew exactly who I could trust.

"Be careful, Annie. It has to be a secret for now."

I nodded and smiled. I already had a plan.

March 6, 1941

Today after my last class, I went to Miss McGhee's room. She was working at her desk and looked up when I cleared my throat.

"Hello, Annie." She smiled and motioned me to come. "I'm glad to see you. How's everything?"

"Real good." I said, trying to remember what I'd planned to say.

"Can I help you with something?" She waited. "How's the writing going?" She continued to smile until I found my tongue.

"The writing's fine, but I need help for a friend."

"And what would that be?"

I was relieved she didn't ask who the friend was, though I was pretty sure she'd figure it out.

"My friend isn't going to be able to come to school for a while." I paused. "Could I take my friend books ... to keep up?" A knowing look came over Miss McGhee's face.

"I understand perfectly, Annie, and I think it's a good idea. Come back tomorrow and I'll have the books ready. I think your friend should have assignments as well as a tablet and pencils. Will that help?"

"Oh, yes ma'am. Thank you. I can't tell you ..." Miss McGhee interrupted.

"You don't have to tell me anything else." She squeezed my hand.

I hope this works out because Buddy wants to go to college and doesn't need bad grades. I hope my uncle finds out something before too long.

March 7, 1941

They had Mrs. Hooper's funeral this afternoon at the Episcopal Church. I'd never been to a funeral. Mama and I sat in one of the back pews. Since we weren't familiar with the service, we stood with the others or sat with our heads bowed. I loved the music and didn't feel sad. When I thought about Mrs. Hooper's life after the accident, I knew she was happier now wherever she was. We didn't go to the cemetery.

March 14, 1941

It isn't hard taking Buddy's assignments to him and returning them to Miss McGhee. I think the teachers know but don't say anything about it. Buddy comes downstairs after dark, eats supper, does homework and sleeps in the spare bedroom. My uncle's house sits a good way back from the road, half hidden by mesquite trees and brush. He keeps the shades down at night. There isn't much traffic on the county road.

At school the kids are beginning to forget about Buddy. Some think he's run away, probably hopped a freight train. There's not much talk about Mr. Longmire.

March 17, 1941

When I came home from school, Uncle Riley was having coffee with Mama. They said Mr. Longmire had been charged with the murder of Mrs. Hooper.

"Did they find the knife?" I asked.

"No," My uncle shook his head.

"They're bound and determined," Mama said.

"Well, he can't remember anything about that night. They say he was the last one, besides her husband and Lucy Mae, to see her alive. Lucy Mae's description of the encounter in the garden doesn't help."

"Does Mr. Longmire know Buddy's at your house?" I asked.

"No, not yet." My uncle paused. "He's had a pretty hard time being locked up." He looked at Mama who nodded.

"Annie, do you know what an alcoholic is?"

"Yes." Buddy had explained it to me recently. Mama looked surprised.

"Well, Mr. Longmire is an alcoholic. He's drunk so much whiskey that his body couldn't do without it." I nodded my understanding. "At first it looked like he wasn't going to make it, but he's sober now, and each day he's doing better. It's still a battle, but he's a different person. First thing he asked about was Buddy. When they couldn't tell him anything, he went into a tailspin, but he's doing okay."

"What are you going to do?" I asked.

"I'm on my way to talk to a Mr. Marcus Claiborne. Seems he's a lawyer from Houston who read about the case and decided to defend Longmire for free when he goes to trial."

"My goodness," Mama said. "That's unusual. From Houston? They better check up on him."

"I imagine the judge will have something to say about that. Anyway I'm going to see Mr. Claiborne after I leave here. When I made the appointment, I said I needed some advice on a matter pertaining to the case. I hope this won't get Buddy shipped off somewhere. I don't know what else to do"

We agreed that Buddy couldn't stay hidden forever, and it might get Uncle Riley into all kinds of trouble to continue hiding him. My uncle promised to stop by after he talked to the lawyer. I had trouble concentrating on my homework and was glad when I heard a truck coming up the lane.

"I think Mr. Claiborne's going to do a good job for Mr. Longmire." My uncle was relaxed and smiling. "He made sure I understand what I'm getting into with Buddy."

"What *are* you getting into?" Mama asked Uncle Riley. She tapped me on the head which means not to interrupt grown-up conversation.

"He was glad to hear that Buddy's safe and sound because Longmire wanted him to start a search for Buddy before they even talked about his situation"

"Claiborne said I'd bent the rules by not turning the boy over to the law, but he thought it could be worked out. He's going to try to get me temporary custody."

"Thank goodness." I breathed a deep sigh.

"Oh, there'll be red tape, but that's what lawyers do. We talked to Chief Miller and he thinks it's a good idea too."

I wanted to dance a jig and holler, but I didn't.

"What if Mr. Longmire is found guilty?" Mama asked.

"First of all, Mr. Claiborne is convinced he's innocent. Second, we'll cross that bridge if we come to it." Uncle Riley sounded sure of himself. I wish I felt as sure, but at least Buddy will be safe and we can walk to school together. I'm going to stand beside him when he faces those kids.

March 18, 1941

At school today, Emile Corse and his bunch kept their distance and the other kids didn't bother Buddy. Betty Lou Lowry got my goat when she pranced up to him with a big smile on her face.

"Oh, Buddy, I'm so glad to see you. I was terribly worried." She batted her eyelids as she looked up at him. "I've missed you."

"Thanks." Buddy said and quickly made his way into the school house. A couple of girls standing nearby snickered, and if looks could have killed, Betty Lou would have been arrested for murder. I ignored them and walked beside Buddy.

Things went fine all day. I think Mr. Perkins and our teachers had something to do with that.

After school, Chief Miller took Buddy to visit his daddy.

March 19, 1941

Buddy and Uncle Riley ate supper with us this evening. Afterward, Buddy and I talked on the back porch.

"I sure was glad to see my daddy, especially with him doing so much better. We talked more than I can remember in a long time. He was really worried about me and I apologized for that, but we agreed I'd have probably ended up in an orphanage if your uncle hadn't stuck his neck out for me. We can't ever thank all of you enough for giving me a place to stay."

"We worried about you from the very beginning," I said. "Miss McGhee, Mr. Perkins and your other teachers wanted you safe too."

"I know."

We agreed that Mr. Claiborne seems to be working hard to find the truth. In the meantime, Buddy is concerned that his daddy is in jail. The bail was set high and no one is going to lend Mr. Longmire money. Most people think he's guilty.

Buddy told me his daddy was the only prisoner in the county jail, except for an occasional fellow who'd been drinking and got into a fight. One man had been in and out for disturbing the peace in Clavin. He calls himself Brother Atkins, a sort of preacher. He wears a sandwich board proclaiming his message: "Repent. The End Is Near," on his chest and "Hell Burns Forever," on his back. Unfortunately, he has a weakness for drink and when the devil is on him, he starts yelling at the top of his voice, threatening sinners with Hell's fire. At that point they put him in jail until he sobers up.

This last time, they'd found him passed out in a ditch on the Clavin-Duddley road. Besides being dead drunk, he'd been beaten and was in bad shape. Doc Bailey said he was lucky to be alive. When he was well enough to leave the hospital, they put him in a cell next to Mr. Longmire.

"Brother Atkins admits he isn't a real preacher," Buddy said. "Didn't go to a church school, but he was in the Great War and made a promise to Jesus one night in a trench, saying he'd spend his life preaching if Jesus would keep him alive. He saw some terrible fighting and came home wounded. After he recovered, he remembered his promise and has been on the road to Heaven ever since." Buddy paused. "Daddy says it was good to have someone to talk to."

"Wonder why anyone would beat Brother Atkins up so bad?" I asked.

"He told Daddy it was his first time in Duddley, he hadn't even walked with his signs. Says he'd had a few drinks, but wasn't drunk. Didn't have much money and was looking for a warm place to spend the night. It was after midnight and all the houses were dark. He decided to go into the yard of a big house with lots of bushes. Said he thought he might find a shed or even sleep under heavy shrubs. He says someone was in the yard, but didn't throw him out, told him to hide and he'd bring him some blankets. The next thing he remembers is a lot of pain. He told Daddy he was going to take his message to Duddley when he got out because someone there needed it."

March 22, 1941

Uncle Riley took Buddy to see his daddy today. It was Saturday and he could visit in the morning and again in the afternoon. Uncle Riley says they're nice about letting Buddy stay longer because they don't have anyone else locked up.

I wanted to go with them to see what a jail looked like. I thought it might come in handy to know how to describe the cells, what the walls looked like, how it feels to be behind bars. Mama put her foot down before I had time to give her my reasons.

"You don't have any business in a jail, young lady."

"Why not? Uncle Riley will be there too."

Mama didn't say another word, but I know that look. It's like a thick piece of glass, and there's no way to get through it.

They had supper with us and later Buddy and I sat on the back porch. He said his daddy was doing much better since he wasn't able to get any liquor, didn't seem to want it either.

"Daddy doesn't think he killed Mrs. Hooper. Says he really liked working for her, but with the shape he was in, he can't be sure of anything. Mr. Claiborne keeps telling him he didn't do it and not to talk like that to anybody."

I don't repeat what Buddy tells me. Not even to Mama. I know she isn't too happy about my best friend being a boy two years older. She's always nice to Buddy and is worried about Mr. Longmire, but she doesn't want me dwelling on it or getting involved.

We went into the kitchen to have some more pecan pie. Mama and my uncle were sitting at the table.

"Buddy, we're just talking about your daddy," my uncle said. "Mr. Claiborne thinks the police are trying to pin it on your dad and get this thing wrapped up. However, he says the pieces don't fit. That blood on the rags they found in your house was Mr. Longmire's and they haven't found the knife that killed Mrs. Hooper."

"What's Mr. Hooper doing?" I asked.

"Mr. Hooper is at the bank every day," Uncle Riley said. He shook his head and pushed away from the table. Buddy did the same.

"Thanks, Mrs. Turner. I enjoyed your supper."

"I'm always glad to have you, Buddy. By the way, your daddy's clean clothes are ready, and since he enjoyed those oatmeal cookies, I'm sending more."

March 24, 1941

I saw something unusual on my way home from the library today. I heard a loud voice coming from down the street, and then I saw a man wearing a sandwich board, the back of which read, "Hell Burns Forever." The tall, skinny man, wearing a suit way too big, was chanting. "Repent! The end is near." I knew it had to be Brother Atkins, even though no one had mentioned his head of wild red hair that looked like a worn out brush. People came out of the stores, gawking, grinning and shaking their heads. Just as the man neared Mr. Jenks' barber shop, Mr. Hooper stepped out the door onto the sidewalk. The two men stopped in their tracks, facing one another. I couldn't see Brother Atkins' face, but Mr. Hooper's mouth fell open and hung there. He looked like he'd seen a ghost. The preacher let loose.

"Oh, sinner! Satan's right hand who leads the weak to Hell! You will burn in the everlasting fire!"

The preacher walked toward Mr. Hooper, yelling, waving his long arms. When Mr. Hooper reached for the Studebaker's door handle, Brother Atkins grabbed his arm. If Chief Miller hadn't come up and steadied him, Mr. Hooper would have fallen. Chief Miller handcuffed the preacher who was still yelling as they drove away. Mr. Hooper got in his car and gunned it down the street.

This evening my uncle and Buddy came for supper after visiting Mr. Longmire.

"Were y'all still at the jail when Chief Miller brought Brother Atkins over?" I assumed that's where Chief Miller was headed.

"What are you talking about?" Uncle Riley looked puzzled. I told him what I saw this afternoon. I'd already told Mama.

"Can't they do something about people like that preacher? In front of children too." Mama isn't fond of preachers.

"They hadn't gotten there before we left, but I'm sure he's locked up now." Uncle Riley smiled. "They'll keep him a day or two and then send him on his way."

"Well, they ought to keep that man locked up a good long time." Mama frowned.

After supper, Buddy and I sat on the back steps, talking about Mr. Hooper and Brother Atkins.

"Why would he pick on Mr. Hooper?" I wondered. "He told your daddy that he doesn't remember much about Duddley. Didn't know who beat him up."

"Doesn't make sense, but that preacher sounds a little strange anyway."

"Wonder what he meant about the right hand of Satan leading the weak to Hell?"

"Sounds like he was accusing Mr. Hooper of something bad."

"Mr. Hooper looked scared of him before Brother Atkins opened his mouth. The sight of Mr. Hooper seemed like gasoline on a fire and that's when the preacher yelled those things at him."

Buddy and I looked at one another, and without saying another word, went into the kitchen where Mama and my uncle were drinking coffee.

"We want to tell you something about Mr. Atkins and Mr. Hooper."

"Sure, go ahead," my uncle said, before Mama could say anything.

"We think it's strange that Mr. Hooper and Mr. Atkins seemed to recognize one another," I said. "You should have seen the look on Mr. Hooper's face, like he knew Mr. Atkins. He didn't say a word, and though I couldn't see Mr. Atkins, he really lit into Mr. Hooper."

"I understand what you're saying," my uncle said. "Tell you what. I'll talk to Mr. Claiborne. It might mean something." He smiled, making me feel better. Mama frowned.

March 26, 1941

Today is my birthday and I'm twelve years old. Mama says she can't believe she's had me this long, but everyday has been a blessing. I feel the same way. Mama and I don't always agree, but we never have bad feelings. I am lucky to have such a good Mama and a good family too. Travis is the only one I have a problem with, but Mama says we'll grow out of it.

Our family doesn't go in for birthday parties. Too many of us, Grandma says. She had me and Mama over for ice tea and cookies after school. She gave me a handkerchief she made. It's beautiful, a small square of linen, bordered by tatting that's as wide as the linen square. Grandma does a lot of tatting. She tried to teach me, but we both gave up. She says I'm intelligent and that will have to do.

Uncle Riley and Buddy came over for supper and helped me blow out the candles on my cake. It was my favorite, chocolate with divinity frosting. Uncle Riley gave me a Waterman fountain pen. Buddy gave me a box of stationery. The paper is creamy and bordered in gold. Mama gave me my gift this morning before I went to school. She made a pleated navy skirt and a bolero jacket. She ordered a white cotton blouse with a lacy jabot from Sears Roebuck. I got lots of compliments at school.

March 27, 1941

My uncle takes Buddy over to see his daddy as often as possible. Afterward, they stop for supper. Mama always has plenty and they like her cooking. This evening we had fried chicken and apple pie.

"How's Mr. Longmire," Mama asked.

"All things considered, he's doing pretty good," my uncle said. "Don't you think so, Buddy?"

"Yes, sir."

My uncle always tries to include Buddy. I can tell they've become close. I don't know what will happen if Buddy has to live somewhere else. The temporary custody is still under consideration.

"Jim's putting on some weight," my uncle said. "Mr. Claiborne thinks he'll do fine through the trial."

"Did you have a chance to talk with Mr. Claiborne?" I asked.

"Yes, and he's interested in what you saw." He turned to Mama. "He'd like to come over and talk with Annie sometime. I think he wants to get all the details, to see if it has any bearing on the case."

"Riley, you know how I feel about Annie getting involved in this thing. I know she's telling the truth, but what significance could it possibly have?"

"Mr. Claiborne said it might give him a line of questioning. Annie didn't see Atkins' face but he went into a tirade when he saw Hooper who was scared sh ... speechless." My uncle cleared his throat. "Claiborne is convinced Longmire is innocent."

Mama interrupted, "Will she have to testify in court?"

"I don't know. You'll have to ask Mr. Claiborne."

Mama was mad at Uncle Riley and worried about me. I decided to say something even though I knew it would probably upset Mama more.

"Please, Mama. If it might help Mr. Longmire, I want to tell Mr. Claiborne what I saw. I promise I won't say anything that didn't happen." I reached across the table. Mama took my hand and squeezed it.

March 29, 1941

Mr. Claiborne came today. I went out on the front porch when I saw a black, dented Ford V8 raising a small cloud of dust. We were expecting him. The tall man seemed to unfold as he got out of the car. His brown and white seersucker suit was rumpled, but his white shirt was fresh and starched. A perfectly knotted blue tie with swirls of white made me think of windblown clouds. Mama came out on the porch and he took off his Panama, bowing slightly. A shock of salt-and-pepper hair fell over his forehead. He was bony, like he didn't eat as much as he should, but when he smiled, he looked almost handsome. I'm guessing he's about the age of Uncle Riley who's ten years older than Mama.

"Mrs. Turner? I'm Marcus Claiborne. Thank you for letting me come out and talk with you and your daughter." He smiled.

"You should know that I'm against Roscoe Ann getting involved in any way with this trial." Mama didn't smile.

"Yes, I understand your feelings and will do my best not to go beyond listening to what she has to say, unless it will exonerate my client." He had stopped smiling, but something made me think he was honest and meant every word.

I began to wonder if Mama was going to invite him in, but finally she opened the screen door and gestured for him to sit on our ugly, uncomfortable horsehair sofa.

"Mrs. Turner, would it be possible for us to sit at a table? Perhaps in your kitchen?" He lifted a scarred, leather briefcase. "I will need to take notes." His unfamiliar drawl was gentle, but firm. Mama sniffed and led the way. I couldn't get over how rude she was to this gentleman.

Mr. Claiborne and I sat at the table. Mama busied herself setting out some pound cake she'd made that morning. While Mr. Claiborne removed a tablet from his briefcase and took a fountain pen from inside his jacket, Mama poured coffee for them and gave me a glass of milk. I was on edge because Mama worried about me telling my story. Mr. Claiborne cleared his throat and looked at Mama.

"As I said, I understand your feelings about your daughter being involved in this investigation. I'm grateful for the opportunity to hear her story." He paused, took the cap off his pen and smiled at me. My nerves settled a bit.

I told him everything I saw that day. His writing looked like chicken scratch, but I figured it was his private shorthand.

"What made you think Mr. Hooper recognized Mr. Atkins?"

"His glasses fell off his nose, his eyes bulged—usually he squints without his glasses on. His jaw dropped and stayed that way, like he saw something scary. Like in a bad dream when you can't make a sound to call for help?"

"Don't you think it might have surprised Mr. Hooper when Mr. Atkins called him Satan's right hand?"

"I've thought about that, but Mr. Atkins didn't call him Satan's right hand until after they'd had a good look at one another. Before that, Mr. Atkins was walking down the sidewalk chanting about the end being near and Jesus coming. He wasn't yelling or saying anything about Satan."

"Did Mr. Hooper say anything to Mr. Atkins?"

"Not a word. He looked like he'd seen a ghost. His mouth was open, but nothing came out."

Mr. Claiborne and I talked for about half an hour. He asked a lot of questions, and I knew he believed me. His calm, reassuring way put me at ease.

"Mrs. Turner, you have a remarkable daughter."

"Thank you." Mama smiled and I could tell she liked Mr. Claiborne better than when he arrived.

"Annie has a good way of describing what she sees and it doesn't change. I'm not sure how significant this information will be, but I'll be in touch."

After Mr. Claiborne left, I helped Mama clear the table and wash the dishes.

"I think Mr. Claiborne will do a good job for Mr. Longmire," I paused. "He's nice too."

I want Mama to feel better about all this and be nice to Mr. Claiborne.

"Yes, I think Mr. Longmire is in good hands." That was all Mama said, but later I thought she might be thinking about our visit with Mr. Claiborne. She hummed and smiled to herself a couple of times.

March 31, 1941

This afternoon Uncle Riley and Buddy visited Mr. Longmire and saw Mr. Claiborne too.

"Well, Laney, seems like Annie's information has given the police a new lead."

"What do you mean?" Mama frowned.

"For one thing, they've put out a bulletin for Atkins."

"Do they think he killed Mrs. Hooper?"

"They want to question him. When they found him in that ditch, they first thought he was dead. The doctor said he was unconscious for such a long time because he'd had a hard blow to the head— probably a club or piece of wood. When he came to, he started raving about the right hand of Satan leading him to Hell and the fires of Hell burning forever. He was so wild they had to tie him down. He'd pass out and then come to, yelling about Satan and Hell. At the time, coming from this guy, it didn't mean anything to the sheriff in Clavin. Mr. Claiborne found out this happened the night Mrs. Hooper was killed."

"And he told my daddy he'd been in Duddley the night he got beat up," Buddy added.

"That's what Mr. Claiborne is interested in," Uncle Riley added.

"What about Mr. Hooper?" Mama asked.

"They've been talking to him all along. Seems he hasn't been doing too good since that day on the street. Told Chief Miller he's afraid the killer might come after him."

I didn't feel sorry for him when I remembered how he treated Mrs. Hooper. I thought about the preacher who is definitely an oddball. From the things Buddy has said about him, and seeing him that day in Duddley, he didn't seem like a person who would kill someone, though he did grab Mr. Hooper's arm.

Buddy and I talked later.

"Do you think Brother Atkins killed Mrs. Hooper?" I asked

"I don't know. Daddy doesn't think so."

"Why not?"

"Because of things they talked about. Daddy says he's a gentle man, a real Christian when he's not wearing that sandwich board. Daddy says when he's not on the road he works in different flop houses in Houston and Beaumont. No preaching, just trying to help drunks and people down on their luck."

"So what makes him walk around with those signs, yelling and threatening people? I don't have much use for preachers who try to scare people into Heaven."

"Daddy asked him and he said, when he remembers the trenches in France and his promise, he has no choice. Says the more he reads his Bible and the newspapers, the more convinced he is that the world is coming to a terrible end in our time. Walking the roads is the best way he knows to reach the most people. Says something seems to come over him when he has that signboard on and sees all the lost souls. He figures it's the Holy Spirit."

"I wish he hadn't come here. Maybe Mrs. Hooper would still be alive and your daddy wouldn't be sitting in jail."

Buddy didn't answer and I could have bitten my tongue. His daddy would probably be sitting in the Happy Days saloon.

April 2. 1941

The investigation continues.

"There are a lot of unanswered questions," my uncle said. "Claiborne can't say too much, but a jury has to be unanimous to convict in first degree murder. He thinks the evidence is weak and he's still looking for what he calls missing pieces."

"Does he have any idea who the murderer is?" I asked.

"All he says is he's certain it isn't Jim Longmire. He's talked to a lot of people. He wants to go into court with as much ammunition as possible."

Buddy is always quiet when they talk about his daddy. He and I have talked, but I wait for him to bring it up. I wish Mr. Claiborne could find the murderer and this would all be over.

April 3, 1941

Uncle Riley and Buddy came over this morning while Mama and I were having breakfast. One look at their faces told us something had happened.

"Buddy and I are on our way to Clavin. Chief Miller came by and said we need to get over to the jail."

"What's going on?" Mama asked.

"There's been a new development, but the Chief didn't know what it was." Uncle Riley sounded worried and Buddy looked scared.

They left and we went back to the table, but couldn't eat.

"I hope it's good news for Mr. Longmire." Mama's voice was sad.

I had a knot in my stomach. We've all been holding in a lot of our feelings, trying not to think about Mr. Longmire being found guilty, hoping against hope. I can only guess what Buddy's going through.

I stayed home. Mama understood I didn't want to face those kids, their questions and their stupid remarks. We got the laundry out to dry and Mama started ironing. I took a book up to my spot in the oak tree, but all I could think about was what might be going on in Clavin.

It was late when my uncle and Buddy stopped by. Uncle Riley knew we were on pins and needles.

"When we got to Clavin, the sheriff had Mr. Atkins in a back room. Longmire was upset, saying that Atkins would never murder anybody. Mr. Claiborne was trying to calm Mr. Longmire. About three o'clock they charged Atkins as an accessory to Mrs. Hooper's murder. Said Longmire and Atkins knew one another before they were put in jail together. That they had planned this." My uncle shook his head.

"How can they do that?' Mama's voice was shrill. "Just make up stuff."

"Mr. Hooper was there with his lawyer. Apparently he told them something that convinced the sheriff the two men were in cahoots."

"What did Mr. Hooper tell them?" I blurted out. Mama didn't correct me.

"The sheriff would only say that they have enough to go to trial."

We sat there, not saying anything for a few moments. My uncle stood up.

"I gotta get home and take care of the herd." Buddy stood up too. "You stay here, Buddy. I think Laney has some cookies that will taste good with a glass of milk." My uncle smiled and patted him on the shoulder.

"Thanks, Mr. Riley." I knew he was worn out when he didn't insist on going.

We sat together on the back steps and without thinking I took Buddy's hand and held it. He didn't pull away. There was no need to say anything.

April 4, 1941

People are all stirred up again. Two men are in jail for murder. One has been the town drunk and the other scares people. They're innocent until proven guilty, Mr. Claiborne says, but people don't always think that way when they're afraid.

Mr. Claiborne was here a while this afternoon. He wanted to go over my story another time. He started off saying he wouldn't call me to testify unless he had to. Mama was nicer.

"I feel like I'm grasping for straws," he said, more to himself than us. "I'm convinced Mr. Longmire's innocent and I have grave doubts about Mr. Atkins being involved in any way, but I don't know where to go from here. Hooper's behavior on the street that day still puzzles me. The sheriff doesn't seem to think there are missing pieces in the evidence." He shook his head. "I expect them to set a trial date sometime this week."

"Did you talk to Lucy Mae Lankins?" The words were out of my mouth before I realized it. Mama glared at me.

"Is that the girl who worked for the Hoopers?"

"Yes," Mama said. "She keeps house and cooks."

"Still?"

Mama nodded. Mr. Claiborne took some papers out of his briefcase and read for a moment.

"There's not much here. The sheriff talked with her. She said she didn't hear Mrs. Hooper get up. That she'd forgotten to make sure Mrs. Hooper took her sleeping pill. That's it."

He paused and looked at me. "Why do you think I should talk to her?"

I told Mr. Claiborne about the day I took the laundry over to Mrs. Hooper's after her car accident, and how she never came to the door after that. Mr. Claiborne said there was some talk about her nervous condition following the accident. I also decided to tell him about my smelling whiskey on her breath. His eyebrows went up and he thanked me. He left soon after and I expected a lecture, but I guess Mama figured it wouldn't do any good.

April 7, 1941

Three days later, Buddy and I were having milk and cookies after school when we heard a car honking. We ran to the front yard and saw Mr. Claiborne's Ford V8. He was grinning ear to ear as he walked toward us.

"Buddy, your daddy's going to be a free man!"

We stood there, too surprised to say a word.

Finally Buddy spoke.

"What do you mean, sir?

"We found the missing pieces. Your daddy didn't murder Mrs. Hooper. And neither did Mr. Atkins." Mr. Claiborne was calm, but you could tell he was happy.

Uncle Riley and Mama had been drinking coffee in the kitchen. They came out on the front porch.

"What happened?" my uncle asked. He walked over to Buddy and put his arm around his shoulder. Buddy looked like he was in shock. I tingled from head to toe, wanting to laugh and cry at the same time.

"Come in the house and sit down," Mama said. "We can have some coffee while you tell us everything."

"Good idea. I'm a bit overwhelmed with the sudden turn of events." Mr. Claiborne smiled at Mama.

Mr. Claiborne told us he'd gone over to Hooper's to see Lucy Mae right after we talked. Mr. Hooper said she had gone to visit her folks for the weekend, but when he drove out, they said she hadn't been home since Mrs. Hooper's murder.

"Yesterday morning, I waited until I saw Hooper leave for church. I rang that bell about a dozen times before Lucy Mae answered. She didn't want to talk to me. She was afraid Hooper would come home, so I persuaded her to come with me. We knocked on Doc Bailey's door and he gave her something to calm her. After a while, she was able to tell me the rest of her story.

"Mrs. Hooper drank, but her husband tolerated it until the day she drove into Booth's gas pump. Hooper was furious and that's when he decided to keep her locked up in her own house. He didn't try to stop her drinking, but Mrs. Hooper sobered up on her own. She read books Lucy Mae got from the library and worked in her garden. Lucy Mae had orders to watch her and call Mr. Hooper if she tried to leave. Mr. Longmire worked for her, and frequently Lucy Mae brought ice tea and cookies to the gazebo where they talked about books and plans for the garden.

"One day Lucy Mae overheard the Hoopers arguing. Mr. Hooper screamed at his wife: 'You drag me into a divorce court and I'll kill you.' Then he called her names that Lucy Mae repeated in embarrassment. After that incident, Mrs. Hooper started to drink again. That's when Lucy Mae began to take care of Mrs. Hooper around the clock."

"Why did he keep Lucy Mae working and living there after the murder?" My uncle asked.

"He wasn't sure if she had seen or heard something the night of the murder. At first he appealed to her good nature, saying he needed her help with the house. He promised her more money. He came into her room one night after the murder, and though he didn't do anything, it frightened her and she told him she was leaving. Hooper went into a tirade and threatened her and her family. He slapped her face. She began to suspect Hooper killed his wife, but she didn't know how to tell anyone or if they would believe her."

"Did she see anything?" My uncle asked.

"She told me that the day after the murder she saw Hooper with a long slender bundle of dark cloth like you use to wrap silverware. He was in the dining room, opening drawers and doors in the large china cabinet. She watched as he climbed on a chair and placed the bundle on top of the tall cabinet behind a decorative false front. Today when the sheriff followed up on Lucy Mae's story, he found a carving knife and its matching fork. The entire top of the cabinet was a hidden compartment with concealed openings. Hooper hid the fork as well as the knife so that nothing seemed amiss. They didn't find it before because a cursory swipe of a hand over the top of the cabinet wasn't sufficient to disturb the openings."

"So what happens now?" Uncle Riley asked

"The sheriff has Hooper in Clavin for questioning, with his lawyer. I expect the charges against Mr. Longmire and Mr. Atkins will be dropped tomorrow. It takes time."

That was good news, but it would have been better if Buddy's daddy were already out of jail.

After chores, Uncle Riley and Buddy came back for supper. Buddy was quiet, but seemed relaxed. As they were leaving, I slipped him a note saying how glad I was about his daddy and how I hoped he'd have a good night's sleep. There are times when I think words are better written than spoken.

April 11, 1941

This has been quite a day. Mr. Longmire and Mr. Atkins are out of jail and Mr. Hooper is in jail. Mr. Claiborne came by this evening to tell Mama and me what had happened.

Finding the knife was important, but Mr. Hooper claimed Lucy Mae must have hidden it, planning to steal it later. The real break came when the sheriff began to question Mr. Atkins. The preacher told how he'd sneaked into a garden looking for a place to sleep. He remembered the gazebo and a large bundle that could have been anything. When Atkins saw Mr. Hooper on the street, his memory started coming back and he remembered Hooper as the man who'd given him a blanket and a bottle of whiskey. Because he was so drunk, some of his memory is gone forever, but he remembered getting into a car with Hooper and being hit several times before he passed out. When Atkins identified his assailant, Hooper fell apart. Mr. Claiborne says that happens sometimes, when a guilty person knows he's been found out.

Mr. Hooper wouldn't have been a bank president if he hadn't married Norah Collins. The house was hers. Her father had reluctantly given Hooper a job in his bank. I feel bad that Mrs. Hooper had such a sad life, but I am happy for Buddy and his daddy.

April 12, 1941

It's wonderful to write some cheerful things. Buddy came over this afternoon and we walked down to the river. The sunshine had a warm, wrap-around feeling. A mockingbird chased us when we came too near her tree. The water ran quickly and noisily over loose gravel and splashed past some large rocks near the bank. We sat on a grassy spot under the willow tree on a small bluff. I brought a thermos of lemonade and some snickerdoodles. I had a lot of things on my mind, but waited for Buddy to say something.

"I'm sure glad it's over," he said. "Daddy's a new person, says the thought of whiskey makes him sick to his stomach."

"That's wonderful." Then I asked the question that had been worrying me. "Are you all going to move back to New York where your daddy used to work?"

"Oh, no. They've offered him a job here at the bank. Mr. Varner is moving into Mr. Hooper's job, and Daddy will become the branch manager."

We didn't say anything for a while. I was trying to think of a way to lead up to his daddy's friendship with Mrs. Hooper. That has puzzled me all along. It wasn't the Mrs. Hooper I knew. Turned out, I didn't have to ask.

"Annie, I want to tell you something about my daddy. He was a good person in spite of the drinking." Buddy told me how his daddy and Mrs. Hooper became friends talking about the garden and books they read. Mr. Longmire never went to Mrs. Hooper's when he was drunk and he never saw Mrs. Hooper other than sober. Though she didn't speak ill of her husband, Mr. Longmire knew about it and felt sorry for her. The last day she talked to him in the garden, he had come in answer to a note she'd written and Lucy Mae delivered. She told Mr. Longmire she was leaving and wanted to thank him for his friendship. The business about his being drunk was something Mr. Hooper told Lucy Mae to say. Hooper saw them and assumed his wife was planning to run away with Mr. Longmire. It was then that he decided to kill his wife.

"Why didn't your daddy tell the sheriff?"

"He did," Buddy said, "but they thought he was lying."

Mr. Atkins has decided to go back to Houston and work with people in the flophouses. He doesn't feel like he has to walk the roads anymore to keep his promise.

Chapter 8

Marcus Claiborne

I was surprised and happy when Mama told me Mr. Claiborne was coming for Sunday dinner. She said Uncle Riley suggested it as a way to show our appreciation for all he'd done. I looked forward to seeing Mr. Claiborne again. He didn't seem to think children should be seen, not heard. Mama wore her pink pique dress and the dark blue apron she saves for special occasions. She washed and put her hair in rollers that morning. Mama is very pretty when she takes the time. I figured she must think Mr. Claiborne was worth it.

Our only white linen dinner cloth covered the well-worn kitchen table. Matching dinner napkins lay beneath our mismatched knives and forks. I set out the everyday plates and glasses, since that's all we had. I'd arranged red, yellow and orange zinnias with a few sprigs of fern from Grandma Dickey's garden. I knew all this would fade once Mama served her fried chicken, mashed potatoes, milk gravy, green beans, sliced fresh tomatoes, her own dill pickles and fresh baked rolls. Lemon meringue pie was her specialty.

I was happy Uncle Riley was going to be with us. He always asks what I'm up to and seems to like hearing my opinion. Mama is more of a closed person and doesn't like having long discussions. She is always on me about interrupting, asking questions and saying what I think. I try not to rile her, but sometimes it pops out before I know it.

Uncle Riley had just come in the back door when we heard Mr. Claiborne's car coming. I opened the screen door and waved. He always wears a brown and white seersucker suit. He was a bit rumpled, but his white shirt was spotless, the collar starched and his blue and white tie perfectly knotted.

Mr. Claiborne's smile said he was glad to see me. I love to hear him say "Roscoe Ann" and I have finally found the right word for his soft, gentle drawl: mellifluous. He is from South Carolina, which explains why he sounds different from us. Voices interest me and I think you can tell a lot about a person from the way they speak, as well as what they say.

Uncle Riley came in from the kitchen and the men shook hands. Mr. Claiborne is tall. My uncle is shorter and muscular. I could tell they liked and respected one another.

I knew it was going to be a good visit and I hoped Mama would relax and enjoy it. When Mama came from the kitchen to tell us dinner was ready, she extended her hand to Mr. Claiborne. He held it longer than necessary and I didn't see her pull away. Mama's brown hair curled around her face from the steamy heat of the kitchen. Dinner was delicious, of course, and the conversation was interesting. Mr. Claiborne told us about South Carolina and cousins he was staying with in Houston.

Mama was more talkative than usual, but that was because Mr. Claiborne asked her about growing up in Duddley. Uncle Riley talked more too. Mr. Claiborne asked about his farm and my uncle said he was going into fulltime dairy operation.

"Besides good local customers, I've recently gotten a small contract to supply milk to the army. Now that able-bodied young men are being drafted for service, I think a dairy will be easier to operate than a farm."

When Mr. Claiborne asked me about school, I told him it was my first year to write for *The Duddley School News*. He said if I wrote as well as I spoke, I would likely have a career in writing someday. I didn't mention that Miss McGhee already had me thinking in that direction.

When we finished, Mr. Claiborne smiled at Mama. "Mrs. Turner, I don't remember when I've enjoyed a better meal."

He had eaten like a horse; not his manners, but the amount. I wondered if he was one of those people who can eat everything in sight and not gain a pound. He's skinny as a rail.

"Laney's the best cook in our family," Uncle Riley said.

"Thank you." Mama smiled. "You men are excused. Annie and I will join you outdoors in a little while."

I watched from the window as Mr. Claiborne took out a pipe and pouch from his jacket pocket. Uncle Riley had his bag of Bull Durham. Mama didn't allow smoking in the house, not even on the back porch. The two men sat in wooden lawn chairs Uncle Riley had made, discussing something important by the looks on their faces.

Mama washed and I dried.

"Mr. Claiborne sure is nice," I said.

"Yes and a gentleman too."

I glanced at her and guessed she was thinking more than that, but I would just have to guess.

After putting away the last plate, we joined them.

"Laney." Uncle Riley cleared his throat. "Marcus and I've been talking about a matter that's been on my mind for some time."

"Oh?" Mama looked puzzled. I slid down in my chair so that Mr. Claiborne, who sat between me and Mama, sort of hid me. If they were going to talk about something interesting, I wanted to hear. Mama doesn't always think I should listen to grown-up conversation, but I love it, even when I don't understand everything.

"You and Annie have lived here going on twelve years, and I always think of this as your place." Uncle Riley's hand swept around toward the house and the back yard. "But if anything happened to me, you might have to move. I don't have a will saying that I want you to have this." Uncle Riley paused, his forehead creased with worry lines.

"That's right, Mrs. Turner. You all have a large family and though everyone is independent and gets along, we never know what circumstances might arise. You and Roscoe Ann need the security of a roof over your heads no matter what happens." I heard concern in Mr. Claiborne's voice.

"I never thought of that," said Mama.

"I have," said Uncle Riley, "and that's why I'd like Marcus to tell you what we've been talking about."

"I've made some suggestions," Mr. Claiborne said to Mama. "In any case, Riley needs to make a will in which he can name you, Mrs. Turner, to inherit this house and some of the surrounding acreage. Or he could sell it to you for a dollar. You, too, should make a will designating a guardian for your daughter in the event you were to predecease her while she is a minor."

"I never thought of that either," Mama said, shaking her head.

"I don't mean to cast doom and gloom, but we don't know what the future holds. These are just suggestions. You all may have other ideas, but whatever it is, put it in writing."

Mama has told me how Uncle Riley came home from the war in France and bought a place that was weeds, mesquite trees, live oaks and prickly pears. He turned it into a farm with a small herd of cows and put in forage crops. His house, the original homestead, had suffered from neglect, but became the nicest on the Clavin Road. The house Mama and I live in was a shack that Uncle Riley rebuilt for us.

After Mr. Claiborne left, the three of us stayed out in the back yard.

"How do you feel about this? Laney? Annie?"

"Riley, you've always looked out for us. I don't have words to say how grateful I am. I want you to do what you think is best for you as well as for us." Mama ducked her head and I thought she might cry. I added my two cents.

"Mama's right. We'd have had a hard time if it hadn't been for you. I was too little to remember when we came to live here, but I love this house and the trees around it. You gave us a home and I thank you with all my heart." I was getting teary too. I thought about Mama's three sisters and their families who had little to spare. Grandpa Dickey left Grandma a big house to live in, but not much else. My uncle took up the slack for all of us.

Uncle Riley decided to sell the house and acreage to Mama. He wanted us to have something of our own, but he continued paying the taxes and helping with the upkeep. He also made Mama sole heir to his estate. One day I heard my uncle and Mama talking about taking care of Grandma Dickey if something happened to him. Uncle Riley will take care of me if anything happens to Mama.

"You're a good man, Riley." Mama put her arms around his shoulders and hugged him. For the first time, I saw my uncle put his arms around his sister.

"You and your mama are my family, Annie." Uncle Riley cleared his throat and looked down at his folded work worn hands, "I couldn't do without you." No one cried, but we were close.

It took a while for everything to be settled. There was a lot of back and forth and before long, Mama and Mr. Claiborne were calling one another by their first names. Mr. Claiborne asked me to call him Clay, as his family did. I said I preferred Mr. Clay. Mama smiled. I asked him to call me Annie.

Uncle Riley and Mr. Clay often had supper with us. I noticed that Mr. Clay began staying after my uncle left. He and mama sat on the back porch or in the lawn chairs under the oak. I liked to sit with them, but Mama usually thought of things for me to do in the house or at Grandma's.

One evening I came back from Grandma's and saw them standing at the back fence, looking toward a beautiful sunset. They didn't hear me coming. Mr. Clay bent toward Mama, said something, and when she looked up he kissed her—a long time. I hurried back to the front yard before they saw me. After I had a minute to think, I went back down the lane and started whistling like I sometimes do. It worked. They were sitting in the chairs when I came into the back yard. Mr. Clay left soon after.

The next evening when Mama and I were cleaning up after supper, I couldn't stand it any longer. You and Mr. Clay seem to really hit it off. I held my breath because Mama doesn't like me to be what she calls forward.

Mama turned and smiled. "Come on, Annie. Let's go for a walk down by the river." We left the dishes in the sink.

The light was still good, though distant clouds brushed across the waning sun. Tiny flashes of lightning sparkled against a darker sky in the distance, but we couldn't hear the thunder. I always like going down to the river, any time of day. Mama seemed to relax and talk more when we sat on our favorite grassy knoll. I hoped this would be one of those times.

"What do you think of Mr. Clay?" Mama looked at me.

"I really like him."

"Why's that?"

"For one thing, I think he likes me too."

"Oh?" She waited for me to go on.

"Whenever he sees me, he smiles in a way that says he really means it. When he talks to me, he looks me in the eye and makes sure I understand."

"Yes, he has that way about him. What else?"

"He wants to hear what I have to say. He doesn't interrupt or talk down to me. I can believe every word he says. He would never hurt anyone unless he was defending someone else."

"Annie, you really are good at observing people as Mr. Clay has said." Mama reached over and took my hand. "He is a fine man. He's sensitive and compassionate. A lot like your Uncle Riley. A lot like Roscoe Turner."

Mama stopped and I knew she was deep in thought. I was on the verge of asking if she'd thought about marrying Mr. Clay, when she got to her feet and pulled me with her. She gave me a hug and we went home. No more about Mr. Clay. I had trouble going to sleep because thoughts swirled through my brain like eggs whisked in a bowl.

Mr. Clay came by the next day to say goodbye before he left for Houston. He didn't know when he would return, but hoped it would be soon. He and Mama shook hands and, as always, held hands for a few moments. I told him I would miss him and hoped he'd be back soon.

"Me too, Annie. Take care of your mother." He looked like he didn't want to leave. Mama would have said it was my wishful thinking.

I imagined the three of us as a family and wondered how it would feel to have a third person in the house. How would it be to share Mama? She was already so busy and it was special when she and I were alone, even if she didn't say a lot. Would we still go fishing or lie on the grass and sing songs?

Buddy and I are best friends, and we talk about everything. He is honest and I can always trust him. We tell one another things we don't tell anyone else. He liked Mr. Clay and had gotten to know him when his daddy was in jail. I decided to talk to Buddy.

The next day I walked to Duddley and stopped at Mr. McGinty's grocery store where Buddy worked for the summer. I found him in the back, stocking shelves.

He heard me coming and turned.

"Hi, Annie. Need something?"

"Yes, but not groceries." I asked what time he got off for lunch.

"At twelve-thirty when Mr. McGinty gets back. I have an hour."

It was just twelve o'clock so I went across the street to the park and waited at a picnic table shaded by a live oak. I had brought peanut butter sandwiches, apple slices and snickerdoodles. We shared a bottle of milk Buddy brought.

"How are you doing?" Buddy asked. He could tell I had something on my mind.

"Okay, all things considered." I didn't know how to begin.

Buddy looked at me and grinned. "Considering Mr. Claiborne wants to marry your mama?"

I didn't answer, though I don't know why I was surprised that Buddy had read my mind again.

"Don't look so surprised." He grinned. "Everybody's talking about it. Some are hoping your mama says yes."

"How do you know that?" I felt anger rising. "Of all things. Those old biddies are at it again."

"Calm down, Annie." Buddy reached over and took my hands. "You know everybody knows everything about everybody in this town. Work in the grocery store and you don't have to have a newspaper or listen in on the party line." He smoothed the backs of my hands with his thumbs. "It's going to be okay."

"You're right. I'm sorry I flew off like that."

"I thought you'd be happy. Mr. Claiborne's a great guy and he really likes you."

"Yes, he's always been good to me and Mama and I like him very much." I told Buddy about Mr. Clay and Mama kissing and holding hands. I told him about being with Mama down by the river, but that she didn't say how she feels or if they were getting married. I confessed that sometimes it seemed like a good idea and other times I wondered if it would change things between Mama and me.

"Your mama has a special love for you, Annie, and she could never love you less." Buddy looked at me closely and our eyes met as he continued. "If I could see my daddy smile and laugh with someone he loved, I'd be the happiest boy alive. Do you realize that before long we're going to be leaving Duddley? After we finish college, we may not come back and live here." He paused. "It's going to be hard to leave my daddy. Even though he's got a life he enjoys, I'd feel a lot better if he had someone to come home to in the evening after I'm away."

"You're right, Buddy. I want Mama to be happy and Mr. Clay is the only man I've seen who I think could do that. I just wish she'd tell me what's going on. She's always been this way, but the older I get the more difficult it is for me."

"I have an idea," Buddy said.

"That's what I came for."

"Talk to your mama." I started to say something, but Buddy shushed me. "Listen. You always say your mama's a closed person, but maybe you are too, where she's concerned. Ask her. Tell her how you're feeling. Take your lumps, if you have to." He grinned.

Buddy was right.

"Thanks," I said. "You're my good friend as always. I'll try."

As we walked back to the grocery store, Buddy spoke.

"Want to go to the picture show tonight?" He looked uncertain. I don't know how I looked at being asked on my first date.

"I'd love to, but I have to ask Mama."

"Oh, sure." He paused. "I'll be out at your place around six to see what she says."

"Come at five for supper." I knew Mama would let me go because it was Buddy—anyone else would get a big no.

From that moment, I began to think of Buddy in a different way.

Chapter 9

The Bradleys

"How was school?"

"Good." I said, like always, but true.

Mama sat in her rocker on the back porch, cooling herself with the bamboo fan I gave her for Christmas. I went into the kitchen, poured myself a glass of milk and found fresh snickerdoodles. I sat in my rocker that's like Mama's.

"You and Travis getting along these days?"

I wondered if my varmint cousin told his mama I knocked him down yesterday when he called me "teacher's pet." Thank goodness there was rapping at the front door and we got up to see who it was. The door was locked because Mama says, "You never know who will show up." A woman and a boy, both slender and tall, stood on the porch.

"Mrs. Turner?"

"Yes?"

"I'm Lorna Bradley and this is my son, Martin." She was nervous and didn't talk like us.

Mama didn't say anything for a moment. "What do you want?" She was on guard.

The woman wore a brown gabardine suit—though pressed and neat, it had seen better days. A white blouse with a crocheted collar reached up to her chin. A small brown felt hat, a bit of veiling around the brim, sat squarely on her head. A knot of graying hair was pulled together on her neck. Tan lisle stockings covered her bony ankles. Brown, polished oxfords followed. She clutched a large, worn leather purse.

Martin was dressed in brown corduroy trousers, a belted chino jacket and new-looking shoes. He wore a crisp white dress shirt, but no tie. His shock of corn-colored hair was neatly trimmed. With a long narrow face, pale blue eyes and slightly humped nose, he favored his mother. Pale thin lips formed their wide mouths.

"We arrived in Duddley yesterday on the evening bus," Mrs. Bradley said. She paused again and took a deep breath. I was afraid she might faint. She had to be hot in those clothes.

"I see." Mama smiled. I could tell she was beginning to feel sorry for them. I couldn't make up my mind.

"We're staying at the Roman Hotel and ..."

Mama couldn't stand it any longer. "Please come in. It's too hot out here." She held the screen door open. Mama motioned Mrs. Bradley and Martin to sit on the horsehair sofa.

"I apologize for dropping by like this," Mrs. Bradley said. "You are very kind to ask us in."

"Annie," Mama said, "please bring us some ice tea." She gave me a look that meant, "Also bring a plate of cookies and napkins." She looked at Martin.

"You may help Annie, if you don't mind." She smiled at him.

I couldn't believe my ears. We didn't know these people from Adam and here was Mama treating them like old friends. What had gotten into her? Martin knew how to help, even though we never said a word. Mama made room on the small table for the tea and cookies.

Mrs. Bradley spoke.

"I asked one of the ladies at the hotel about finding a job and a place to stay. She said you might be able to help." Mama looked puzzled. The woman continued. "I understand your mother has diabetes and requires care?" She paused, took a breath. "I took care of my husband for several years, he had cancer. I'm recently widowed."

"I'm so sorry." Mama paused. "As a matter of fact, my mother was just recently diagnosed with diabetes. She's on a strict diet and I give her insulin twice a day." Mama didn't say what a job it was to take care of Grandma, keep up with her laundry business and help Uncle Riley. Grandma was a handful and my three aunts weren't much help. Uncle Riley was busy with his growing dairy, though he did as much as possible. I could see Mama was giving Mrs. Bradley some thought.

"I tried to get work in our little town, but the depression has almost destroyed it. We decided it was time to make a new start." She looked at Martin as though she expected him to confirm her words. He wore no expression at all. I began to wonder if he was all there.

"Where was this?" Mama asked.

"Mesaville, near the Mexico border in the southwestern tip of Texas."

I'd never heard of it and I doubted Mama had either.

"Why did you decide to come to Duddley?" Mama asked. I wondered about this because the depression was hard on us too.

Mrs. Bradley took a sip of tea and smiled for the first time—although not a full smile—and continued.

"We have no immediate family anymore. One of my cousins, now deceased, was married to a man who was in oil exploration; they lived all over Texas. They were here for a while, and I received several letters from her saying what a charming little town Duddley is. How friendly and helpful its people are. She loved it here. I never forgot that."

It was true that some years ago, people looked for oil all over Texas, but didn't find any in Duddley.

"Are you planning to settle here?" Mama asked.

"I'm not sure. It will depend."

Mrs. Bradley seemed to relax and Mama told her she'd have to discuss it with Grandma. Mrs. Bradley didn't insist and that made me feel better.

Martin ate more cookies and I poured him another glass of tea. I could hardly hear his, "Thank you." Mostly he looked out the window.

In a short while, Mrs. Bradley got up and spoke to her son. "We've taken up enough of these good people's time." She paused and nodded at him. Martin looked my mother in the eye and said a firm, "Thank you. I enjoyed the tea and cookies." Mama reached out and shook his hand. I could tell she liked them both. I wasn't so sure.

After they were gone, I asked, "What are you going to do?"

"I'm going to talk it over with Riley and your grandma. You heard her. She needs a job and a place to stay. I can use the help, as you well know."

"What do you think Grandma will say?"

"It's hard on your grandma to make changes, but she may like having someone around who will listen to her chatter and be at her beck and call. Mrs. Bradley seems like a kind person who knows how to care for the sick. What do you think?"

"Grandma gets lonesome." I decided not to tell her about my doubts. If they came from Texas, why were they wearing such heavy clothes? And, the evening bus doesn't come from the western part of Texas, where she said they were from, it comes from Houston. I didn't say anything because Mama had more experience judging people, and she needed help with Grandma.

Mrs. Bradley and Martin moved in with Grandma and in no time Grandma was saying how much she liked Mrs. Bradley living with her and helping out. Mrs. Bradley took care of the house as well as Grandma. Martin worked with Travis in the yard, but before long he was doing it all, which didn't surprise me. He worked harder than Travis, knew about plants and kept the grass watered in the hot weather.

Martin was two grades ahead of me. We got along, but weren't real friendly. I was surprised when he said he wanted to talk with me one Saturday morning when I went over to Grandma's. We sat in the farthest part of the yard where Grandma has a small rose garden. There's a bench shaded by an oak tree. He swore me to secrecy.

This is how I remember his story.

—

It was early afternoon when Mama and I rode down the dry, rutted road away from our farm in Nebraska. I whisked the reins over the rump of the horse. The things Mama told me to load were tied to the wagon bed. Papa was nowhere in sight.

Mama's face hadn't changed since she came down to fetch me from the field where I'd been plowing. Her voice was raspy and whispery, like she had something caught in her throat.

"Son, I need you at the house."

She and Papa had one of their arguments at dinnertime about me going back to school in the fall. Papa yelled and cussed like he always did, calling both of us bad names. Mama motioned me to leave. Later I saw him go down to the pasture where he was clearing brush.

Ordinarily Mama smiled when she spoke to me, but that day her lips were pulled into a hard line, eyes half-open and unblinking. I'd never seen her like that.

"I got to get this field plowed before sundown," I said. "You heard Papa."

"You do as I say." She turned and strode back to the house. Mama wasn't likely to say she needed me unless she did. I looked toward the pasture but I didn't see Papa, and figured he was working down in the dry creek bed. I finished the row and headed toward the barn.

"Well, Jeremiah," I told the horse. "You got off easy today." Unharnessed, our only horse plodded to the water trough, dust rising from his tracks. There hadn't been any rain in months. We worried how we'd get a good corn crop if it didn't rain soon.

I went into the house, thinking about Mama. When she was upset or angry, she could be quiet for a long time, but I'd never seen her like this. I looked out the back door and was relieved not to see Papa coming.

"Come upstairs," she called. As I climbed the stairs to our bedrooms, I glanced into the parlor and was surprised to see the wooden mantel clock sitting on top of Mama's small pump organ that was rolled into the middle of the room. A narrow rug, which usually lay in front of the davenport, was folded up next to the organ.

In less than an hour, we were ready to leave. We'd changed into our Sunday clothes and Mama packed a valise. A wooden apple box was covered with several of Mama's embroidered tea towels. She'd wrapped pieces of harness leather around the box and rigged a carry-strap at the top. I found out later, it contained a few dishes, kitchen utensils, salt and pepper, bed linen, towels and bars of homemade soap.

"Mama," I said, "please tell me what's going on. Papa's gonna strap me when he sees I didn't ..." She cut me off.

"Go harness Jeremiah to the small wagon and bring it around to the front of the house. Be quick."

I loaded the valise, the box, the clock and the rug into the wagon. We rolled the organ out to the edge of the front porch, but the two of us couldn't lift it. I went to the barn and found some rope and a long, wide plank, heavy enough for the weight of the organ. We made a bridge from the porch to the wagon. I tied a rope around the organ. Mama pushed and I pulled until it slid onto the wagon bed. We spread a quilt over it and I wound the rope around several times and tied it to the wagon seat.

Mama went in the house and returned with a carpetbag in which she kept her sewing. She handed me a flour sack that had my books, tablet, pencils and an exercise book I'd kept when Papa made me drop out of school.

I was scared, but I quit asking questions because I wanted to get away before Papa came back, I knew he'd be mad about the unplowed field and no supper on the table. When he discovered we were gone with the horse and wagon, all hell would break loose. I didn't want to think about him catching us.

Mama looked straight ahead, sitting stiff as a board and holding her head high. I was confused and scared. Mama and Papa had some go-rounds, but nothing like this. I didn't know what to do except be quiet and get Jeremiah up to a good trot.

Most of the time, Papa didn't say much, but when he gave orders, he meant exactly what he said and no arguments. I was afraid of Papa when he was angry, especially if he was drinking. He didn't strap me often, but when he did, I'd be black and blue for days and hurt something bad. He wouldn't let Mama help me unless I was bleeding. One time he hit me in the head so hard, I was out for a minute or two. Mama told him that would be the last time, and it was. I learned not to cross Papa and stayed out of his way. When Papa took me out of school, Mama tried to change his mind. Every time she brought it up, he yelled and cussed, but no matter how loud and vile Papa got, Mama didn't give up. Until that day.

When we reached Sanborn, the sun was casting long shadows. All the stores were on one side of the street and railroad tracks on the other. When we came to Hoffman's General Store, Mama told me to pull over to the hitching posts.

"Wait here," she said. Soon Mr. Hoffman and his son, Dan, came out. The tall, broad-shouldered men had no trouble lifting the organ and carrying it into the store. I took the clock and carpet. Mr. Hoffman gave Mama some money and we were on our way in less than ten minutes. I couldn't believe she sold the three things she treasured. Several blocks further, Mama told me to pull up to the depot.

"Put our things on the platform." When she climbed down, I realized what she had in mind, but was too surprised to say anything. I guess I was relieved to know we wouldn't be staying in Sanborn where Papa could find us. Mama gave me some money. "Take Jeremiah and the wagon over to the livery. Tell Mr. Lowery your papa will come get them. That's all he needs to know."

The livery was across the street from the depot.

"You and your mama going on a trip?"

"My paw'll come get the horse and wagon." I dropped the money on the counter and walked away, making out like I didn't hear his questions. Just as I got to the depot, we could see the train coming. Mama said nothing. I looked back where we'd come from and breathed easier when I didn't see Papa.

—

Martin stopped talking and when it looked like he was finished, I said, "That's quite a story."

"It's the truth, Annie. You got to believe me." He looked like he might cry.

"I feel bad for you and your mama, having to leave your home and all." I wasn't surprised they had come from Nebraska.

"Remember, you promised not to tell anyone."

"I won't tell." But, I thought Mama ought to know. What if Mr. Bradley found them? And us?

"I don't know why I told you all this stuff. Guess it's kinda been building up like a head of steam. Mama won't talk about it. It wasn't the first time she and Papa had a fallin' out over my schooling. I can't figure what made Mama leave."

"Well, your Papa may show up one of these days," I said.

"I don't know if he'll have much luck finding us." Martin shrugged his shoulders.

"What do you mean?"

Martin continued his story.

—

We got to Omaha, Nebraska and stayed overnight in a hotel. Mama asked the man at the desk if he knew a good hotel in Kansas City, Missouri with reasonable rates. He wrote down several names and she put the piece of paper in her purse. The next morning she bought tickets for Tulsa, Oklahoma and we stayed there three days, in different hotels. Mama used different names each time. When we got to Dallas, she found a rooming house and we stayed two weeks. Mama gave the landlady a story about needing a place to stay until she found a house to rent. She went out every day, saying she had to take care of our affairs. I stayed in the room, reading. We ate at different cafés far from the rooming house. The day before we left Dallas, she told me she'd gotten official papers saying we were Lorna and Martin Bradley.

—

I was so surprised, I interrupted.

"Your name isn't Martin Bradley?"

He shook his head and bit his lip.

"Did she show you the papers?"

"No, but she had a big envelope from a lawyer's office. She said we were going to live a new life, so we needed new names—legal ones. I asked her what Papa would say if he found out." He paused, looking as miserable as I've ever seen anyone. "Her face got all stone-like and she whispered, 'He will never know.'"

He was in a daze that afternoon and I felt sorry for him, but I was worried that I couldn't tell my mama any of this.

"You know, Martin, I think your mama ought to tell my mama why y'all left your farm in Nebraska."

"You promised you wouldn't tell." He looked scared.

"I haven't told anyone," I reminded him. "But I think it's only right that my mama knows who you are and why you're here …" Martin interrupted, raising his voice.

"My mama doesn't want me to talk about it and if you tell your mama, we'll probably have to leave." He brushed tears away with the back of his hand.

"Martin? Annie?"

Involved in our conversation, we didn't see Mama until she spoke. We nearly jumped out of our skins. Martin turned white and I thought he might faint. My heart was racing because I had no idea how much she had heard.

"Annie would never tell anyone whatever it is you've told her and no one is going to make you and your mama leave." She waited for us to say something.

Martin began to sob. Mama put her arms around him, and I put my arms around them. He told Mama the story, and she shared Martin's fears about his mother's reaction. Mama said she thought Mrs. Bradley was brave for leaving. She promised to keep his secret.

A week later, Uncle Riley came and took us to Grandma's. He wasn't sure what all happened, but the police had come and taken Mrs. Bradley away.

When we got to Grandma's, Dr. Bailey was coming down the front steps. He told us not to worry. Grandma had one of her nervous spells, and he was going to the drugstore and have them bring something to calm her down.

My aunts were there, all talking at the same time. Mr. Mathews, our math teacher, had taken Martin to the police station so he could be with his mother. Uncle Riley went to see Mr. Claiborne, since it looked like Mrs. Bradley would need a lawyer. The police didn't say much, but it had something to do with her husband in Nebraska. Mama and I didn't say a word. My stomach churned like never before.

In a little while, Mr. Mathews and Martin came. My friend was pale and looked worried, but he smiled at Mama and me. I nodded my head to let him know we hadn't given away his secret. He lifted his hand to say he understood.

Aunt Fritzi spoke. "Oh, you poor boy."

Martin cringed.

"Don't start that," Aunt Geraldine snapped, then turned to Martin. "What can we do for you, son?"

"I'd like to go to my room, please." Without waiting for permission, he opened the door just off the kitchen and closed it firmly behind him. In a few minutes, Mr. Mathews came looking for Martin. He knocked a couple of times.

"Martin? May I come in?" He entered after a muffled, "Yes, sir."

No one said anything, not even Aunt Fritzie. Aunt Judy was upstairs with Grandma. I was worried about what would happen to Mrs. Bradley and Martin. They had become like family. Mrs. Bradley was good for Grandma, getting her to eat right and take an interest in her garden.

Uncle Riley returned and took Martin and Mr. Mathews to talk with Mr. Claiborne. Martin looked better, not so pale. I was thankful Mr. Mathews was there. He had taken a special interest in Martin, helping him catch up with his schoolwork and putting him on the baseball team.

Mama and I spent the morning with Grandma making sure she took the medicine Dr. Bailey ordered for her. It made her sleep and that was good for all of us.

"What do you suppose Mrs. Bradley did?" I asked.

"I can't imagine," Mama said. "From what Martin told us, it doesn't seem like she'd have had time to do anything except pack up her few things and leave."

"I hope she can come back. She's really helped Grandma."

"Yes, she has a way of calming those around her."

As it turned out Mr. Claiborne took Mrs. Bradley's case. He met her bail and arranged for them, including Martin, to go back to Nebraska where she would be charged with killing her husband. We were dumbfounded.

Mr. Claiborne explained. Three days after Mrs. Bradley and Martin left the farm; a passing neighbor heard the cows in the field making quite a racket. They hadn't been milked and he couldn't find anyone at home. The sheriff came out and discovered Martin's father dead in the basement. They were going to charge Mrs. Bradley with manslaughter. He'd been drinking and lay at the bottom of the cellar stairs with a broken neck. The prosecutor said they had a fight; she pushed him down the stairs and didn't bother to see if he was hurt. He said she ran off and left her husband to die.

Mr. Claiborne called when they reached Sanborn, to let us know they were okay. We didn't hear any more for three weeks until he called to say Mrs. Bradley had been found not guilty and they were coming home. We were relieved and happy beyond words.

When they returned, we all gathered at Grandma's.

"We have some explaining to do." Mr. Claiborne smiled and looked at Mrs. Bradley. "Siegfried?"

We looked at Mrs. Bradley in surprise.

"Yes," she said. "That is my real name. Siegfried Lindstrom." She smiled and gestured toward Martin. "This is my son, Edvard, or Eddie as he was called before." She paused. "Please continue to call me Lorna, but Eddie hates being called Martin." We all nodded and murmured, with a few chuckles.

"Tell us about the trial," someone asked.

"Yes, I want to do that," Mr. Claiborne said. "You all have been part of this—taking Lorna and Eddie in and making them part of your family. Without your love and trust, this latest ordeal would have been even more onerous. The prosecutor assumed the verdict was a foregone conclusion, even though Mr. Lindstrom physically abused and mentally tormented his wife and son, especially when he was drunk. He refused his intelligent son an education, threatening to beat a mother if she continued to teach her son. The prosecutor was correct in that the law does not permit a woman to leave her husband, cruel as he was, to die on a damp, cold cellar floor, even if his being there was the result of defending herself. She could have gone for help.

"I've never tried a case that seemed more conclusive until I put Eddie on the stand. His memory was clear and he answered all the questions with confidence. It was obvious to all he had no idea that anything had happened to his father before they left Sanborn. I asked him about the cellar and Eddie explained that his father made whiskey in the cellar and kept a padlock on the door. He allowed no one else to go down there and carried the key on his chain at all times.

"I asked if Mr. Lindstrom had been drinking the day they left. Eddie explained that his father worked very hard during the day. He only drank at night after supper. For dinner, he drank milk and a cup of coffee and had done so the day they left. I asked if the cellar door was locked when he came in the house to help his mother pack. Without hesitation, he said, 'Yes.'" Mr. Claiborne paused and sipped his ice tea. I was on pins and needles.

"I established that Mr. Lindstrom couldn't have been drunk at the time they left. I concluded he returned at supper time, found his wife, son, the horse and wagon gone. He went into a tirade, proceeded to get drunk and probably went for more whiskey, fell down the steps and broke his neck. By that time, Eddie and his mother were on the train out of Sanborn. The key to the cellar was on the chain in his pocket when he was found."

No one said anything. Mr. Claiborne smiled at Mrs. Lindstrom who spoke.

"As Marcus said, you gave us the strength to get through this. I didn't know how we were going to prove my innocence, but knowing all of you were praying for us made the difference. I apologize for the lies I told and I ask you to forgive me."

At that point, everyone began to talk at once, reassuring the Lindstroms they were welcome to stay. Grandma told Mrs. Lindstrom she couldn't live without her. Eddie didn't say much, but he looked relaxed and happy.

Several days later, Eddie and I sat in the swing in Grandma's side yard.

"I'm sorry my mama had to go through a trial, but it sure is easier having the truth known."

"It shows," I said. I wondered how he felt about his daddy being dead and it was as if he read my mind.

"I feel bad that my papa died the way he did. I hope he was unconscious the whole time. I was scared of him, but I always hoped things would be different when I got old enough to work like he did. He was a hard worker and our farm was a good one."

"What's going to happen to your farm?"

"A man from Sanborn wants to lease it. He's farming a small tract and wants something bigger. With things the way they are, we aren't going to ask a lot of rent. We just hope he'll take care of things. I want to go back some day and run the farm myself."

Chapter 10

Piano Lessons

The Spencers moved to Duddley when I started seventh grade. Mr. Spencer was the new band teacher. In fact, he was the first band teacher Duddley ever had. Soon everybody was excited about blowing horns and beating drums.

"Oh, Annie," Doris enthused. "It'll be like in the movies. We'll have uniforms with braid, tassels on our hats, marching down Main Street before the football games. Lena Bastrop and June Carney already know how to twirl and toss a baton, so they'll be majorettes. What are you going to play?"

"I'm not," I said. "I don't want to blow a horn or beat a drum. Or, show off in some uniform."

"For goodness sakes, Annie, you don't have to be such a sourpuss." She flounced away to sign up for clarinets.

I didn't want to be in the band because I wanted to play the piano. I dreamed of making those lovely sounds. I never said anything because I knew Mama didn't make much money washing and ironing linens. Even if I wanted to be in the band, a uniform and instrument would cost too much.

I wasn't sure about Mr. Spencer either. He was tall, athletic and had wavy blonde hair. Doris thought he was handsome and I guess he was, but I couldn't stand that little yellow mustache under his nose. He had five children, four girls and a boy. Mrs. Spencer was tall, skinny and plain. She always looked sad or scared. I figured those five kids were enough to scare anybody and make her sad most of the time. Especially Frank, Jr., called Frankie.

I didn't see much of him until school started, but I heard Travis and some of his friends talking one day. I was reading on the upstairs porch off Grandma's bedroom, when they gathered in the garden swing below.

"Boy howdy, that Frankie really knows some stuff." I recognized Junior Pearce's voice.

"Yeah, and he says his old man doesn't even care if he smokes a cigarette once in a while." My cousin Travis snorted.

"My paw would kill me," Joe Rainer said. They all laughed.

"How about those picture playing cards he carries around?" Elray Barnes asked. "Says they're straight from Paris, France. Says his uncle brought them home from the war. Says he's going to give the girls in Duddley a good ole time." They snickered and snorted. Those boys are all like Travis. Disgusting. Now there would be another one. I wondered what Frankie Spencer had in mind for the girls in Duddley.

That night at supper, Mama brought up the school band.

"It might be fun," she said.

"I've thought about it, Mama, but I'm really not interested in horns or drums."

"That surprises me. I know you love music and you have a good singing voice. I thought you'd be eager to join."

"I bet those uniforms are going to be expensive," I said, trying to sound sincere, not stubborn.

"I can manage the uniform and we can rent an instrument until you're sure which one you like." She cocked an eyebrow, waiting for my answer.

It was now or never.

"I want to play the piano, Mama, like Mrs. Terry." I told her how much I loved hearing Mrs. Terry play at Sunshine Club. When Miss McGhee played her Chopin records, it was the most beautiful thing I'd ever heard. "I know we can't afford a piano, but maybe Grandma will let me use that old one in her parlor."

"I had no idea." Mama looked deep in thought, but we didn't talk about it anymore.

When school started, Mr. Spencer organized the Duddley Consolidated School Band. About fifty kids showed up for the first practice because no one was going to have to pay for the instruments. Mr. Spencer knew about a special program for school bands. After a few practices, there were twenty-eight band members.

One day during the second week of school, Mama was ironing when I came home.

"How was school?"

"Good."

Mama folded a bed sheet and disconnected the iron. "How does it feel to be a seventh grader?" Mama smiled, but I knew this wasn't the real question.

"It's okay. Miss Larsen makes it interesting and doesn't give too much homework."

"Do you think you'd have time for piano lessons?"

I couldn't believe my ears. Mama chuckled when she saw the look on my face.

"Oh, Mama, I'll practice every day."

"I talked to Mrs. Terry and she's not able to take more students, but she heard Mr. Spencer is offering private lessons. I went to school today and talked with him and he'll be happy to have you as a student. Your uncles will move Grandma's piano out here. She says it's all yours."

"Oh, Mama." In that moment I knew I wanted to learn to play more than anything, even with Mr. Spencer for my teacher. Mama said Uncle Riley wanted to pay for my lessons.

I began as soon as the piano was moved to our house. It was out of tune, but Mr. Spencer arranged to have someone from Houston tune the two school pianos, four church pianos and several private ones. Uncle Riley put ours on the list. There's not much space left in the front room. We had to put Mama's sewing machine in her bedroom, but she says it's cozy, not crowded.

I loved touching the keys and hearing the beautiful sounds. I practiced an hour every day and I liked Mr. Spencer. He never raised his voice or was impatient if I had trouble with a piece. When I played well, he praised me. I forgot all about the blonde mustache.

I liked school, but recess and lunch weren't always pleasant. That's when Travis and his gang—there's no other word for them—went around showing off and picking on the small, shy boys. Sometimes older country boys weighed in on Travis' bunch, but that didn't stop them. As I expected, Frankie Spencer fit right in. He not only picked on the little kids, he aggravated the girls. He knew he was good looking. Tall for his age, he had his dad's blond hair. A constant smirk took away from his good looks. Travis and the others tried to swagger like Frankie, but never succeeded. He was smarter than the others too. I heard him call Elray a boor one day and they ate it up. What idiots.

Of course, some of the girls liked Frankie's attention even if they didn't know what to expect. I stayed out of his way. One day he asked Sue Anne Markey if she wanted to see something really good and pulled out a couple of those cards from Paris, France. Her face turned red, she squealed like a stuck pig and ran off crying. Travis and his bunch laughed like hyenas. Sue Anne wouldn't tell anyone what she saw. Another time, Frankie cornered Lydia Conklin, saying he wanted to tell a secret in her ear. She also squealed and ran off, but told us later that he stuck his tongue in her ear.

I knew Travis was dying for Frankie to "get Roscoe Ann." I have a reputation for disliking boys, except for Buddy. I wasn't surprised when Frankie came over as I was talking with Doris and Iris.

"Hi, ladies." He smiled, pushing his fingers through his wavy blonde hair. "Y'all are looking as beautiful as the Venus de Milo." He ran his eyes up and down the three of us and we knew he was imagining no clothes and no arms. Doris and Iris reddened. I glared. Just as I was about to tell him where to go, he touched the front of my blouse. Before he found bare skin, I grabbed his shirt sleeves, pulled him as Buddy had taught me, and brought my knee up between his legs as hard as I could. He fell, grabbed his crotch, screamed and cursed a blue streak. Every eye on the playground turned on us. Doris, Iris and I shrugged and walked away as though we had no idea what was wrong with him. I threatened Travis if he dared tell his mama or anyone in the family. It didn't end their shenanigans, but those cretins didn't bother us again.

One day after spring arrived, Doris, Iris and I were eating lunch on one of the benches near the gym.

"There he goes," Doris said. We followed her gaze to the side door of the gym which went into a large storage room. It was Mr. Spencer.

"What's wrong with that?" I asked.

"Just wait," Iris said.

The bell rang, telling us it was time to go back to class. I started to get up. Doris pulled me down onto the bench and whispered.

"Here she comes."

I was surprised to see Miss June Duggan, the chemistry teacher, hurrying toward the same door Mr. Spencer had entered. Doris kept her hand on my arm and I didn't move. The door closed behind Miss Duggan. Without a word, we hurried to get to class on time.

After school, I invited Doris and Iris to walk over to Grandma Dickey's for milk and cookies. Out in the garden swing, I got right to it.

"What's going on with Mr. Spencer and Miss Duggan?"

"We're not sure, but I think they're having some kind of love affair," Doris said. Iris nodded, her mouth full of cookies. We weren't sure what all a love affair included, but we went to the movies enough to know a married man didn't do that with someone who wasn't his wife. Today was the second time Doris and Iris had seen them.

"I can't believe Mr. Spencer would do something like that," I said. "And Miss Duggan, she's so ..."

"Homely," Iris finished. I didn't correct her. Miss Duggan was short and square. Her arms were muscular and her legs bulged down to her ankles. She had beautiful black hair that curled all over her head, but that was about it. Her face was pudgy and red most of the time. Mrs. Spencer was no beauty, but I wondered what Mr. Spencer saw in Miss Duggan.

We witnessed the same thing the next week on three consecutive days. I was completely disillusioned. I managed to get through my piano lesson, but Mr. Spencer noticed.

"Are you all right, Roscoe Ann?"

"Yes, sir."

He didn't say anything else. I guess he chalked it up to growing pains. I didn't mention it to Mama because she'd give me a lecture about spying on people. I hoped with all my heart that Mr. Spencer and Miss Duggan were pure as the driven snow in spite of what I'd seen.

When the band gave its spring concert a couple of weeks later, we were surprised to see how the stage in the gym had been rebuilt to look like the outside of a Greek Temple. The columns, though flat, were painted to look round. The carving along the top looked almost real. Large containers between the columns held fake palms and bright lights from the back of the gym shown down on the band causing the uniforms and instruments to glitter and glisten. Before the concert began, Mr. Perkins, the principal, welcomed everyone and thanked Mr. Spencer and the band members.

"In addition I want to thank Mr. Frank Spencer and Miss June Duggan for the spectacular background they've created for our stage. Not only is it fitting for this concert, it will lend itself to future programs as well. A big hand, please." He motioned for Miss Duggan to join Mr. Spencer in front of the band. I never clapped so hard in my life.

Two days before the last day of school, the Spencers left Duddley without saying a word to anyone. I was devastated. No more piano lessons.

"Why do you think they left like that?" was the question everyone asked.

"I think Frankie did something to disgrace his family."

"Oh, Doris," Iris said. "How could he do something that bad?"

Some of the older girls snickered behind their hands. The school board called a meeting to discuss finding a new band teacher. I hoped they'd find one who also taught piano.

Chapter 11

Evangeline Latimer

After Mr. Spencer left, I continued to practice, but it was hard to know if I was improving. Mama encouraged me, but I needed a teacher. One evening at supper, Uncle Riley asked how my piano playing was going.

"Okay," I said, "but I need a teacher and Mrs. Terry still can't take me."

"Today when I was making deliveries to Mortenson's in Clavin, I happened to see a notice on their bulletin board. It caught my eye because it had a picture, done in Crayolas, of cows, trees and bluebonnets, like it could be a pasture around here."

"What did it say?" Mama interrupted.

"Oh, yeah," my uncle chuckled. "It says Mrs. Evangeline Latimer has time for piano pupils. I got her phone number." He handed Mama a piece of paper.

"But that's over in Clavin," she said.

"I deliver over there twice a week. It takes almost an hour and I thought she might be able to give Annie her lesson on a day I make deliveries." He paused. "You want a lesson every week, don't you?"

"Yes, sir."

The next week I had my first lesson with Mrs. Evangeline Latimer. I admired how tall and slender she was. Her brown hair, beginning to gray, was pulled back into a smooth twist that lay down the back of her head. I've discovered it's called a chignon. Wispy curls fell around her face and onto her neck. I guessed her hair curled when not pulled into the chignon. Her eyes were deep blue and though a few winkles formed around the corners when she smiled or laughed, her skin was smooth and creamy.

She asked me to call her Miss Evy at our first lesson. "Mrs. Latimer is too formal and Evangeline is a mouth full," she chuckled. She was a good teacher, like Mr. Spencer. I looked forward to my lessons.

Before long, Mama started driving me to Clavin. Uncle Riley had a large herd and it was hard to find help. With the threat of war, good jobs were available in big cities and people were leaving Duddley to find better pay. My uncle taught Mama to drive so she could make the deliveries in Duddley and Clavin.

One day when Mama dropped me off, Miss Evy was standing on the front porch.

"Hello, Annie." She watched Mama drive off in Uncle Riley's small truck. "Has your mother been driving very long?"

"No, ma'am," I said, puzzled by the question. Ordinarily she never asked about my family. "She learned so she can make deliveries for my uncle and bring me for my lesson."

"I've wondered how it might be to drive an automobile, and come and go as I please." She watched until Mama turned the corner.

My lesson went well and when we finished, Mama hadn't returned. I usually waited on the front porch, but today Miss Evy invited me to wait in the parlor.

"Would you like some lemonade?"

"Yes, ma'am."

"I'll be right back. Make yourself comfortable." She smiled and pointed to a wing chair sitting with three others around a polished table of inlaid woods. "You'll be able to see your mother."

I couldn't stop looking at the room. Four heavy ceiling beams matched the dark wood book shelves and window frames. Three comfortable chairs sat next to tables with a lamp for reading. I would have loved to look at the books, but controlled myself.

Miss Evy returned. "Annie, I hope you enjoy plain iced tea. I thought I had lemons, but they're all gone." She placed a small silver tray on the table with two tall glasses and a plate of sugar cookies.

"I love iced tea," I said, putting a "d" on ice as she did. We always say ice tea, and Mama says that's Texas talk. Before I had time for a second cookie, Mama pulled up.

"I hope your mother can join us," Miss Evy said and was out of the room and down the front walk in no time. She spoke to Mama through the truck window, and then they walked up to the house.

"I'm so glad your mother is finished with the deliveries," Miss Evy said as she pulled a velvet cord hanging near the door. A young colored girl appeared.

"Angie, please bring Mrs. Turner some tea. In fact, bring the pitcher too."

"Thank you," Mama said. "Ice tea is perfect on a day like today." She smiled at me and patted my hand.

Even though I wasn't involved in their conversation, I felt grown-up.

"Annie tells me you've recently learned to drive," Miss Evy said. I don't think Mama expected that, but she didn't let on.

"Yes, as a matter of fact, I learned so I could help my brother and bring Annie to her lessons." Mama explained about the deliveries she made for Uncle Riley.

"Was it difficult to learn?"

"The hardest part is shifting gears," Mama said. "Riley's truck has quite a few miles on it. My brother is a patient man." Mama chuckled as she told about scraping the gears and Uncle Riley trying to stay calm with, "Easy, Laney, easy." We laughed when she described how my uncle stomped on the floorboard when he thought she was going too fast.

"I mentioned to Annie that I've often thought how nice it must be to come and go when you please."

"Yes, I enjoy driving; starting up the motor, deciding when to turn, how fast to go and when to stop. Does that sound silly?"

"Not at all."

They'd forgotten I was there.

"I haven't said anything to Riley, but I've started a savings account so I can buy a car one of these days."

My mother surprised me.

"What a good idea," Miss Evy said. "When I lived in Baltimore I didn't need an automobile. There were buses, trains, streetcars and cabs. Here I feel isolated and limited. My basic needs are in walking distance, but I would love to drive out in the country, go to Houston for a concert—go where I want to when I feel like it."

"I agree."

I was seeing a new side of Mama.

"May I ask you something?" Miss Evy paused. "And please be honest. You won't hurt my feelings."

"What is it?" Mama smiled.

"Would you teach me to drive?"

I couldn't believe my ears. Mama didn't say anything for a moment.

"I'd love to, but I probably wouldn't be a good teacher since I haven't driven very long."

"I've watched you and you drive with confidence." Miss Evy smiled.

Mama shook her head and laughed softly.

"Riley's truck won't make it easy for you."

"Oh, I have a car. It belonged to my uncle who died two years ago. It has a few years on it, but not many miles. I thought I might ask the local garage man to take a look at it and see what he thinks. If you'd consider using it?"

That's how Miss Evy learned to drive.

Miss Evy's car was a black Chevy coupe. It ran like new after the tune-up. I rode in the small back seat. We had hilarious times and some scary ones too. One time Miss Evy put the car in reverse instead of second. Fortunately, she found the brake before she hit a fence. Another time she almost ran off the road when a large truck came toward us.

"Remember," Mama said, "half the road is yours."

Mama and Miss Evy became close friends. I was glad because by this time I loved Miss Evy. One day after my lesson, Mama invited Miss Evy to dinner.

"Thank you, Laney. I'd love to, but I always eat dinner with my mother." There was a tightening in Miss Evy's face. I'd never seen her mother, but one day as I was going out the front door, I'd heard her call, "Evangeline Mary Louise." After searching my thesaurus, I decided it was a querulous voice.

"We'd love to have her too," Mama said.

"That's very kind of you, but Mother is confined to a wheelchair and never comes downstairs." She paused. "Perhaps you and Annie can have dinner with us sometimes. We have a small dining room upstairs." Something in her voice made me think she was just being polite. On the way home, Mama was deep in thought. I broke the silence.

"I'm sorry Miss Evy can't come for dinner."

"I am too." Mama paused. "Have you seen her mother?"

"No. Like she said, her mother stays upstairs. But I heard her call for Miss Evy one time." I didn't mention the querulous voice because I didn't want to speak unkindly of an old lady in a wheelchair.

One day Miss Evy stopped by our house with two baskets of linens.

"These haven't been out of the closet since I left for Baltimore, more than twenty years ago. They need washing and ironing. If they fall apart, don't worry about it." We all laughed. Mama said she'd bring them when we came for my next lesson.

The day we arrived with the linens, the front door was open as usual, but before Mama could call out, we heard a loud scream from upstairs. Then Miss Evy's voice, "No, Mother, no."

There was a loud thud and crash of something falling. We dropped the baskets and raced upstairs. Upon reaching the landing, we heard Miss Evy sobbing. "Oh, Mother, Mother." We entered the bedroom where an old lady lay on the floor halfway under a wheelchair. Her eyes were closed and blood flowed from beneath her head. Miss Evy's hand was covered in blood. She held her mother to her chest. A pair of pointed sewing scissors lay on the floor.

"Annie, do you know where the phone is?" Mama was calm in spite of everything.

I ran downstairs and told the operator what I'd seen. In a few minutes, though it seemed longer, an ambulance and a doctor arrived. Two policemen came minutes later. Clavin is the county seat with a hospital and a good sized police department. If we'd been in Duddley, it would have taken longer to get the kind of help we needed.

A policeman took our names and asked questions. Because we weren't family, he told us to go home. We waited in the truck until Miss Evy and her mother left in the ambulance.

"They'll probably keep Miss Evy overnight," Mama said as we drove home. "I'll call later this evening to check."

There was no answer when Mama called from Uncle Riley's after supper. When she called the hospital, they told her Miss Evy was in no danger, but her mother was critical.

Mama called Miss Evy's the next day. A woman, who said she was a cousin, told Mama Miss Evy's mother died at the hospital and Miss Evy was at home resting. They planned a private service in Clavin. I worried about Miss Evy's hand, hoping it wouldn't affect her piano playing.

One afternoon, two weeks later, Miss Evy came to see us.

"Laney, Annie, I've missed you so."

We hugged as the tears flowed. Mama took Miss Evy's arm and guided her to a chair in the kitchen.

"How are you getting along?" Mama asked.

Miss Evy was thin and pale, her hair grayer.

"I'm doing better each day."

Mama got ice tea from the refrigerator. I put sliced pound cake on a plate. Miss Evy's left hand had a small bandage, and when she saw me looking at it, she smiled.

"It's not serious. The scissors pricked a vein and the blood made it look worse. It'll be good as new." She paused. "Thank you both for the thoughtful notes and beautiful flowers. You'll never know how much it comforted me." She dried tears that lingered on her cheeks. "I placed your flowers on Mother's grave. She loved working in her garden before her illness."

"We appreciate your coming over like this," Mama said. "You've been in our prayers every day." Mama and I aren't much for going to church, but we say a prayer every night before I go to sleep. Not long ones. Just thank you, bless those in need and get us through tomorrow.

I was full of questions, but didn't want to be rude. Miss Evy must have read my mind.

"You are my best friends and I want you to know the story."

"It's all right, if you don't feel up to it," Mama said.

"No, I'll be fine. I'd have come over sooner, but there was so much to do. A cousin from Meisner, an attorney, helped me take care of everything." She paused and sipped her tea. "The story is sad, but I want to tell you all of it. May I?"

We nodded.

"I met Quentin Latimer when I attended Juilliard in New York City. It was love at first sight, and we planned to marry after finishing school. He signed up when the United States entered the war and, too soon, he had orders for Europe." She paused and took a deep breath.

"You don't have to put yourself through all that," Mama said.

"I want you to know." Miss Evy paused. "There wasn't time to marry, so we said goodbye on a New York pier and I didn't see him for two years. He was badly wounded toward the end of the war and his return was delayed. When I saw him again, he was in a wheelchair. He'd lost both legs. He looked ten years older and his hair was snow white, but his spirit was the same and his smile as bright as always. We loved one another more than ever."

"We decided to make our home in Baltimore where Quentin grew up. His Aunt Maude, who'd raised him after his parents died in a boating accident when he was ten, still lived in the family home. She was a dear lady. I found a job teaching at a girls' school. When I told my mother our plans, she forbade me, though I was in my twenties and independent. You wouldn't want to hear the details, but suffice it to say, Quentin and I married and made our home with Aunt

Maude. My mother refused to come for the wedding and vowed never to speak to me again." Miss Evy reached for her glass.

"Surely she didn't mean it," Mama said.

"She was terribly hurt and angry. In my youth and love for Quentin, I didn't understand. Aunt Maude helped me through that time and eventually I began to see things through my mother's eyes, though it was hard to understand her way of thinking. She had been a widow most of her life and I was her only living child. My brother died when I was five. Mother was never close to her family, most of whom lived in Meisner and Houston. My father grew up in an orphanage and was not accepted by all members of Mother's family. It's sad, but Mother's death has brought her family back into my life and they have helped me through this time. A gift beyond measure."

"Being family is sometimes hard," Mama said.

"So true, Laney. Eventually my mother and I reached a tenuous rapport. We exchanged letters and telephone calls. Because Quentin understood, I spent most of every summer with her. It wasn't always easy, but I learned to avoid topics that upset her and kept my emotions in check. We loved one another, but liking was sometimes difficult." Miss Evy paused and looked at me. "Annie, I realize I'm talking about matters that might perplex you, but you're very mature for your years. When I see you and your mother together, I wish I had been like you."

"Yes, we get along for the most part," Mama said. "Mainly because of Annie's nature." She patted me on the hand. Mama had never said anything like that before. I am glad we don't have problems like

Miss Evy and her mother had, but I wish we could talk more about things that bother me. Mama tries, but maybe I expect too much.

"After our marriage," Miss Evy said, "I continued teaching, and Quentin took private violin students. He became a member of the Baltimore Symphony Orchestra. Our life was filled with music, friends and happiness. We were deeply saddened when Aunt Maude died." She paused and took a breath. "One morning three years later, I found Quentin slumped in his chair. He'd had a massive heart attack." Miss Evy's eyes filled with tears, but she went on.

"I sold the house and settled into a new life. I loved teaching and that helped. Two years ago, I had a call from Mother's doctor, asking me to come. He thought Mother was slipping into dementia. During my last visit, I noticed her general health had declined, but I hadn't detected her mental failure. Her doctor was very kind, explaining that Mother's age was the primary cause. She was becoming more and more difficult for the nurses who cared for her. When I saw how changed she was, I decided to move back to Clavin. For some reason, even after all our difficulties, Mother responded to my requests. As the dementia progressed, there were times when she thought I was one of the nurses. That's what happened the day you came." Miss Evy drank some tea.

"The nurse who was scheduled to be there had called to say she'd be late. I was settling Mother in front of her favorite window where she could see the garden. I don't know how she got the scissors. They were kept in a sewing box in another room. As I tucked in her lap robe, she began striking out with the scissors and hit my hand. Because she was so frail and erratic, the wounds weren't deep, but a vein was hit, causing all the blood. I'm sorry you had to see such a sight, but you'll never know how thankful …" Miss Evy shook her head and Mama put her arms around her. I took a wash cloth from a basket of folded laundry and rinsed it in cold water. Mama patted Miss Evy's face and throat. Just as our friend was getting herself together, there was a knock on the front door.

"Laney?" It was Uncle Riley.

"Come on in," Mama called. "It's just my brother, Riley," she said to Miss Evy.

"I should go," Miss Evy said, but Mama put her hand on her arm.

"Please stay. I want you to meet him. He's been worried about you too." I thought that was stretching it a bit, but he had asked about her. Miss Evy remained seated.

My Uncle was dressed in crisp khaki trousers and shirt with a black necktie. He'd gone to Meisner on business that morning. He must have recognized Miss Evy's car, so I was surprised he stopped by. My uncle's a shy man and not comfortable around women outside his family. Mama introduced him.

"Pleased to meet you" Uncle Riley smiled.

"I'm glad to meet you." Miss Evy smiled too.

I fixed another glass of tea and he sat down at the table.

"I was sorry to hear about your loss, Mrs. Latimer."

"Thank you. Your sister and niece have been a great help to me."

"I guess you don't remember me."

Miss Evy took a moment before she spoke.

"Please forgive me, but I'm afraid I don't."

"I was that mean little boy who sat behind you in fifth grade and pulled your pigtails." My uncle grinned. "One day Miss Simms saw me and made us trade desks. I couldn't pull your braids after that." He chuckled and shook his head.

"Now I remember," Miss Evy said, laughing. "That was a long time ago."

"I wondered why you didn't tell on me. The other girls liked to see me get in trouble."

"I was afraid of my own shadow in those days."

"I didn't see you the next year because Duddley built its own school and I had to transfer."

"You have a good memory, Mr. Dickey."

I tried to imagine my uncle as a brazen fifth grader picking on a girl who was probably the prettiest in the class. Mama and I listened as they continued. Miss Evy asked about Uncle Riley's dairy farm.

"Yes, it's something I always wanted to do. My father helped me in the beginning. Now, I almost have more than I can take care of."

"In a way your good fortune has been mine as well," Miss Evy said. "When Laney took over the deliveries, we three became close friends."

"Well, I couldn't do without either of them." Uncle Riley smiled at Mama and me. "They're my family as well as helpers with the dairy."

"I really must go," Miss Evy said.

Mama invited her to Sunday dinner and this time she accepted. Uncle Riley walked Miss Evy to her car, opened the door and closed it carefully after she was settled. They talked for a moment, but I couldn't hear from the porch. My uncle stood and watched until she reached the county road, waving as she turned toward Clavin.

"I'm so glad she came by," Mama said.

"She's a nice lady." My uncle paused. "By the way, I came to tell you I bought a bigger truck over in Meisner."

"That's good news," Mama said.

"I found a used one with low mileage that's been taken care of. It'll be ready on Tuesday afternoon and I was wondering if you could go with me to pick it up? I'm going to keep the old one just in case we need it sometime."

Mama asked me to finish the ironing on Tuesday after school. I don't mind ironing and I knew we had to get Mrs. Martin's things ready or she'd throw a fit.

"Oh, by the way, Laney. Would there be room for another plate on Sunday?"

"Of course. I meant to say something. It slipped my mind when we got off on the new truck."

"Thanks," he said and was gone.

Chapter 12

Hugh McMillan

School started after Labor Day. I was in the eighth grade. I got home that first day, and an unfamiliar car was parked in front of the house. I went around to the back porch as always. Mama called from the front room.

"Annie, please come in here." She paused. "We have company."

A nice looking well-dressed man, about Mama's age, sat on the ugly sofa. I didn't remember seeing him before, but he looked familiar. He stood, smiling. His hair was reddish blonde, freckles dotted his straight pointy nose, and his eyes were green—just like mine. When he put out his hand, I stepped back.

Mama spoke hurriedly. "Annie, this is Mr. Hugh McMillan. An old friend."

"Yes." He paused. "Your mother and I were college classmates."

My face got hot and my hands shook. Thoughts spun through my head. My daddy was supposed to be dead, and here was this "friend" who looked like me. Before he could say anything, I ran to my room and slammed the door. I heard their voices, but had no interest in knowing what they said. Many times I'd thought about Roscoe Turner, the man Mama told me so little about, wishing we were a family—Daddy, Mama and me. I had stopped asking about him because she always found a way not to answer—now this man, who looks like me, shows up. I was furious at Mama, at that man, at everyone who'd never told me the truth.

There was a tap on the door, but I didn't get up from the bed to answer. The door opened.

"Annie, I'm so sorry." Mama's voice quavered.

"Leave me alone," I mumbled, not looking at her.

"I should have told you. I was waiting until you were old enough to understand."

"That was a long time ago." I glared at Mama. "You never want me to know anything, but I had a right to know about … your friend, Mr. Hugh McMillan." I spat his name and tears rushed down my face. Mama tried to put her arms around me, but I pulled away. There was a knock on the door. "Laney? May I come in?

"No," I yelled.

"Come in, Hugh. I've made such a mess of things. I need your help and so does Annie."

He pulled up my desk chair and sat facing me.

"Annie, I'm sorry. I didn't intend to shock you. I'd just arrived and before your mother could get over her surprise, there you were. I am sorry with all my heart."

He didn't try to touch me. He sounded sincere and his face was marked with worry. I calmed down and stopped crying. The three of us sat in silence for some minutes. My stomach churned.

"Annie, I want you to know I didn't come here to shake up your world. I imagine that's how it feels." He paused and looked at Mama who nodded. "I came to visit your mother because at one time we cared very much for one another. I had no idea I would find someone who looks like me."

I knew he was telling the truth. He spoke softly like Mr. Clay, with a touch of our Texas twang. "I'm going now, your mother wants to tell you our story. I hope the three of us can talk tomorrow." He looked questioningly at Mama and she nodded. "It may not be easy, but we have to set things right for you."

He got up to go and smiled. "I look forward to seeing you again, Annie."

Mama saw him to the door. They had a few more words, which I didn't try to hear. When Mama returned, she reached for my hands. I put them in my lap and didn't look at her.

"Please believe I'm sorry you had to find out like this. I wanted to tell you so many times, but I couldn't find the right time or the right words. You realize by now it's hard for me to talk about some things. That's no excuse, but it is the way I am. Today you have borne the brunt of my cowardice, my selfishness. Please forgive me."

In spite of Mama's words, I felt like I'd been snatched up by the wind and whirled around until I'd never be able to think straight again. I didn't hate her, but I was heartsick to think she hadn't trusted me enough to tell the truth when I asked about my daddy.

I spoke clearly and deliberately. "I want to hear the whole story. Right now."

We walked in silence to our favorite place on the river. I didn't notice things as I usually do. One minute I wanted to yell at her, the next I wanted her to wrap me in her arms and make everything good again. We sat some minutes before she began. I didn't say anything until she finished. Her voice no longer quavered and she didn't hesitate.

These are Mama's words as best I remember.

—

Growing up I was like you. I loved school and worked hard so I could go to college and be a teacher. I didn't know what I wanted from life, but I knew an education would enable me to see the world beyond Duddley. When I graduated from high school, your grandma thought I was too young, seventeen, to be away from home. She had her eye on a young man in Duddley who had gone into his father's business and could offer me a secure life. He had his eye on me too. Your grandpa saw differently and arranged for me to attend a school in San Marcos where I could earn a teaching certificate in two years. He expected me to return to Duddley. I didn't mention my ideas.

I loved college, living with other girls from all over Texas. There were lots of young men on campus. I was naive and awkward around them. I went to movies and parties with my friends and sometime boys would join us, but I didn't date.

I met Hugh McMillan in the spring of my freshman year. Hurrying, late for a class, coming around a corner in the hallway, I ran into him. We fell to the floor, books went everywhere. I think he was ready to give me a piece of his mind until he realized I was hurt.

He was very sympathetic and helped me to the infirmary. My ankle was sprained and I had to use crutches. By the time we reached my dorm, we were talking like old friends.

Hugh came every day, carried my books and walked me to my classes. After I no longer needed the crutches, we continued to see one another, studying at the library, going to special events on campus. He was finishing his second year, planning to attend the University of Texas so he could teach high school. His family wanted him to attend law school and practice with his father.

Soon we were planning to spend the rest of our lives together. Since he had two more years and I had one, we couldn't marry right away. Hugh came from an old family in Houston who would never agree to our marrying before their only son finished his education. I wondered at the time how they might feel about their only son marrying someone from the sticks. When I mentioned it to Hugh, he laughed and said they would love me at first sight. I knew my family would love Hugh. We planned to visit our families and announce our engagement after school was out for the summer.

One evening on our way from the library, we walked along a less-traveled, heavily wooded path that took a little longer. We stopped and sat on the grass, talking, touching, kissing. After all our vows to wait, I can't explain why it happened, but it did. Hugh and I became lost in one another. He didn't force me. Do you understand what I'm saying?

I nodded.

I was frightened. Hugh was distraught as I'd never seen him. We talked until time for me to be in my dorm, promising to meet after our last class the next day. Annie, I never saw him again until today.

During the night he had awakened with a high fever. His friends took him to the infirmary and he went into a coma. His best friend came to tell me what happened, but I wasn't allowed to see him. His family took him to Houston in an ambulance that same day.

My telephone calls were cut off as soon as I said my name. I wrote letters that were never answered. His friends received the same treatment.

I was beside myself with worry, hurt and shame. Spending the summer in Duddley was the last thing I wanted. I confided in my best friend, Janet, who lived in Ft. Worth and was planning to work in her father's business as a clerk. She asked me to come and spend the summer with her, working for her father.

I visited my folks for two weeks. Though they were disappointed I wasn't coming home for the summer, they agreed it would be good experience and the money would help. I promised to come for a visit before school started.

After I started my job, I didn't feel well. A visit to the doctor revealed I was pregnant. Oh, Annie, I was so frantic. I couldn't bring myself to go home and tell my family I was expecting a baby whose father had disappeared.

When it came time to return to school, I told them I'd decided to stay on with my job until I had enough money for the second year of school. We had a long discussion, but they agreed. I said I would come for a visit later, that things were too busy right then.

I couldn't continue staying with Janet because her parents would have been scandalized and notified my family. I found a home for unwed mothers run by a Catholic order. They were always kind and caring. I worked mainly in the office and kitchen.

When I think back on that time, I cringe. How stupid I was to not trust my parents. They'd have disapproved, been disappointed in me, but would have helped me. My father would have found Hugh and his family. I was scared and not thinking. Annie, I hope you will always be able to come to me, regardless.

The sisters didn't judge me and I felt safe. The one point of contention was their policy of putting the babies up for adoption as soon as possible. I didn't say anything as first, hoping they would make an exception. I loved you so much already, and I couldn't face giving you away. The sisters also cared for young children who hadn't been adopted or had been left because of a family crisis.

I asked Mother Margaret if they would keep you until I could go back to school, get a teaching job and come for you. She gently refused and while she tried to calm me, I yelled something angry and ran from her office, tears streaming down my face.

There was an older man in the hallway with a wide, long-handled mop, cleaning the floor. He tried to move the mop out of my way, but I stumbled and fell. He knelt and took me in his arms, trying to calm me. Annie, in an instant I felt the most remarkable peace and my tears stopped as though a faucet were turned off.

I recognized the janitor who worked there. I'd seen him in the yard with the children, laughing, playing their games and pushing the swings. He also spent time in the nursery giving bottles, changing diapers and rocking crying babies.

That's how I met Roscoe Turner who became my friend and protector. In a short time he asked me to marry him so I wouldn't have to give you up. Mother Margaret talked with us and in the end gave her blessing.

After our marriage, Roscoe rented a small apartment. He found a better paying job with a janitorial service. We were happy, and each day I realized I was falling more in love with him. We talked endlessly about you and our plans as a family. Those were some of the happiest days of my life.

My friend, Janet, had decided not to go back to school and offered to receive my letters and take any phone calls from my family, making an excuse so I could call later. I became very good at hiding the truth, but it was wrong to involve my staunchest friend. I regret that.

When Christmas came, I pretended I was planning to come home for the holiday. Then I called, said I was in bed with the flu and wouldn't be able to make it. Fortunately, the weather was bad and my dear mother and father were relieved I wouldn't be on a bus traveling treacherous roads. Another lie.

You decided to come two weeks early on a Saturday morning. Roscoe was more excited than I'd ever seen him. He asked me over and over if I had everything in my suitcase, if I was okay. When it was time to go to the hospital, he called a cab. You took your time getting here and since fathers weren't allowed in the delivery room, Roscoe spent ten hours in a waiting room. They took you to the nursery, but not before I saw your beautiful face, the wispy red hair and those green eyes. I had a difficult labor and delivery with some problems so I was taken to surgery.

When I awoke from the anesthesia, I was surprised your daddy wasn't there. The nurses said he'd watched you through the nursery windows and they'd seen few fathers as happy and proud. When he was told I wouldn't be awake for some time, he left saying he hoped there was a florist open. It was eight o'clock by then. He never returned.

You and I were in the hospital for a week. Janet tried to find him, but there wasn't a trace. He hadn't been to the apartment. All of his things were there. The sisters hadn't seen him. I called the police. They said a city bus hit a man on that date when he dashed out between parked cars near the hospital. He was unconscious for a few minutes, but came to before the ambulance arrived. He looked around for a minute, jumped up and ran. The police were unable to find him. I learned later there were flowers scattered on the street.

After you and I returned to the apartment, I continued to check with hospitals and police stations in Dallas as well as Ft. Worth. Nothing. When you were five months old, your grandpa Dickey had a stroke. It was his second. They hadn't told me about the first because it had been mild and he seemed to recover. The second was nearly fatal. I packed us up and came home to Duddley.

That's when I concocted my story about meeting this young man, Roscoe Turner, who was home on leave from the army. We'd had a whirlwind romance and marriage before he left for duty in The Philippines where he was killed in an automobile accident. It was a flimsy story and I don't know how much the family believed, but with Daddy so sick, you and I didn't get a lot of attention.

Six months later my dear father died, and we stayed for a while with your grandma. It wasn't a good arrangement, but we managed until your grandma suggested it would be better for us to have our own place. The hubbub and constant activity of a young child was too much under the circumstances. Your Uncle Riley fixed up the little house for us and I started doing laundry.

I made no more effort to find Hugh. In fact, I never wanted to see him again. I pushed it all out of my mind. I told Riley the real story and he went to Ft. Worth and Dallas to see if Roscoe Turner had appeared. Nothing. I grieved for Roscoe and I still feel sad, but I am convinced he must have been the man hit by the bus. Head injuries can cause amnesia. Some people recover. Some don't.

—

The next day Hugh McMillan was at the house when I came home from school. I'd thought about him almost constantly and decided he was honest and hadn't left my mama on purpose, but I planned to keep my distance. This man couldn't just come in and take Roscoe Turner's place in my heart. I wondered how Mama felt toward him after all this time.

They were sitting at the kitchen table having coffee and pound cake. After I put my things in my room, I sat with them. Mama poured me a glass of milk.

"Your mother tells me you're a good student."

"I guess so."

He smiled. "I didn't get interested in school until I took Mr. Stewart's American history class in eighth grade. Not only did I learn to love history, he took me under his wing and before I knew it, I was enjoying math and English as well." He paused. "Do you have a favorite teacher?"

Without hesitation, I told him about Miss McGhee, mentioning I'd written a couple of stories she'd helped me with. I hadn't shown them to Mama. I thought it might do her good to realize how it feels to not know things.

"I'd like to read your stories sometime, if you don't mind. Thanks to Miss Evans, an English teacher, I started a journal when I was in high school and still write things I want to remember clearly. One day I may try to write a book." He grinned. "What do think about that?"

"I think it's great." I was surprised at how much we were alike. Mama must have decided the conversation had gone far enough because she broke in.

"Annie, I've told you what happened to us all those years ago. Hugh would like to tell you about his life following his illness. How do you feel about that?"

I wasn't sure, but said it would be okay. Mama suggested Mr. McMillan and I sit at the table and talk. She went out to work in the garden.

I was alone with my real daddy.

"I loved your mother from the moment she knocked me down." He laughed and I noticed how his eyes crinkled at the corners, like he laughed a lot. "She was the girl I wanted to spend the rest of my life with. But it wasn't meant to be."

I wrote his exact words as nearly as possible.

He said he nearly died, and the doctors never agreed on a diagnosis. He was in a coma for months. When he regained consciousness he had no memory. They called in specialists and therapists and over the course of a year he regained most of his memory, though there were still blank areas. His two years of school where he met Mama returned in bits and pieces. His family told him Mama hadn't made any attempt to see him or find out what had happened to him.

"Annie, when I finally remembered your mother I had finished my degree at the university, graduated from seminary and decided your mother must have made her own life. I did not recall the evening that put you in the picture. Eventually I met Virginia. We fell in love and married. Our boys, David and Luke, are five and three."

He took a picture from his wallet and I saw a pretty lady who had blonde hair. Two boys looked like their daddy and me. Mr. McMillan wore the collar of a priest.

He continued.

"We live in San Antonio where I'm vicar for an Episcopal Church. After my illness, I wanted to know why I was here, what I was supposed to do with my life. Why had God let me live? But that's a story for another time."

I couldn't take my eyes off the snapshot. All kinds of thoughts churned inside of me. I'd never thought about how it might be to have brothers, but I wanted to meet David and Luke more than anything.

"They have our red hair and green eyes." He laughed.

I handed him the picture, but he insisted I keep it.

"Thank you, Mr. McMillan," I said, holding back the tears.

"About my name," he said. "I don't expect you to call me Daddy or Dad, but how about plain Hugh?" He took my hand.

"Plain Hugh doesn't sound right either. May I call you Hugh?" We laughed and hugged.

I called Mama and we continued our visit in the kitchen. Hugh explained that while he was visiting friends in Clavin, he saw a milk bottle with Uncle Riley's brand name, Dickey's Duddley Dairy. Hugh remembered Mama's name was Dickey and she had come from Duddley. It seemed like an omen.

"I hesitated, wondering how you'd like an old boyfriend turning up, and now that I know the truth, I am overwhelmed with your understanding." He looked at Mama.

Mama smiled. "My life has been good. Roscoe Ann made all the difference." She reached across the table and took my hand. Hugh placed his hand over both of ours.

He stayed for dinner and told us about his life in San Antonio.

"I have a small church on the south side. Most of the congregation is Latino."

"Do you preach in Spanish?" I asked.

"I have two services on Sunday, one in Spanish and the other in English."

Hugh was a great talker. I didn't have to ask many questions. Some of the stories made us laugh, but there was no question about how much he loved what he did. After dinner, Mama washed the dishes, Hugh dried and I put them away. For a little while, it felt like a family, and I wondered why it couldn't have always been like that.

Hugh asked Mama and me to come visit him and his family in San Antonio. He said he wanted to bring his family to Duddley too. Then they started laughing.

"I'll have some explaining to do," Mama said.

"You're not the only one." Hugh chuckled. "Fortunately I told Virginia about my time with you at school. She'll be surprised to learn she has a stepdaughter, but I have no worries. My wife is wise and has a heart as big as the sky. By the way, is there a picture of you two I can have?"

Mama gave him a couple of snapshots taken last Easter when the family got together at Grandma's for dinner. I gave him a picture from school this past year.

"Goodbye, Annie." He held out his arms I welcomed his hug. He kissed the top of my head. "I'll write and we'll figure this out." He and Mama hugged too.

After Hugh left, Mama and I went out on the back porch to watch the sunset. I was still trying to take in all I'd been told.

"Mama, I'm glad you and Hugh told me what really happened, but there's a lot I don't understand."

"I can appreciate that, Annie. Remembering how you came to be has made me see some things differently." She paused and I was afraid she wouldn't continue. "I wish I had trusted my parents. Before my dad died, he said, 'Learn to live with the truth.' I think he guessed my real story."

"But you'd never have met Roscoe Turner." I smiled. "What would you have named me?"

"Not Hugh Ann." Mama laughed.

"Do you still love Hugh?"

"No." Mama thought for a moment. "I don't have the same feelings I had all those years ago, but I am happy to be his partner in raising you. He is a kind, caring person and being a vicar has nothing to do with it. He told me he's felt guilty all these years, even though he had no inkling he had a daughter. He thinks he should have tried harder to find me. I believe his family had a lot to do with that.

"Hugh said he always felt something lay between him and his mother. He's going to Houston soon to talk with her. His father died several years ago and she's frail, but her mind is good. She may be the reason he never received my letters. He doesn't look forward to broaching the subject and wouldn't if it weren't for you. He is hoping she will find comfort in knowing she has a beautiful granddaughter. Regardless of what happens, Hugh loves you and looks on you as an undeserved blessing. 'Grace in my life,' are his words."

"What do you think happened to my daddy Roscoe?"

"I wish I knew. I believe he was that jaywalker, but why he ran and we never heard from him haunts me."

"Do you think he's still alive?"

"Part of me says 'yes.' Part of me says 'no.' I don't like to think he may be dead, however if he is okay, it seems he would have found us by now. He loved you so much, Annie." Mama stopped and I felt her sadness.

We sat for a while, not sharing our thoughts, but there was love between us as never before.

"Mama? When is Mr. Clay coming back?"

"He plans to return as soon as he wraps up some business in Charleston. He hopes it won't be more than a month. Why do you ask?"

I thought carefully before I spoke.

"Do you think you and Mr. Clay might get married one of these days?" I held my breath and waited to get my lumps.

Mama sighed. "Annie, that's a forward question, but considering all the hurt I've caused, I will try to do better." She reached over and took my hand.

"I won't tell anyone," I said, relieved she hadn't given me any lumps. "Promise."

"The honest answer is I don't know. Marcus and I have become more than good friends and he's the first man I've been interested in since Roscoe Turner. After you and I came home to Duddley, I continued to make inquiries to the police in Ft. Worth and Dallas. Riley went up there a second time, but the information was on someone else. Recently Marcus hired a private investigator to make a final search. There's nothing." She held my hand tightly. "I'm so sorry, Annie."

"I know, Mama,"

We rocked for a bit and Mama continued.

"To try to answer your question, Marcus and I are talking about marriage. He's been married before. His wife died just three years ago, after a long illness. They'd been married twenty-four years, but had no children. His grief was so intense that he closed his law practice and traveled. He came to Houston to visit cousins. That's when he read about Mr. Longmire's arrest. He told me he couldn't get the story out of his head. He felt that Mr. Longmire was being accused because of his drinking. On talking with Mr. Longmire, he was convinced of his innocence. Marcus said he felt it in his bones." Mama smiled at me. "He always mentions what a help you were."

"Mr. Clay's a nice man," I said.

"May I ask you a question?"

I nodded.

"Do you think you would like having Mr. Clay as your step-daddy?"

I didn't say anything for a moment. Remembering my conversation with Buddy I thought of Mama being alone when I went off to college, and how it might feel to be a real family. I decided to say what was on my mind.

"I think Mr. Clay would be a wonderful step-daddy. We like one another and I especially enjoy our conversations." I paused. "But in my heart, Roscoe Turner will always be my real daddy. You said he loved me so much before he ever saw me. That means everything."

"What about Hugh?"

"He's one of the nicest people I know. He calls me his daughter, but doesn't insist I call him Daddy. He wants me to know my brothers."

Mama smiled. "Roscoe Ann Turner, you are my wonderful girl—wise beyond your years."

We sat a good while, rocking and humming our favorite songs. Lightening bugs flickered everywhere.

—

On his return, Mr. Clay rented a room at Mrs. Rich's boarding house and office space upstairs in the Duddley Farmers Bank Building.

"I plan to stay," he announced while having Sunday dinner with us. "Duddley needs me and I need Duddley." A slow smile was his way of saying one thing and meaning another. Mama was Duddley.

Mama had told Mr. Clay about Hugh McMillan before he appeared on our doorstep. When she told him I was almost a carbon copy of Hugh, he chuckled.

"It's not funny, Marcus." I'd never heard Mama snap at him before.

"No, but it's important to whether you want to acknowledge Annie's roots." He reached across and patted Mama's hand. She relaxed.

"Did you discuss this with Hugh?" he asked.

"Yes, but we haven't decided what to do." Mama shook her head. "Hugh thought it was humorous too."

Mr. Clay asked, "What does he want to do?"

"He wants to acknowledge Annie and have her get to know her brothers and stepmother, Virginia. There's no denying that Annie and his boys are related."

"I can see where that's a problem for a priest."

"He plans to talk with his bishop. It may or may not cause him difficulties."

Marcus asked if she planned to tell her family.

"Yes. I've told too many lies about Annie and me. Concocting more is ..." Mama's voice cracked and tears gathered in her eyes. Mr. Clay got up, took Mama's hand and gently pulled her to her feet.

"Let's go out in the yard, maybe some fresh air will help," Marcus said. We sat under the oak in the lawn chairs for quite a while, each with our own thoughts. Mr. Clay held Mama's hand and they didn't seem to mind I was there.

Mr. Clay broke the silence.

"As I see it, Laney, you have two choices. You can tell your family the truth, all of it. They're good people who took you in and have stood by you all this time, not asking too many questions. You could have taken the easy way and come home without Annie, but chose to love and nurture her. You can do this too."

Mama nodded. I began to see my mother in a different light. I had mistaken her courage for stubbornness and pride.

"Your other choice it to keep your secret, maintain the status quo and hope for the best. Either way, I suggest you and Annie decide this together."

I was glad he included me, because I had some strong feelings about what we should do. Mama and I looked at one another, her beautiful face drawn and pale. When she finally spoke, each word came as if jerked by an unseen hand.

"I want to stop the lying, Annie. I'm so sorry. Can you ever forgive me?"

I jumped up and hugged my mother as hard as I could. We held on, not crying. My heart was light and happy.

Grandma was shocked at first because she'd never doubted Mama's story. She cried to think Mama had gone through so much.

Telling her sisters was more difficult. Even though Mama was the youngest, they always looked up to her for the way she worked and took care of me. They didn't seem too surprised, but they asked a lot of questions about Roscoe Turner and Hugh. They told her how much they loved and admired her. Aunt Fritzi brought up Marcus, saying how lucky Mama was to get another chance. Mama didn't want Duddley to know, so the sisters agreed the children shouldn't be told until the time seemed right. It worked because Travis and his gang never mentioned it to me.

—

One evening we were sitting in the back yard after supper, trying to cool off when Eddie Lindstrom came.

Mama asked him to sit down.

"Thank you, ma'am, but I can't stay. I came to tell you a long distance call came for you at Mrs. Dickey's. They left a number. Said it was important."

"That's strange," Mama said. A worried look came over her face. "Did they say who was calling?"

"Mama didn't tell me a name. They said it was important. Said to call collect."

Uncle Riley's truck was in the drive, so he took us. Grandma met us at the door, questions pouring out like an overturned bucket of water. Mama hurried to the phone and placed her call. Grandma stopped talking and we stood around while Mama waited for the connection.

"Hello." Mama listened. "Oh, Hugh." I could see it wasn't good news.

"How's your family?" She listened again. "It'll be hard for Annie and me too." My stomach did several flips and I swallowed hard. I hoped my brothers were okay. Mama listened for several minutes.

"Yes, Hugh. We'll keep all of you in our prayers."

Mama hung up, turned around and held her arms out to me. I let her envelop me in her warmth.

"That was Hugh McMillan. He's been called to active duty as a naval chaplain and will be reporting to San Diego next week. He sends his love to everyone."

Mama told us he'd signed up a year ago as the war threat increased. Now that it seemed war was even closer, all the services were building their ranks. He looked forward to serving, but it was hard to leave his family.

I started praying for my daddy's safety that night and continued until it was no longer necessary.

I heard from my daddy frequently. Virginia wrote telling me about my brothers. I sent one of my stories to daddy and he returned it with good suggestions. He encouraged me to write more. He never commented when I started calling him Daddy.

One day I received a letter saying Daddy was going to sea. He couldn't name the ship and didn't know their destination. Marcus said he thought they were sailing because the Japanese had gone into China, killed many people, taken territory. Our government worried about their next move.

Hitler was gobbling up Europe. We sent supplies to England and Russia, but the German U-boats were sinking lots of ships. We listened to the radio every evening and I tried not to worry. Some of the boys in Duddley had been drafted into the army and others joined the navy or marines. I was glad Buddy wasn't old enough and Uncle Riley and Mr. Clay were too old, having served in The Great War.

Mr. Clay spent a lot of time with us. Mama always looked pretty now that she took more time for herself. I liked the idea of Mr. Clay being my stepfather and was anxious for them to marry.

"Hold your horses," Buddy told me one day. "It will happen when it's supposed to."

Chapter 13

Roscoe Turner

One day, I was doing Uncle Riley's bookkeeping when the telephone rang. I answered, hoping it was Buddy.

"Hello, ma'am." I didn't recognize the man's voice. "I'd like to talk to Lanelle Dickey, please. My name is Roscoe Turner."

"Who?" I wasn't sure I'd heard right.

"This is Roscoe Turner. Is Lanelle Dickey there?

I couldn't say a word.

"Hello? Are you Lanelle Dickey?"

"No," I said.

"May I speak to her, please?"

"She's not here." I couldn't believe what I was hearing. At that instant Uncle Riley came into the room. He said later, I looked like I'd seen a ghost.

"What's the matter, Annie?"

I handed him the phone and he barked. "Who is this?" He listened for a moment. "What are you trying to pull? You've scared a little girl half to death." I'd never seen him so angry.

Miss Evy came into the office, took one look, put her arms around me and held me close. She told me later she'd heard Uncle Riley from the kitchen and knew something was wrong.

"What makes you think there's a connection?" My uncle continued to shout. If the man on the phone was my daddy, why was Uncle Riley was so mad?

"I'll meet you tomorrow at the police station in Duddley. At ten o'clock. Don't call here again." He turned around and his face was red as a beet.

"Who was that?" Miss Evy asked.

"Some guy says he's Roscoe Turner. Says he might be Annie's uncle."

My world tipped this way and that. My heart pounded. I was scared to death. If that man was Roscoe Turner, how could he be my uncle?

"Why did that man say he was Roscoe Turner?" I asked.

Uncle Riley looked uncertain, but explained that he claimed to be the brother of the man Mama married.

"He says he's Roscoe Turner, and his brother is Paul Turner. Says he's been looking for him to settle some family business."

"How did he find Laney?" Miss Evy asked.

"He hedged and said it was complicated. That's when I told him to meet me at the police station tomorrow. I thought that might scare him off if he's up to no good, but he agreed and said he looked forward to meeting me." Uncle Riley shook his head.

"Do you think he'll show up?"

"I'm going to call Chief Miller right now, so they'll be on the lookout for him. They might be able to do some checking too." He turned to me. "Don't you worry, Annie. We'll get this straightened out. It's going to be okay."

My uncle put his arms around me and gave me the longest hug ever. Miss Evy and Uncle Riley decided to go over and tell Mama right away. Mama was ironing and Mr. Clay was working on some papers at the kitchen table, as he often did. I was glad he was there, because half way through my uncle's story, Mama began to cry.

"Why do you think he called?" Mr. Clay asked.

My uncle paused. "I wonder if he might try to get some money from Laney. These days you never know."

"Why would he think she has money?" Miss Evy asked.

"She owns property and the dairy has her name on it," Mr. Clay said. "To some people that means money."

"If he's Roscoe Turner, who did Laney marry?" Miss Evy asked.

"I hope we get answers to that and everything else tomorrow." My uncle shook his head.

I hoped we'd find our Roscoe Turner. I hoped he was alive.

The next morning, Uncle Riley and Mr. Clay met Roscoe Turner at the police station. Mama, Miss Evy and I waited at our house so we could do the laundry that was due that day. Uncle Riley and Mr. Clay returned around one o'clock.

"Hi, ladies," my uncle called as he got out of his truck. He waited for Mr. Clay to join him. They were smiling and I figured that was a good sign.

"Things went better than I expected," my uncle said.

"There are some problems, but we can work it out," added Mr. Clay.

"Is he going to make trouble for Mama?" I couldn't hold it any longer.

"Oh, no, Annie. Nothing like that." I noticed Mr. Clay take Mama's hand and hold it.

"Come on," said Miss Evy. "Let's go in. I'm sure you two haven't had a bite to eat."

Over coffee and sandwiches, Uncle Riley told us everything.

"Roscoe Andrew Turner is from Ladalily, Arkansas. He had identification. Chief Miller made some calls and is checking everything, but it looks good. He's the younger brother of Paul Adam Turner."

"What does he want?" Mama asked.

"He wants to get the record straight for one thing. Says he's been looking for his brother off and on through the years. Because the Turners have always lived in Arkansas, that's where he's looked."

"Why did he come to Texas?" Miss Evy asked.

"He's a welder and when a new plant opened in Ft. Worth, he applied for a job. During the hiring process they ran a security check and came up with a Roscoe Andrew Turner who had a Ft. Worth police record of arrests for vagrancy, public drunkenness and disorderly conduct covering several years until 1927. The next record was for employment in 1928 and 1929 at a janitorial service. Then nothing. Until this Roscoe Turner can prove his identity, the company is holding up his employment."

Mama asked, "How did he find me?"

Uncle Riley continued, "He went to Austin looking for his brother's death record, assuming he was dead. Instead, he found a marriage license for Roscoe Turner and Lanelle Dickey, as well as a birth certificate for Roscoe Ann Turner. It wasn't hard to find the Dickey family in Duddley."

"How did he know to call Uncle Riley," I asked.

"He got the Duddley operator and she gave him my number." Uncle Riley paused. "To get the job in Ft. Worth, he must prove his brother assumed his identity. He hopes Laney will be the key. Otherwise, it will take more searching and some legal representation."

"We have to find out what happened," Mr. Clay said. "Laney, can you think of a reason why the man you married used his brother's name?"

"I've racked my brain, but can't remember anything in particular. He never talked about parents or brothers and sisters. I assumed he was estranged from them or they were gone. He told me he'd been married before, but his wife was dead and there were no children." Mama paused. "We weren't together that long and we mostly talked about bringing our baby safely into the world. He would have been a wonderful father. I know that's true, regardless of anything else."

We sat for some minutes not saying anything. My thoughts were going a mile a minute. I wondered about my birth certificate. Was Roscoe Ann Turner my name? Was Mama really married if her husband used someone else's name? I figured Mr. Clay would help with that. In the meantime, I wondered what the real Roscoe Turner was like and decided if they really were brothers, no doubt he would be a good person. I was sure *my* Roscoe Turner had a good reason for taking his brother's name.

"The next day Mama, Mr. Clay and Uncle Riley went to the Duddley police station to meet with Roscoe Turner. I wanted to go, but they said they needed to find out what he had in mind and get a better idea of the kind of person he was. Frankly I thought they'd already done that, judging by yesterday's conversation. I had that feeling of not being told everything again, but there was no use in being angry.

When they came home, Mama looked tired, but she was smiling and gave me a hug. No one said anything about their morning in

Duddley until we were seated at the table, eating vegetable soup, fried chicken and potato salad. Miss Evy saved me from having to ask a forward question.

"What kind of a person is this Roscoe Turner?"

"He seems honest and straightforward." My uncle looked at Mama and Mr. Clay. "Don't you think so?"

"Yes," said Mr. Clay. "I feel better about him than I did yesterday. It took courage to face us, to be open about his life and ask our help in straightening out a difficult situation. He realizes the problem is also Laney and Annie's and doesn't want to make it any harder than it is already."

"I was pleased that he asked about Annie, calling her his niece." Mama smiled at me.

I've tried to remember what Mr. Clay and Uncle Riley told us they learned that morning.

Paul Adam Turner was the oldest of five children. Roscoe Andrew was the youngest. Their father owned a large farm and worked hard, but there were droughts, and boll weevils ate the cotton crops two years in a row. Paul wanted to leave the farm, look for other work and send money back home until things got better. He was fourteen and his father forbade him, took his belt to him for thinking such a thing. As the oldest son, it was his place to stay and work the farm with his father, to do as he was told because one day the farm would be his. Roscoe Turner, even though he was about four at the time, remembered the loud voices and slamming doors. For years the family talked about Paul defying his father and slipping off in the night. They never saw him again.

Times got worse and when the bank took the farm, the family had to move. Roscoe went to live with his mother's brother who was childless and took him in as his own. The uncle made sure he learned a trade—welding. Roscoe saw his parents from time to time. On a visit shortly before his father died, the sick man made Roscoe promise to find his brother and tell him his father was sorry. He's looked for his brother off and on for years. Roscoe decided his brother was probably dead and was shocked when his name turned up in the background investigation. Mr. Clay thought the plant was making something for the military and that was the reason for the background check.

"I believe this fellow is who he says he is," Mr. Clay said. "It will help if we draw up a statement for you to sign, telling how you met and married Paul Adam Turner, thinking he was Roscoe Andrew. We will include how he disappeared and any other details pertinent to proving Roscoe's identity. He plans to go back to Ft. Worth and search for information on the man who was hit in front of the hospital the day Annie was born. I hope this will satisfy the company."

"What will we need to do about our records?" Mama asked.

"We'll have to wait for Roscoe to complete his work. I don't know all the steps, but it will mean changing your marriage certificate and Annie's birth certificate. If you change the name to Paul Adam Turner on your marriage certificate and put the changed name on Annie's birth certificate it may cause Annie some problems later on.

He was not her father the day she was born." Mr. Clay looked at me. "If Hugh McMillan is on the birth certificate, it may cause some problems too, but it is the truth. I understand your feelings, Annie. The decision is up to you."

I thought for a moment before speaking. Through all this, I began to realize that although the man I'd called Daddy had loved me and Mama very much, he had deceived us and caused his brother serious trouble. I gave him the benefit of the doubt, because in our conversations we all thought he'd probably had amnesia when Mama met him. If he was the man in the street, a hard blow to his head could have sent him in all kinds of directions. Mama insisted he wouldn't have knowingly taken his brother's name.

"It feels like I'm losing someone I love very much. But, I am Roscoe Ann McMillan."

Marcus smiled and said he would set things straight.

Miss Evy fixed supper at Uncle Riley's the evening before Roscoe Turner caught a bus to Ft. Worth. We talked a good while. He told us about his family of three boys and two girls. His wife was a nurse and already had a job waiting in Ft. Worth. He remembered how Paul looked out for him since he was the youngest, and his older brothers sometimes picked on him. He asked Mama about his brother and admitted he had been angry until he heard about the good things Paul had done. Mama also told him about her time with Paul. Even though Roscoe didn't look like his brother, Mama said he had his mannerisms and voice.

Eventually everything was taken care of. My birth certificate was changed and I received a letter from my McMillan family in San Antonio, promising a visit. Mama's marriage to Roscoe Turner was annulled because he had used a false name and the marriage had never been consummated. Mr. Clay explained what that meant. I didn't tell him I knew.

Two months after Roscoe Turner's appearance, he wrote to say he'd been able to establish his identity and was working at the plant. His family had moved and they were getting settled. He hadn't found anything to connect his brother with the man who was hit by the bus in front of the hospital. He said he would continue looking and keep in touch.

Chapter 14

Thanksgiving 1941

I was still Roscoe Ann Turner. We didn't intend to have Duddley know the story. As Mama said, "It's no one's business, outside of the family."

Daddy was a chaplain serving aboard ship. He was sick until he got his sea legs. My brothers and Virginia missed him but were doing well. I was anxious to meet them, but we decided that would have to wait until Daddy came home. Calling Hugh "Daddy" had came naturally.

Buddy and his daddy lived in a small house in Duddley. Mr. Longmire said he tended his garden in memory of Mrs. Hooper. Buddy and his daddy fished the river on Uncle Riley's place and often shared their catch. Sometimes Mama persuaded them to stay for supper. Buddy loved the way Mama fried fish and served it with greens and cornbread.

Mama and Mr. Clay spent time together when they weren't working. I had given up on them getting married. In the meantime we became better friends than ever.

One day Mama and I took clean clothes to Grandma. While they visited, I took my book and settled in the swing. I was absorbed in the story when a noise startled me. It was Mr. Clay clearing his throat and smiling.

"Must be a good book."

"It's Sherlock Holmes. Mrs. Wilson said I might like it, and I do."

"He's one of my favorites. May I sit with you?"

"Oh, sure." I loved talking with Mr. Clay because he was interested in what I had to say and was never preachy.

"Is your Mama inside?"

"Yes, we brought over Grandma's laundry"

"Well, I'm glad I saw you. I was on my way to your house. Now that things are settling down, I've wanted to have a private conversation with you." My curiosity sprang into full gear, but I didn't say anything.

"I know you are aware that your mother and I care very much for one another." He paused, looking at me.

"Yes, I've noticed." I hoped I didn't sound smart.

"How do you feel about my asking her to marry me?"

A shiver went through me and I couldn't answer right away. He smiled and waited.

"I would like that," I said, and went on to tell him that I wanted Mama to be happy and would love to have him as my stepfather. "I had doubts in the beginning, but I don't feel that way anymore."

Marcus smiled. "I can see you've given this much thought and that's good. Your feelings are important to me and I thank you for being so forthright. We're a good team. I hope your mother will feel the same way. Caring about one another and being married are two different things."

It dawned on me that he hadn't asked Mama to marry him. He was asking me before he proposed. For once, I knew something first.

"I plan to take your mother to dinner in Clavin tomorrow evening and, with your blessing, give her this." He took a small velvet box from his jacket pocket. It held a ring with a single bright diamond. I caught my breath.

"It's beautiful, Mr. Clay. That will look perfect on Mama's hand."

Just then Mama came around the corner of the house. I could tell she was surprised to see Mr. Clay.

"What are you up to?"

I hoped she hadn't heard any of our conversation.

"Just good friends spending good time together," Mr. Clay said. He slipped the box into his pocket like magic. He drove us home and came in for coffee.

"Laney, would you have dinner with me at the Cornelius House in Clavin tomorrow evening?" He paused. "Take off one Sunday from cooking."

"My goodness," said Mama. "That's a nice place. What do you think, Annie?" She thought he meant both of us.

"I think you'd have a good time."

Mama looked at me questioningly. I thought as fast as I could.

"I was going to ask if I could spend tomorrow with Buddy and his daddy."

"Doing what?" Mama frowned.

"They want to go fishing and have a picnic down by the river. Buddy wants me to know his daddy better." I crossed my fingers behind my back. "Please?"

Mama was puzzled that I wanted to be with Buddy and his daddy, rather than her and Mr. Clay at a nice restaurant, but she smiled and said it sounded like fun. She couldn't see Mr. Clay when he held up his hand, making a circle with his thumb and forefinger.

After my invented story, I asked to go over to Uncle Riley's to catch up on bookkeeping. I called Buddy and told him the whole thing. He was happy for me, but wanted to know how I got to be such a good liar.

Buddy told his daddy my good news, and we had a great time on the river. Mr. Longmire is quiet, but good company.

Mama and Mr. Clay came home late. I've never seen Mama so happy. Her eyes sparkled and her cheeks were rosy. She held out her hand.

"Marcus says this will come as no surprise to you." We hugged and shed a few tears. Mr. Clay never quit smiling.

Mr. Clay said he was tired of Mrs. Rich's boarding house and suggested they marry before Thanksgiving. Mama wanted it to be simple. They decided the wedding and reception would be at

Grandma's because it was difficult for her to get out. The living room was large enough for the number of guests, and the dining room would be just right for the reception buffet. Mrs. Lindstrom insisted on making all the preparations. Uncle Riley was best man and Miss Evy was maid of honor. When I told Buddy I hoped my uncle would notice how beautiful Miss Evy was in her bridesmaid dress, he accused me of being a matchmaker.

The ceremony was on Saturday before Thanksgiving, a sunny, crisp afternoon. Mr. Longmire transformed Grandma's house into a garden. A friend of Miss Evy played "I Love You Truly" and "Annie Laurie" on her violin. Before I knew it Mama was Mrs. Marcus Claiborne.

Mrs. Lindstrom's table was magnificent, and I'm sure none of the guests had ever enjoyed a more elegant repast. Mr. Clay toasted Mama with champagne, and there was sufficient for all who preferred it to sparkling cider. The ceremony was short, but the reception lasted until people had to go home and look after stock and such. Grandma enjoyed herself, but when the last guest was gone, she sighed and said she thought they'd never go home.

Mama and Mr. Clay left about an hour after the ceremony. Miss Evy caught Mama's bouquet. Someone tied cans to Mr. Clay's car and wrote *Just Married* on the trunk. We threw rice. They had reservations in Houston, a two-hour drive.

"You can stop worrying," Buddy said, grinning. "You have a great daddy and a wonderful stepfather. What more could you want?"

Buddy ducked his head, like he does when he's embarrassed, then looked up at me. "Would you like to go to the movies tomorrow night?" He paused. "Clark Gable's in it."

"I'll have to ask Aunt Evy, but I think she'll let me. For some reason she likes you." I grinned.

Buddy and I didn't call it a date, though some of our friends tried to make something of it. I've never understood why people don't realize that a boy and girl can be just friends.

—

We celebrated Thanksgiving, at Grandma's as always, two days after Mama and Mr. Clay returned. They kept it simple since we'd just had a big wedding reception. We named our many blessings.

After dinner, Mr. Clay asked me to walk with him. He said he needed to "walk off some of that turkey." We didn't say anything until he stopped and looked at me.

"Annie, I'm the happiest man alive today. I am married to the most wonderful woman in the world and you are my daughter. However, I don't expect you to call me Daddy. Hugh is truly your daddy and you are blessed." He paused. "I would like to have you call me Marcus. Please."

"Oh, yes," I said and nearly knocked him down with a big hug. He chuckled and hugged me back. We walked to the park and sat in the gazebo, talking about everything. He was more than a stepfather. He was my true friend and we loved one another.

One evening Marcus came home with plans for a house and Mama didn't seem surprised. The house had a living room, dining room, kitchen, bedroom and bath on the first floor. The second floor had three bedrooms and a bath. Marcus asked me what I thought about it.

"It looks real nice," I said. "Where will you build it?" I loved our little house and was afraid they planned to tear it down.

"Because your uncle was so generous when he sold this property to your mother there's sufficient space to build to the west and still have a good yard, without tearing this house down. There are some large oaks over there too." Marcus paused. "I would like to do some renovation inside this house to accommodate my law practice."

"And a bathroom." Mama said.

"I thought we might make a small library in your room, Annie, for my overflow of law books as well as a place for you to write and store your book surplus."

I couldn't wait.

Chapter 15

December 1941

On December 7, 1941, Mama, Marcus and I finished dinner and sat at the table discussing plans for the new house. Mama and Marcus would have the downstairs bedroom and bath. I was excited about having a larger bedroom and a bathroom to myself upstairs. Another upstairs bedroom was to be Mama's sewing room and guest bedroom. The third room was extra for now. I hoped there might be a brother or sister one day, though I knew better than to say it out loud.

There was a knock on the back screen door. Uncle Riley called, "Laney? Marcus?"

"Come in." Mama went out to the back porch. "Good grief, Riley. Did you run over here?"

"Pretty much." My uncle's face was red and he was out of breath.

"Sit down." Mama got him a glass of water.

"Is something wrong?" Marcus asked.

"The Japanese bombed Pearl Harbor."

I knew Pearl Harbor was in Hawaii, a long way from Japan, and wondered how they got there.

"They don't know what all happened, but most of the Pacific fleet was in the harbor and has been sunk or set on fire. The Japanese planes came over Oahu and bombed the airfields, destroying planes on the ground so our boys couldn't even get up there and fight them."

He gulped the water and caught his breath—worry lines creased his face. I'd never seen my uncle like this. He had been in The Great War, and I wondered if this brought back memories. He never talked about his time in France, but he'd been there during the trench warfare.

Marcus turned on our small radio. The news was on, and some of it was difficult to understand, but we heard enough to realize our lives would never be the same. The ominous cloud that hung over us these last two years poured down in a torrent. President Roosevelt called it, "A date which will live in infamy." I was scared and thought about my daddy, praying his ship was still out to sea.

War was soon declared between the Allied nations, America, Britain and France, and the Axis countries, Germany and Italy. There would be more joining the fight. We listened to the radio every evening hoping somehow it wouldn't be as bad as we feared, but it got worse.

A week before Christmas the war came to our house. Marcus received a call from Washington D.C. He was too old to be recalled to military service, but he was being recruited to serve as a civilian. Mama was upset, though she tried not to be. Marcus explained that he could not turn down the request.

It was decided that Mama and Marcus would go to Washington and find a place for us to live. It would be hard because the threat of war had already caused a housing shortage. I didn't like the idea of being separated from Mama, but she needed to be with Marcus and I didn't want to change school in the middle of the year.

Mama worried about this sudden change in our lives.

"Annie, I hope you understand how important it is for Marcus to take this job. The request comes from someone he worked with in The Great War, and now that person is one of the president's closest advisors. It would be impossible for him to refuse, even if he wanted to, and he feels like he needs to do this." She smiled and hugged me.

"I understand, Mama. I'm glad you can go with him, but I want to finish this year in Duddley."

"I thought you might feel that way, and I've been talking to your grandmother."

"I know. She wants to teach me to embroider and quilt."

"Don't you want to stay with her?" Mama looked surprised.

"No," I said, feeling terrible.

"You'll have a nicer room. You won't have to walk so far to school. You'll see more of your friends." Mama smiled. "It's only until May."

"I love Grandma, but she talks about things that happened years ago, over and over. She asks questions about things I don't want to talk about. How would I practice piano every day?"

"I understand, Annie, but your aunts don't have room for you and you can't live out here alone even though your uncle's nearby."

"Why can't I stay with Uncle Riley?" I'd thought about that from the beginning, but wasn't sure how he might feel about having me underfoot. Uncle Riley's used to living alone and seems to like it that way.

"Riley?" Obviously Mama hadn't thought about that either. "Maybe. It wouldn't be for long." She paused. "You could come over here and practice, look after things. Riley certainly isn't going to talk your ears off or ask too many questions." She was giving it some serious thought. "We'll see what he thinks about it." I crossed my fingers.

Marcus thought it was a good idea. "She'll be able to continue doing the bookkeeping." He smiled at me.

Mama's leaving was a problem for my uncle because she and I did all the paperwork in addition to her making deliveries twice a week. Mama and Marcus decided to talk with my uncle at supper that night.

"Riley, I feel like I'm leaving you in the lurch going to Washington on such short notice," Mama said.

"I'm going to miss you, no doubt about it. However, I have some news that might make you feel better." Uncle Riley sipped his coffee. "Cal Higgins' boy is home. He was hurt in a training accident at Ft. Hood last year. He lost part of his left leg. Cal says he's learned to walk with an artificial leg. He can drive and needs a job."

"That's wonderful, Riley. I'm glad you can hire him, but can he handle the cartons and crates?"

"Cal thinks he'll do fine. Says Ben is big, strong and determined to live a normal life. He's got a nice girlfriend over in Clavin and they plan to get married. He's coming over next week so we can talk."

I guess Mama figured this was a good time to talk about me.

"Riley, there's something else. If you don't want to do it, please tell me. It won't hurt my feelings." Mama paused, looked at Marcus as though she expected him to say something, but he smiled and nodded as if to say, "You're doing fine." She took a breath.

"Annie wants to finish the school year here. I think it's best too, however, she needs a place to stay and ..."

Uncle Riley grinned. "Would you like to live with me, Annie? Think you can stand an old bachelor who's set in his ways?"

My hugs always make my uncle squirm, but he got one anyway.

On Christmas Day we had our traditional family get-together at Grandma's. But, it was different. Without saying anything, we knew this was the last of an important part of our family's life. We realized how much we loved one another in spite of any differences we'd had.

Two days later, Aunt Fritzi's husband, Lou, loaned us his Buick so I could go along when Uncle Riley drove Mama and Marcus to Houston. Saying goodbye was harder than I'd expected.

On the way home I told Uncle Riley how I much appreciated him taking me in.

"I'm looking forward to it," he said. "You remember Buddy spent several months with me when his daddy had all that trouble? I enjoyed his company and missed him when he went home. You and your mama have been good to me, but there are times my house seems like a tomb." He didn't take his eyes off the road, but I could see he was smiling.

"Besides keeping up with the dairy's paperwork, you need to do as much around the house as you can," Mama said. "You're a good worker. I know you'll do fine."

I was concerned about doing Mama's share of the paperwork, but that was solved when Uncle Riley hired Ben Higgins' girlfriend, Leatrice, to do the bookkeeping and paperwork. She had finished a course at business school.

I washed and ironed our clothes and the linens over at my house. One Saturday just as I was setting up to iron, there was a knock at the front door. It was Mrs. Gorsham.

"Oh, Annie. It's you." She looked and sounded disappointed.

"Yes, ma'am." What else could I say?

"I saw the house open and hoped your mother had come back from her ... uh ... honeymoon?" She actually lifted her upper lip on the word honeymoon—as though she smelled something bad.

"No, ma'am." I wasn't going to make it easy for the old biddy. I remembered her conversation with Mrs. Hooper about how strange Mama and I were, and how they wouldn't give my name to a dog.

"Well, I haven't been able to find anyone reliable to do my laundry. The good ones have gone off to the factories. I wonder, could you help?"

"You mean me? Do your laundry?" I tried to sound incredulous, emphasizing *your.*

"Well, yes. Of course. I'd pay you the same rate your mother charged." She hadn't liked my reply. "Surely you can use the money." She thought she had me.

"It'll probably come as a surprise to you Mrs. Gorsham, but I don't need the money. However, I do need time for school work."

I wanted to slam the door, but didn't want to miss the look on her face. She stood for a moment, lips pursed, cheeks puffed, eyebrows arched. She turned on her sensible heels and stomped toward her shiny black car. Then I slammed the door.

Chapter 16

Uncle Riley and Miss Evy

Living with Uncle Riley was a happy time for me. Though he was quiet and undemonstrative, I knew he loved me like I was his own. Miss Evy came over nearly every day to help with cleaning and cooking so I'd have more time with my friends after school.

I noticed that Uncle Riley was more talkative when Miss Evy was there, though they were about as different as two people could be. They say opposites attract, but I think what matters most is when two people are kind, respectful and explore their differences. My uncle learned to appreciate classical music. Miss Evy learned to ride a horse.

Another thing I liked was seeing Buddy almost every day. On Saturdays Uncle Riley invited him to stay for supper. Buddy always brought a change of clothes and showered in the barn. Most Saturdays we'd walk to Duddley after supper to see the movie.

"I'm glad you're staying with Mr. Riley," Buddy said one evening.

"Really?" I said, wondering.

"I get to eat more of your cooking." He chuckled.

"Thank you." I liked to cook and be complimented.

"Yeah, my daddy and I can put a decent meal on the table, but nothing like yours or your mother's." I knew Buddy's favorites were Mama's fried chicken and lemon meringue pie.

"Thank you," I said.

"Know something else? Mr. Riley invites me a lot more than he used to."

"That's because he likes you. He told me he missed you when you went home."

Buddy didn't say anything for a moment.

"Oh? I thought he wanted someone to keep an eye on you."

Buddy grinned and I punched him on the shoulder.

"Think you're so smart," I snapped, but my heart flipped.

Buddy was on my mind a lot. Moving to Washington D.C. meant I wouldn't see him for a long time, maybe not until the war was over. No one knew how long that would be. I could tell he liked me. I liked him, but thought I should keep him guessing. In the movies, and in stories I read, the girl who got the boy played hard to get. Now, I wondered if Buddy would become interested in another girl if I weren't around. I'd seen Barbara Hanson stop him and straighten his shirt collar as she talked to him. He moved out of reach and didn't tarry, but it bothered me. I never said anything to him.

After the movie, we walked along the county road. As we approached my uncle's place, we saw Miss Evy driving away toward Clavin.

"Wonder why she didn't wait to say hi?" Buddy asked.

"That is strange," I said. "I asked her to supper this evening, but she said she had some calls to make."

We walked on and when we got to the front porch, I spoke.

"Want to come in for more apple pie?"

"Sounds good, but my dad and I are getting up early so we can go fishing at Eagle Bluff Lake."

Before I could say another word, Buddy gave me a peck on the cheek and loped out to the county road, swinging his flashlight. I placed my fingers where his lips had touched. A shiver ran through me. I watched until he was out of sight, wondering how it would feel if he kissed me on the lips.

Uncle Riley was sitting in the front room. He looked up from the newspaper.

"How was the movie?"

"Okay. I've seen better."

"Did you ask Buddy to come in?"

"Yes, but he says he needs his sleep, working for you."

I grinned so he'd know I was teasing. Uncle Riley chuckled, but before I could tell him the real reason, the telephone rang. I knew it was Mama because she called every Saturday about the time she thought I'd be home from the movie.

"Hi, Mama. I'm so glad to hear from you." I struggled to keep my voice steady. Even though Uncle Riley and I were doing fine, I missed her more than I ever dreamed.

"Oh, Annie, you have no idea how lonesome I am for you. If we find a house soon, I may come back earlier than I planned." She told me about their house search. Some of the places sounded awful and everything was high as a cat's back. She asked about school, Miss Evy and my piano lessons. Marcus came on, but talked briefly because he knew how much Mama and I needed to visit. Uncle Riley whispered that he wanted to talk to her when I finished.

After a while, we said goodbye. I gave the phone to my uncle and went into the kitchen. Uncle Riley told Mama about Ben and Leatrice, and how good everything was going. He lowered his voice but I heard him tell Mama that Miss Evy was thinking about going back to that girls' school in Baltimore.

"They want her to be head of the music and arts program," my uncle said. "She hasn't made up her mind. She's really torn. As much as she wanted to leave Clavin all those years ago, she says these last months have made her want to stay forever. I guess money is a problem after her mother's long illness."

Mama said something.

"She came over to tell me this evening."

Mama said something else.

"I thought she just wanted to talk it over with somebody. That's all."

After that, Mama was on the line, with "yeah" and "I know" coming from Uncle Riley.

"You're right, Laney. But I don't know how to say those things. You know me."

Mama talked again. Then my uncle.

"Oh, Laney, I've never felt like this about anyone before." His voice shook. "Will you call her?"

The conversation continued, but I went to my room. I didn't want my sweet uncle embarrassed to find his niece taking it all in. The prospect of losing my dear friend and teacher plus my uncle's reaction made me want to cry.

Sunday morning I fixed pancakes and sausage, Uncle Riley's favorites. He thanked me but was preoccupied and picked at his breakfast. Puffy circles under his eyes told me he hadn't slept much. I kept his coffee cup full while wracking my brain, trying to think of some way to cheer him up.

"Uncle Riley?" He didn't seem to hear me. "Uncle Riley?"

"Yes?" He finally looked up.

"May I call Miss Evy and ask her to come for supper tonight?"

"That would be fine." He emptied his coffee cup, leaving most of the pancakes and sausage.

I called Miss Evy, trying to make my invitation sound ordinary. She thanked me but said she had promised to visit her family over in Meisner. She expected to be home quite late.

I was disappointed and told Uncle Riley when he came in at noon for the light dinner I'd fixed.

"That's too bad," he said in a monotone. After a few bites he got up and went into the living room.

I finished cleaning up and looked in on him. He hadn't turned on the radio, so I expected to find him napping in his chair. Instead, he sat staring at the wall. I hesitated to disturb him, but I was going over to my house and didn't want him to worry.

"Uncle Riley?" No answer. "Uncle Riley?" He turned toward me and I could tell he had been deep in thought.

"Yes?" He smiled as though it was an effort.

"I'm going home to practice. Maybe do some cleaning?"

He nodded and sighed.

When I returned several hours later, I saw my uncle's truck turn in from the county road. Miss Evy was with him. I waited on the porch.

"Hi Annie," my uncle said, smiling ear to ear as he got out of the truck. I watched as he went to the other side and opened the door for Miss Evy and gave her his hand as she stepped from the running board. Miss Evy was all smiles too. I wondered what happened to her trip to visit her family.

"Come on," my uncle said, "let's go in the house."

In the living room Uncle Riley and Miss Evy sat side by side on the sofa. They were cheerier than I'd ever seen either of them.

"Annie ..." My uncle was looking for the right words. "You know we get along really good, Evy and me. "He looked at Miss Evy who hadn't taken her eyes off of him. I knew that look.

"You're going to get married," I blurted. "Oh, I'm sorry. I shouldn't have said that." I felt my face getting hot and I wanted to bite my tongue, but it was too late.

"Exactly." My uncle grinned. "I couldn't have said it better myself." He reached for Miss Evy's hand. She leaned over and brushed her lips against his cheek, then turned toward me.

"I'm going to love being your aunt."

"This is the best news since Mama and Marcus got married," I said, smiling and laughing at the same time.

It seems my uncle drove over to Miss Evy's before she left for Meisner. I would never know what all happened, but my uncle told Miss Evy how he felt and asked her to marry him. She told me years later she'd almost given up waiting for him to speak. She had no intention of taking that job in Baltimore, but hoped it might make him think about life without her.

They told me Miss Evy would move to Uncle Riley's house after they married, so I could stay put. Permanent arrangements would be made after I moved to Washington. I wondered about their wedding plans and Miss Evy seemed to read my mind.

"We're going to be married at my house in Clavin because it's large enough for our families to gather, and if the weather is good we can celebrate out of doors too."

Miss Evy was radiant. Remembering Mama, I was amazed at how love transformed people. I checked my uncle and he was downright handsome.

Six weeks later they were married in the parlor against a bank of spring flowers. My aunts did a beautiful job. One of Miss Evy's students played the piano, a friend played the harp and a cousin sang "I Love You Truly." I had goose bumps.

Miss Evy's long sleeved gown was fine lace over yellow silk. Falling softly over her bosom from a round lace collar, it outlined her slender form, draping to the floor in a modest train. A narrow wreath of tiny yellow roses rested on her silver upswept hair. She carried a small bouquet of yellow roses nestled in baby's breath.

When Miss Evy asked me to be her attendant, I was thrilled beyond words. We shopped in Meisner and found a floor length crepe dress cut in a princess style. It was the palest green I'd ever seen. A V-neck and long sleeves were trimmed in ivory piping. I wore Grandma's pearls. My white slippers had a slight heel, giving me some height.

"You're a knock-out," Buddy whispered.

Uncle Lou was best man, Buddy and Eddie were ushers. They wore dark gray suits with a small yellow rose in the lapel. Mrs. Lindstrom worked her magic again to include a three tiered wedding cake. The day was sunny and warm so we visited on the veranda and in the garden as well as in the house. Miss Evy's family, the Dickeys and a few friends made a good sized gathering. We missed Mama and Marcus, but I wrote Mama and she said it was almost like being there.

A violinist and bass player joined the piano and harp in the parlor, playing popular songs for dancing. All the furniture had been moved to the side and the carpets rolled up. I discovered my uncle knew how to dance. He and Aunt Evy made a striking couple. Buddy and I went to dances at school and weren't bad either.

"Two weddings in three months," Buddy said. "We're getting to be social butterflies." He grinned as he spun me out and gathered me in.

"I love it," I said. "I wonder who we can persuade to get married next." I was trying to be humorous.

"I can think of a couple," Buddy said. "But it may take a while."

"Why?" I wasn't thinking.

"They're not old enough to get a license."

I looked up at his smiling face. "Oh."

My heart pounded and I was afraid if I said anything, I'd sound like an idiot. I put my head on his shoulder and he tightened his arm around my waist. His heart was pounding too.

Chapter 17

Spring 1942

After the wedding, I began thinking about the move to Washington D.C. Some days I was excited about a new house, new school, and living in a big city with museums, theaters and historical sites. I couldn't wait to see Mt. Vernon, the Lincoln Memorial, Arlington Cemetery, the Washington Monument, all the things Miss McGhee had told us about. The Atlantic Ocean wasn't that far. I could hardly wait. Then it would hit me. I'd be leaving my friends, especially Buddy. Grandma wasn't doing well. Uncle Riley and Aunt Evy were like second parents. Would I find a piano teacher as good as my aunt? Mama tried to prepare me whenever we talked on the phone.

"Annie, Washington is a beautiful city with many things to see and do, but you have no idea the number of people—they're all in a hurry. Because of shortages, stores are always full of shoppers looking for food, clothing and household items. Rationing makes it difficult to plan meals. I'm learning how to make everything last as long as possible. We had some of that in Duddley, but here it's almost overwhelming. I told Marcus I hope we can find a house with enough yard so I can plant vegetables. Some folks turned their flower gardens into vegetable gardens. There are also areas set apart where people lease a space. They call them Victory Gardens."

Mama couldn't tell me anything about school because it would depend on where they found a house. She and Marcus had a small apartment in Arlington, Virginia. Marcus rode a bus to his office every day. Sometimes he had to wait for a second bus because so many people were riding instead of driving. The gasoline shortage was acute and Marcus wasn't sure they would even try to buy a car. Finding one would be a problem too.

They decided to look for a house in the District because Marcus would be working downtown as soon as his clearance came through. When I asked what a clearance was, Mama laughed.

"They want to make sure he isn't a spy in a seersucker suit planning to steal military secrets."

The war news was discouraging until April 19. The day before, General James Doolittle and his crew, along with twenty-four other crews, bombed Tokyo and other war targets in Japan. It was a while before we learned they had taken off from an aircraft carrier about eight-hundred miles from Japan. Some of the planes reached China, some crashed in the China Sea and one landed in Russia. There were many unanswered questions, but the idea of our planes striking Japan in retaliation for Hawaii made everyone feel like we would win the war. President Roosevelt spoke over the radio and warned that even though our pilots had struck a powerful blow against Japan, the war was far from over.

After this, several young men who were waiting to be drafted signed up. Mr. Mathews announced he was going into the navy after school was out. He would go to officers' training before being assigned to duty. We hadn't heard from my daddy in several weeks, which wasn't unusual, but I prayed as hard as I could for his safe return.

At our last assembly, Miss McGhee announced that she was joining the Women's Army Auxiliary Corps. We were stunned at first and then clapped wildly. Afterward she spent time with those of us who wanted to know more about her plans. She told us that on May 14 Congress passed a bill creating the Women's Army Auxiliary Corps, and on the next day President Roosevelt approved the bill and authorized a strength of 25,000 women to serve in the army at jobs that would release soldiers for combat.

"Are you going to get a gun?" someone asked.

"No."

"Will you wear a uniform and march in parades?"

"Yes. But first I will be interviewed and have a physical to make sure I'm healthy. If I'm accepted, I'll report to Ft. Des Moines, Iowa in July for training."

"Where will you go afterward?"

"I have no idea."

When we asked how she found out about the WAAC, she said she had followed the progress of the bill to create the corps when it was introduced in May 1941 by Congresswoman Edith Nourse Rogers. The idea of a women's army had been discussed for years following the Great War. Miss McGhee said she hoped she could pass the various hurdles. We assured her she would be an outstanding WAAC. I was happy for her, but felt sad because it seemed our lives were drifting apart. I stayed behind to give her my good wishes, and said I hoped we would see one another someday.

"We will, Annie. I promise. And I want you to promise me something too."

I looked at her questioningly.

"Keep writing. Even though I won't be able to help, you have made giant steps and are ready to go on alone. Promise?"

"Oh, yes, ma'am. I promise. I'm keeping my journal and when I see you again, you can help me find the stories."

We hugged and I didn't cry.

Several other young women in Duddley signed up for the WAAC. I overheard some remarks one day when I was at the grocery store. Mr. Hoseman was talking with a couple of older men.

"Yeah, them gals don't know what they's getting' into. Army's a rough life."

"Maybe they figure it'll be worth it." Mr. Loakie snickered.

"Whadda you mean?" asked Goody Barmis.

"They's old maids. Couldn't make a catch in these parts. The grass is always greener, you know."

They laughed and snorted until they started coughing and hacking. I gritted my teeth.

On our next phone visit, Mama told me they'd found a house.

"It's a row house in the northwest section of the District."

"What's a row house?"

Mama explained there were five two-story brick houses on our block, built side by side, with common walls. Ours would be an end house with windows on the west, a bay window facing the street and three bedrooms and a bath on the upper floor. The living room, dining room, kitchen and pantry are on the ground floor. We'll move in on July 1." Mama sounded happy and excited.

Mama planned to come as soon as she could get a reservation. Marcus couldn't get away. His clearance had come through and he was working ten hours a day, five, sometimes six, days a week. Mama said she hoped it wouldn't always be like that.

"Washington is like a beehive, so many people rushing here and there. It's a different world, Annie." I wondered if Mama was happy in her new world. I hoped being a family again would help. Even though I was well taken care of, I knew she worried about me.

Mama arrived the first week of June. We were beyond happy to see one another, laughing and crying at the same time. I realized I couldn't possibly stay in Duddley, though I loved living with my aunt and uncle. After Mama rested from her trip, Aunt Evy invited Miss McGhee for lunch. Uncle Riley was going to be in Clavin all day.

"We're having a hen party," Aunt Evy chuckled as she greeted Miss McGhee.

"Your husband is one of the most patient people I know," Miss McGhee said, "but I'm glad he won't have to listen to our chatter." We laughed.

I felt special to be included and vowed not to pop up with something forward. The conversation quickly centered on Miss McGhee and her approaching departure.

"I must admit I'm excited and scared out of my wits," she said. "I wake up in the middle of the night and think, 'What have you gotten yourself into?'"

"It sounds like an opportunity to do something important for our country and see what goes on in the world," Aunt Evy said. "When I was your age, I was on the verge of volunteering for duty with the Red Cross in Europe when the news came that my fiancé had been badly wounded and would be returning." There was a catch in my aunt's voice.

Miss McGhee told us she applied for a commission based on her education and work experience. She had been chosen to go to officers' training and would graduate as a first officer. The WAAC was an auxiliary corps and not part of the army, but merging with the regular army was in the works.

"I'll be a captain. And guess what, Annie?" She turned to me, smiling. "We'll get to see one another from time to time because I'm being assigned to Ft. Meade, Maryland, about thirty miles from Washington."

Doubts about being happy in my new home began to melt away.

Mama and I sorted through my things and decided which should go to Washington and which we'd store in our little house. Leaving some of my things in the little house softened the anxiety of leaving.

Even though our new house had six rooms and a bath, Mama said the rooms were small and closet space was limited.

"The good thing is we won't have to buy so much furniture." Mama laughed.

"Will there be room for a piano?" I asked.

"We'll find room."

The hardest part was leaving Buddy. After Mama arrived, I didn't see him every day and he didn't come up to the house as often. One Saturday, I found him cleaning out the milking stalls. He was talking to himself, but I couldn't make it out. I spoke.

"Hi."

He jumped like he'd been shot.

"Having some deep thoughts?" I asked.

He blushed, smiling slowly.

"Not hardly. Just wool gathering."

"I was wondering if you can stay for supper this evening? Mama's in the kitchen and it's going to be fried chicken and lemon meringue pie." I had asked Mama to fix his favorites.

When he didn't answer right away, I was afraid he would say, "No." He glanced down for a moment. He looked uncomfortable.

"Thanks, Annie, but I don't want to horn in on your family. Y'all have lots to talk about …"

I cut him off.

"Since when can't you stand to listen to us talk?"

"I didn't mean that."

I knew he didn't. "Then it's settled. We'll expect you at the regular time." I turned to go and then remembered. "Do you have some clean clothes with you?"

He frowned. "Of course, I do."

"How about the movie afterward?" I smiled to let him know the teasing was over.

"Sounds great." He smiled.

Supper was delicious and everyone got into the conversation. Aunt Evy asked Buddy about the calf he'd helped pull the week before when my uncle had been in Houston on business. The veterinarian hadn't expected it for a couple of weeks, but all of a sudden it was coming and Buddy was the only one there. The calf and the veterinarian arrived at the same time. After it was over, Doctor Ford said he couldn't have done better.

"It was scary," said Buddy, "but there's something wondrous about a little critter taking its first breath, crying and snuggling up to his mother."

"Think you might become a veterinarian?" Mama asked.

"I don't know." Buddy paused. "Maybe."

Buddy and I walked into Duddley to see the movie. We always went dutch except for popcorn and cokes. That was his treat. Afterward we walked home along the county road. It was barely light.

"I'm going to miss you," Buddy said.

"I'm going to miss you too."

"I mean really, really miss you."

His voice cracked and I realized we were talking about more than missing one another. I didn't know what to say.

"Ever since that day you whacked Emile Corse with your book bag, even though he was bigger, you've been special, Annie."

"You've been special ever since then too."

"I wish you weren't going away."

"I have to. It's my family."

"I know."

We walked on in silence and soon turned into my uncle's lane. Just outside the yard gate, Buddy stopped and took my hands.

"I'll always be here, Annie, no matter how far away you go. I'll wait."

Chapter 18

Washington D.C.

Marcus met us at Union Station the day before we were to move into our house. He had been able to buy essential furniture, kitchenware, linens and groceries. It was hard to find some things because of shortages, but in a way, it was fun. We felt so clever when we tracked down items such as an electric toaster, rubber doormats and metal curtain rods. Marcus used the third bedroom for a study and we made bookshelves from cinder blocks and boards.

The first Saturday after Mama and I arrived, we called Uncle Riley and Aunt Evy. Mama talked a bit, but soon gave me the phone. She knew I was bursting to tell them everything. It happened that Buddy was there, so we talked too. I missed him, but didn't want to say it with Mama and Marcus right there. Buddy said he missed me, so I said, "Me too." I figured my aunt and uncle weren't there to hear him. When I looked around, Marcus and Mama had gone to the kitchen. I told Buddy how much I missed him in spite of all the excitement in my life. He said he would try to call me the next Saturday.

Mama seemed to enjoy putting our new home together, but she tired often, and we rested when she felt like it. I helped her prepare vegetable beds in our small front yard before winter set in. Many people had gardens because the war reduced food supplies for civilians. We planted carrots, green beans, yellow squash and tomatoes. The summer was hot and promised to be longer. Trips out to Maryland's countryside gave us vegetables and late blackberries.

People at a roadside stand told us to be sure and return for apples and cider in the fall.

The public schools were crowded because of a teacher shortage. Parents in Marcus' office suggested he look at private schools. He found a small girls' school, Norwynn Hall, within walking distance of our house. We went together for my interview.

"Don't be anxious, Annie. You'll do just fine. Be yourself. After all, this isn't just to see if *they* like you. You may not like *them*." He chuckled.

"Then what?"

"We'll look elsewhere."

The principal and two teachers talked with me for about an hour. I was anxious at first, but they were soft spoken and smiled. Soon I was my talkative self, but I thought about what I was saying and made no off-the-wall comments.

"I think they liked me," I told Marcus on the way home.

"And?"

"I liked them too."

School would begin in September and I looked forward to it. I hoped the girls were as nice as the teachers.

One morning Mama and I were watering the garden when I heard a thud. It was Mama, lying on the ground with her eyes closed. I took a handkerchief from my pocket, soaked it in the water can and began wiping her face.

"Mama? Mama? What's the matter?"

She opened her eyes but took a few minutes before she spoke.

"My goodness. What happened?" She tried to get up.

"Stay put, Mama,"

I knew she shouldn't stand up. We sat for a while and I continued to bathe her face. Finally she took a deep breath.

"I think I've got my bearings. Help me get up and I'll be fine." Her voice was stronger.

I put my hands under her arms and kept her from toppling over. At thirteen I was as tall as Mama and strong. Slowly we made it up the steps and into the house. I insisted she lie on the sofa while I went into the kitchen for ice water and a damp cloth. I thought the heat had been too much for her, so it seemed right to keep her cool.

"I'm feeling better, Annie. I'm going upstairs to rest." She said she'd be okay, but I went with her and made sure.

After finishing in the garden, I went to see about Mama. She was asleep. I fixed egg salad for sandwiches and put glasses and plates on the table. When Mama finally came down, she looked like herself and was smiling. I poured ice tea, placed bread and a bowl of egg salad on the table. We sat down to lunch, as they called it in the East. I was also learning to call supper, dinner.

I'm sorry if I gave you a scare," Mama said.

"I have to admit, you did. Are you feeling better now?"

"Yes." Mama paused. "In fact, I am feeling on top of the world." She chuckled.

I was surprised by her comment and wondered if she really was okay. I thought about how tired she always seemed to be.

When I didn't say anything, she continued.

"Are you ready for a bit of news?"

"I guess so."

"I believe I'm going to have a baby." She took my hand and squeezed it.

A baby. "Oh Mama," was all I could say. I hugged her.

"Maybe I shouldn't have told you like this, but I know you've been worried about me. I want you to know how happy I am."

"Does Marcus know?"

"He will this evening. I've had my suspicions, but today I know it must be. The signs are all there."

"I'm happy for you, Mama, for all of us." I hugged her. I cried because Mama told me first.

When Marcus came home, I went up to my room. Before long, they called me and we had a laughing, crying, hugging session like never before.

At first, I couldn't fathom how it would be having a brother or sister. An only child for thirteen years, my life would be different, but as I pondered, a feeling of contentment and joy spread throughout me. I had two half-brothers I'd never seen, and now I would have a brother or a sister I could hold and love from the beginning.

Marcus took Mama to see a doctor several weeks later. Dr. Berlinn told Mama she should be careful and not overdo. He gave her something to build up her blood and help with morning sickness. He predicted the baby would arrive in April. Marcus and I were alone one afternoon while Mama was asleep upstairs.

"Well, what do you think about all this?" He smiled. "The idea of a brother or a sister seems to please you."

"Yes, I'm very happy. Waiting is going to be hard."

"I agree. Of course, I'm going to be a bit old for a new father, but it has given me a deeper understanding of family, and I feel closer to you and your mama than ever. I didn't think that was possible."

"You're going to be a wonderful Daddy. You've made me feel like your daughter."

We sat with our thoughts for a few minutes.

"I'm more at ease now that Mama's seen a doctor. I hope she minds about not overdoing. That day in the yard, I was scared to death seeing her lying there with her eyes closed. I couldn't tell if she was breathing. The worst thing I can imagine is something happening to Mama." I suddenly remembered finding Mama after Brother Ralph hurt her. I must have made a sound.

"Annie, are you all right?"

"Yes. I was just remembering."

"Do you want to tell me about it?" Marcus took my hand and I saw the concern on his face. Mama and I never talked about that afternoon and I never told her how my friends helped me get Brother Ralph to leave town, but at that moment I wanted Marcus to know everything. When I finished, he kissed me on the cheek.

"Annie, you are the bravest and most remarkable person I've ever known—almost like David and Goliath. I can see those innocent faces looking up at that sorry excuse." He paused. "Your mother told me about Brother Ralph's 'pastoral visit' some time ago. I think she should hear the rest of the story. What do you think?"

Mama said she was glad she hadn't known what I was up to.

—

School started the day after Labor Day. As I expected, someone asked about my name.

"Roscoe is my daddy's name," I explained. "Mother added 'Ann' so people would know I'm a girl." There were no more questions. One thing I began to appreciate was the good manners that generally prevailed at my new school.

When October came, the days were noticeably shorter and cooler. Trees changed color and soon those leaves covered the ground. I did the garden chores and leaf raking. Mama seemed to be doing well, but she got tired easily.

Marcus rented a spinet piano. One of my Norwynn teachers, Miss Tugwell, just out of college and energetic, took students after school. Soon I looked forward to my lessons and practiced every day. I knew I'd never be a professional, but I loved learning new music.

Mama was over most of her morning sickness, but she had no stamina. Dr. Berlinn prescribed special vitamins, but Marcus and I didn't notice much improvement. Mama kept saying she felt just fine, that we should realize having a baby was hard work.

One day in early November, I came home from school and called out to Mama. When she didn't answer, I went to the kitchen. She was lying on the floor, some blood on the front of her skirt, her face white as chalk. When I bent down, whispering her name, she opened her eyes and stared at the ceiling, not saying a word. She was gasping for breath.

I found the emergency numbers Marcus had put on a pad by the telephone and called for an ambulance. I checked on Mama and she hadn't moved but was breathing a little better. I called Marcus, and he stayed on the line until the ambulance arrived. He told them about Mama's condition and where to take her. I wanted to go with Mama, but Marcus told me to stay near the telephone and he'd call from the hospital. It felt like my world collapsed as I watched them close the ambulance doors and speed away.

I was scared. What would I do without Mama? The only time we'd been apart was when she and Marcus came to Washington after they married. I'd missed her every day. I began to remember the times I was angry with her and acted ugly. I managed not to cry because I knew Marcus would call as soon as he could, and I didn't want him worrying about me. I wanted to call Aunt Evy in the worst way, but didn't want to tie up the phone.

After what seemed like forever, Marcus called.

"Annie, are you all right?"

"Yes," I answered as calmly as possible. "How's Mama? The baby?"

"The doctor's with her and she's stable." He paused and I heard him take a deep breath. "But ... the baby ..."

"Oh, Marcus."

"They're doing all they can. It'll be a while before we know."

"They have to save our baby, Marcus. They have to."

"Annie, I want you to come to the hospital. I don't know how long we'll be here, but we need to be together." He paused. "There's a number for a cab company on the telephone pad."

"Yes, sir."

"Call a cab and come to the George Washington University Hospital on 23rd Street. I'll be waiting at the main entrance."

I thought the cab would never come as I stood shivering on the curb. The driver was concerned when I gave him the name of the hospital. I explained my mother was very ill and my father was waiting for me. He got us there in what he called, "jig time." Marcus was waiting, and he gathered me into his arms.

I couldn't see Mama because the doctors were with her. Marcus and I went to a cafeteria in the hospital and tried to eat dinner.

"Did you see Mama?"

"For a few minutes, but she was unconscious."

"Oh, Marcus, when I saw her lying on the floor, I thought she … her face was white as chalk and I couldn't tell if she was breathing. She opened her eyes, but I knew she didn't see me."

Marcus reached for my hand.

"You kept your head, Annie, and though I'm not surprised, I am very proud of you." His eyes looked teary, but he didn't cry. "The doctor said he thinks your mother can get through this, but not to get our hopes up about the baby."

We sat in the waiting area for more than an hour before Dr. Berlinn came. I listened as he spoke to Marcus in clipped sentences. He'd have been more reassuring if he hadn't worn a deep frown.

"Your wife is holding her own. The baby is weak, but viable. The next twenty-four hours are critical." He paused and looked at me. "Is this your daughter?"

"Yes," Marcus said, putting his arm around my shoulder.

The doctor looked at me, unsmiling.

"You sit here while I talk with your father," sounded like a military order.

Marcus gave me a hug and I deliberately stood up while they walked to the other side of the room. In a while, they returned.

"The nurse will take you to her room. You can see her for a few minutes. Then go home. Return in the morning." The unsmiling doctor turned on his heel and disappeared through the swinging doors.

We found Mama asleep. Her brown hair lay lank and dull around her pale face. The veins in her hands stood out blue and puffy. Deep gray hung beneath her eyes.

"She's medicated, but resting well," the nurse said. "Why don't you go home and get some sleep? She'll be glad to see you in the morning."

We kissed Mama lightly on the cheek and left.

In the cab, we held hands and talked about Buddy, Aunt Evy and Uncle Riley. It was the only way we could keep from crying. At home I warmed some milk, and we sat at the kitchen table. Without Mama, the house was like a tomb.

"Well, Annie, all we can do is hope and pray. Your mother is very sick and the doctor doesn't think the baby will make it."

I shivered as the cold words washed over me and at the same time, I realized Marcus was telling the truth, not keeping me in the dark.

"Tomorrow they will do tests to see what might have caused this. Dr. Berlinn said your mother lost a lot of blood." He paused to take a breath. "She'll be in the hospital a week or longer. If our baby survives, your mother will probably have to stay in bed during the remainder of her pregnancy."

I swallowed hard, held back my tears and reached for his hand. We sat for several minutes.

"I love you, Marcus."

"And I love you." He squeezed my hand. "I've given you a lot to think about, but we'll get through it."

The cold feeling slipped away.

Marcus pulled out his pocket watch. "It's midnight in Duddley. We'll wait to call Evy and Riley tomorrow after we know more. What do you think?"

"I agree ... oh, I just remembered. I have a history test tomorrow."

"You're not going to school, much less take a test. I'll call. I'm sure you'll be excused." He smiled and stood up. "Let's try to get some sleep. We want to be at the hospital early."

I fell asleep as soon as my head hit the pillow, but about five in the morning, I awoke and couldn't go back to sleep. My thoughts were on Mama and our baby. I repeated my prayer. "Please God, let them be all right." I wondered how God felt about getting these frequent, fervent prayers from someone who rarely went to church. Brother Ralph had shaken my faith, but I still believed God, or some being out there, watched over us. Mama never talked about God and I didn't ask her, because I figured Brother Ralph had shaken her beliefs too. My real daddy, a priest, said nothing to us about believing in God during the short time we'd seen him. He was off to the navy soon after, and there was no telling when we'd be together again. Knowing he believed in God and was risking his life to be with those young sailors made me think there probably was a God. I always felt better when I told Him how worried I was and asked Him to keep Mama and our baby safe. I decided I would talk with my daddy about religion and believing in God when he came home. I wondered what Marcus believed.

Mama came home a week later, feeling and looking better. Dr. Berlinn was amazed at how she and the baby had responded, but he hesitated releasing her until he was sure we could take care of her. He insisted someone be with Mama during the day until Marcus came home in the evening. I offered to take care of Mama after school because sometimes Marcus was very late.

"Young girls have too many other things on their minds," was how Dr. Berlinn put it, barely glancing at me. "I can give you names of people licensed for home care." I bit my tongue, deciding not to argue with Dr. Berlinn. I wanted him to take good care of Mama. What he thought of me didn't matter.

"Your wife can carry to term if she follows my orders. She must have complete bed rest, except for the bathroom and meals." When he found out her bedroom was upstairs, he insisted she eat upstairs. She could sit at a table, but only for a short time. She was never to be out of bed without someone in the room. "A fall could be fatal."

That is how Mrs. Roberts came into our lives. She had recently moved from Atlanta, Georgia to live with her daughter, whose husband was overseas. She was soft spoken and qualified to care for Mama. She also cleaned, did the laundry and made a good dinner for us. Mama and Mrs. Roberts liked one another.

—

Thanksgiving came and we didn't do anything special because we didn't want Mama to get involved with preparations. She hadn't gained a lot of weight, but she was beginning to show and took a long nap every afternoon. Mrs. Roberts insisted on baking a chicken with the trimmings. Uncle Riley sent us pecans, and I made our favorite pie. We invited Mrs. Roberts and her daughter to have dinner with us. At first, Mrs. Roberts hesitated and I was afraid she was going to refuse, but I blurted out, "You're one of our reasons to be thankful. Please?"

She smiled and I realized she'd not been sure we meant it. We were white. She was colored. We were all from the South. To tell the truth I'd forgotten about Mrs. Roberts' color after the first couple of days, but I guess when your color is considered the different one, you never forget.

Her daughter was at ease and good company.

It took planning and coordination, but we managed dinner in Mama's room. After we'd eaten, Mrs. Roberts' asked if she could say a few words.

"My daughter and I thank you for your sincere hospitality and kindness. May God bless and keep you." She paused. "And please, call me Bertie." She giggled and we laughed with her.

—

Marcus and I talked one day about racial barriers.

"Growing up in Duddley, I didn't pay much attention because the colored people lived in a section called Crow's Nest or were scattered along the county roads on small farms. When I was very little, I once told Mama that I liked the name Crow's Nest better than Duddley and thought we should move there."

Marcus said, "In South Carolina, when I was a boy, the line between the races was very definite and brooked no crossing, one way or the other. My family owned slaves before the Civil War. Afterward, the Reconstruction nearly destroyed everything they owned and feelings were bitter toward the federal government and black people. When the Reconstruction ended, political and economic power reverted to white hands, and some took revenge on black people. Jim Crow laws were enacted and black lives were almost as circumscribed as before the war."

"It seems that colored people here have a good life," I said. "There are colored girls at Norwynn, and our differences seem unimportant."

"You're right. Some are doing well, but acceptance and opportunities are still uneven. Success doesn't travel well. If they return to the South, they are discriminated against like those who live there. Even in the North, there is subtle discrimination. The harsh sting is they never know when or where it will rear its ugly head."

"I knew our schools were separate and, except for those who worked at menial jobs for white people in Duddley, I rarely saw colored people. As I grew older it didn't make sense, but that's the way it was. I never heard anyone in the family talk about it and I never asked. We did our own house cleaning and yard work. Except for Lucy Mae, Mrs. Hooper's maid, I don't think I ever had a conversation with a colored person—until now."

"As long as there is segregation in schools and public places, Jim Crow will continue to rob and impoverish. But times are changing and I expect some of those changes to come more quickly as a result of this conflict we're mired in."

Marcus gave me a couple of books to read. "Take your time. Tell me what you think."

—

Mama followed Dr. Berlinn's orders and did well. I always spent time with her after school. She liked hearing about my day, and sometimes I read the newspaper because it wasn't easy for her. She enjoyed hearing me practice and I tried hard to play well. I began to know my mother in a new way. She told me more about her childhood, and we had some good laughs about things she, her sisters and Uncle Riley did. We grew close as she told me how she felt about life. I came to see a spiritual side of my mother that didn't include going to church, but was a strong force in her life.

When Marcus came home, I always went to my room so they had time together before dinner. Marcus and I visited when possible, but with his long hours, we had to snatch moments whenever they presented themselves. Even though I missed Duddley, Buddy, Aunt Evy and Uncle Riley particularly, I was where I wanted to be.

I continued to enjoy Norwynn. Our teachers were interested in us and made our classes challenging without piling on tons of homework. Anita Mason and I became good friends very quickly. She was easy to talk to and fun to be with.

One evening Marcus came home with a big smile on his face.

"Annie, you'll never guess who I met today. Miss Ethel McGhee."

"My teacher?" I couldn't believe it. "Where is she?"

"She finished her training about two months ago and has been assigned to the staff of the WAAC director, Oveta Culp Hobby. Mrs. Hobby is moving her office to Washington."

"That's wonderful. Will she be able to come over?"

"Not only that. She's going to spend Christmas Day with us."

"Oh, Marcus," Mama said. "That's the best news I've heard in a long time."

Marcus told us they had run into one another in Virginia at the Pentagon, an office building for the War Department that was going to be the largest of its kind in the world. It was about half finished, and government workers were moving into parts that were ready. Mrs. Hobby was looking at a possible place for her offices.

"Does that mean Miss McGhee will be here all the time?" I asked.

"Yes. My office may move there too."

"It would be nice if she could come sometime before Christmas," Mama said.

"I asked her and she said she wanted to come as soon as she could. I gave her our phone number and my office number. She expects to be here permanently by Christmas."

I couldn't believe my favorite teacher would be nearby. Living in Washington D.C. was getting better all the time. If Buddy came for Christmas, it would be perfect.

The next day, when I got home from school, Bertie was on the phone and I knew at once it was bad news. She looked at me, sadness across her face.

"Yes, Miss Evy. She just walked in."

Bertie handed me the phone. My hands shook.

"Hi."

"Annie, I have sad news. Mr. Longmire died this morning, a heart attack. Buddy is here with us and, all things considered, he's doing well. He wants to talk with you in a moment."

I felt like someone had dumped a bucket of cold water over me. I shivered and tears formed when I thought about Buddy being all alone now. I took a deep breath.

"Oh, Aunt Evy, that's terrible. I can't believe it, after everything Buddy and his daddy have been through, when their life was so good." I paused to get a grip on my emotions. "I wish I were there."

We talked, but it was hard. Buddy told me not to worry. Everyone was taking care of him. I barely heard him whisper, "I miss you."

Marcus went to Duddley for the funeral and to handle Mr. Longmire's affairs as executor. He flew into Houston and Uncle Riley met him. I wanted to go, but we couldn't both be away from Mama. Marcus knew I would take care of her.

Each day was consumed with thoughts of Buddy. I wanted to see him, to know he was really okay, to put my arms around him, to share his grief. He called again the day Marcus left.

"I'm doing better today," he said. "I hated to see Marcus go, but I know he has to get back to you all. He said your mama is having a little trouble, but you and Mrs. Roberts are doing a good job looking after her."

"It is a job some days, believe me. You know Mama, but now that the weather is getting colder and wetter, it's easier to keep her happy and snug in her bed. This is a lot different than Texas." I paused. "Are you going to be okay?"

"Marcus took care of everything."

"I knew he would."

"I didn't know it, but Marcus and Daddy arranged for your uncle Riley to be my guardian until I reach eighteen. Marcus said it seemed like Daddy had a premonition and insisted on it. Of course, no one said anything because they didn't want me to worry. We're going to keep the house for now and try to rent it. When I'm eighteen I'll inherit and can decide then what to do. Yeah, who knows? I might have use for that house some day." He paused. "You suppose?"

"Yes, you might."

"In the meantime, I moved in with your aunt and uncle. They're very good to me. I'm going to be spoiled. I have to walk further to school, but when I finish chores, I'm home."

We talked about school in Duddley and at Norwynn. I told Buddy that I missed going to the movies and fishing down on the river. He said he missed all that and more. We visited a little longer and he whispered, "I miss you—a lot," before hanging up. I always felt lonesome when I heard the click.

It was getting harder and harder to get a telephone line and sometimes, we would be cut off in the middle of our conversation, so Buddy and I wrote letters. When I asked him to come for Christmas, I could hardly wait for his answer. I was disappointed when he explained that though they were trying to get tickets from Houston to New Orleans to Washington, it didn't look good. We stopped mentioning it, though I know we thought about it every day.

Miss McGhee came over for dinner on a Friday evening. Bertie stayed to serve a delicious fried chicken dinner and clean up afterward. We ate upstairs with Mama and though it was crowded, it was fun. "Cozy," Mama called it.

Just as we were finishing dessert, Dr. Berlinn came by to check on Mama. He often came in the evening after he finished at the hospital. He and Marcus had become good friends. He treated Mama with care and respect, but I was the invisible daughter.

When I heard his voice downstairs, I immediately wondered how he would act toward Miss McGhee. She was dressed in her uniform, looking beautiful as well as impressive. Apparently, Dr. Berlinn thought so too. The next day, he called Marcus to ask how he felt about his getting in touch with Miss McGhee. Marcus gave him her telephone number.

Soon Dr. Berlinn and Miss McGhee were a twosome and spent time with Mama and Marcus, which was good for everyone. Dr. Berlinn began to look at me when he spoke and smiled once in a while. They asked us to call them Ethel and Josh. I managed not to call him anything for a long time. Calling my former teacher by her first name came easier.

By the time Christmas arrived, Mama was doing well enough that Dr. Berlinn allowed her to sit for short periods in a comfortable rocking chair. He agreed to let Marcus carry her downstairs on Christmas morning as long as she rested on the sofa and went back upstairs after the midafternoon dinner we planned.

Christmas Eve was a quiet evening with Marcus, Mama and me enjoying a dinner Bertie had fixed for us. We didn't exchange gifts. Marcus suggested we make a donation to the USO, an organization that sponsors entertainers who visit military installations in the United States and overseas. Daddy told us how much it meant for the young men far from home and under fire. Our gift to one another was to reminisce about the good things in our life, past and present. We had a serious a discussion on naming the baby, but no decision.

Christmas Day Ethel and Josh came over. Ethel and I prepared a southern dinner of fried chicken, mashed potatoes and gravy, green beans, ambrosia salad and Parker House rolls. The day before, I baked two pies, apple and pecan. Marcus surprised us with champagne and Josh let Mama have a little bit. Everyone enjoyed the meal and good conversation. Josh relaxed and forgot he was a doctor for a little while. I missed Buddy.

We weren't able to talk to our Duddley family until several days after Christmas. They gave Buddy and me as much time as possible. The goodbyes were getting harder.

Chapter 19

Journal, January 1943–April 1943

January 1, 1943

We spent a quiet day with Ethel and Josh. Bertie was with her family. Ethel and I prepared a Southern dinner of ham, cabbage and black-eyed peas. This is supposed to make you healthy, wealthy and wise through the New Year. Josh is from Boston and had never heard this. The lemon meringue pie made up for any cultural differences.

Mama was happy to be downstairs. Josh says she is doing well and he expects a healthy child and mother in mid-April. They left around five for a party at one of Josh's friends with whom he'd gone to medical school. His friend is in the army working at Walter Reed Hospital. Josh was turned down for military service because of a heart murmur.

We were unable to get a call through to Duddley. I knew they were trying as well. The last time we talked, Buddy mentioned enlisting in the navy when he turns seventeen in April. Boys who are juniors, and have their parents' consent, automatically receive their high school diploma. I was relieved that Uncle Riley refused to sign for Buddy. Some of his friends wanted to join because they were afraid the war would be over before they were of age. I hope the war is over by the time Buddy graduates. My uncle pointed out that we are involved in two wars, one in Europe and one in the Pacific. Both are fierce and the Germans and Japanese seem determined to fight to the bitter end. Uncle Riley never talked about his service in the trenches of France during The Great War, but I was sure he didn't want Buddy to go to unless it was necessary. Having my daddy in the thick of things is enough.

January 8, 1943

It's good to be in school again. I told Marcus I work harder at Norwynn, and feel like I'm learning more than I would have in Duddley. He teased me, saying I'd better because it was costing enough. Marcus said Duddley gave me a good start and that's why I am doing well.

I've submitted a piece to *The Student Voice,* Norwynn's publication of nonfiction, fiction and poetry. I'm interested in history and wrote a fiction piece on Betsy Ross. If this is accepted, I'm thinking of doing more on women in history.

We finally got through to the family on Tuesday. There wasn't much time, but it was good to hear everyone's voice. Grandma wasn't able to talk to us. Aunt Evy said she was aware of things, but getting weaker. Grandma said to give us her love. Afterward Mama cried and Marcus spent a good while with her until she was able to sleep.

Josh says Mama's doing well, but some days it seems like she has trouble staying awake and is weaker when she's up. I talked with Bertie because I don't want to worry Marcus. She said that sometimes this is nature's way of saving up strength for the delivery. I hope she's right. Bertie also told me Mama doesn't always ring the bell when she needs to get up. I will talk to Marcus.

I had a letter from Buddy yesterday. He's working hard at the dairy. Uncle Riley's business has grown since the war started. He's hired another man to work with Ben, and a friend of Buddy's, Jimmy Price, is working after school too.

Buddy misses his daddy, but is happy living with my aunt and uncle. They seem to know when he wants to be alone and when it's time to keep him busy. He says he misses me more than he ever expected and he is trying to figure a way to come see me this summer. I hope it works out. Getting train tickets shouldn't be as difficult as it was for the holiday.

January 18, 1943

My piece on Betsy Ross was in *The Student Voice* today. It's encouraging to see my work in print. Several of the older girls said they enjoyed reading my story because it felt like they were there with her. Marcus read it to Mama, and they said I'd made Betsy Ross come to life. I can't wait to show it to Ethel.

I want to be a writer but I don't know how to plan for that as well as a life with Buddy. I'm crossing my bridges before I'm anywhere near, but something has happened since I've been away from Buddy for nearly a year. I remember those quick kisses and the hints about us being together, like needing his house someday. I'm not sure I want to live in a house that's in Duddley. He's serious about becoming a veterinarian and working with Dr. Ford. I see myself working on a newspaper or a magazine in a large city, like Houston. I might go to New York City someday and get a job writing for a newspaper or magazine, or selling books in a shop while I write a novel. I hope those bridges take us to the same place.

January 26, 1943

Today was a sad day. Grandma Dickey died last night in her sleep. Aunt Evy sent a telegram saying Grandma went quietly; she seemed to feel better yesterday than she had in a long time. We'll know more details when Aunt Evy is able to call.

Mama and I spent most of the day trying not to cry. I was supposed to take a test in civics, but Marcus called and I will make it up. He went to his office for several hours and was home before three.

The hard part is none of us can go to Duddley for the funeral. Marcus, Mama and I talked a good while before dinner and that helped. We reminisced and some of the things we remembered made us laugh.

"Grandma had a good heart, but sometimes she made life difficult for those around her," Mama said. "Except when I brought Annie back to Duddley with no husband and a flimsy story. Your grandmother put her arms around us and never asked a question." Mama wiped away tears.

"She and Dallie Pickens used to have good gossip sessions," I said.

"Yes, and you shouldn't have been listening."

I didn't defend myself because she was right, but I remember one day in particular when I stopped to visit Grandma after school. Grandma liked to visit and tell me all the news she thought I should hear. That afternoon she had a visitor, Miss Dallie Pickens, who was somewhat younger than Grandma and had never married. She was short, almost as wide as she was tall, with orange ringlets hanging to her shoulders tied back from her face with a black ribbon.

Miss Dallie, an only child whose parents died long ago, lived alone in a large house several blocks down the street. Grandma said she had relatives living in the valley, but it was a long way, and Dallie didn't know them very well. Walley and Betts, a colored brother and sister whose parents had worked for Miss Dallie's folks, lived in a small house on the back of the lot and saw to Miss Dallie. The bank looked after her affairs and she lived as she always had.

That day she was wearing a flowered print dress that made her look like a bouquet squashed into Grandma's large overstuffed chair. White stockings puffed over the sides of Mary Janes. Her cheeks were rouged and her small puckered mouth was painted scarlet. She smiled and her chirpy voice greeted me.

"Why, if it isn't Roscoe Ann. Lordy child, I haven't seen you in a month of Sundays. You're getting to be quite the girl." She stared at my developing bosom. My face got hot and I wondered if I was as red as I felt.

"Say 'Hi' to Miss Dallie," Grandma prompted me.

"Hi, Miss Dallie." I was afraid Grandma was going to tell me to give her a kiss on one of those rosy cheeks, but I guess she forgot.

"Why don't you go in the kitchen and have some cookies? There's lemonade in the icebox. You'll be comfortable in there."

She meant I was not to come back. I was relieved, because as I left the room, Miss Dallie said, "You're gonna have to keep an eye on that one."

"She's a good girl, Dallie." Grandma was emphatic.

I hurried so as not to hear more, my cheeks burning. I knew what Miss Dallie was getting at. The girls at school couldn't talk about anything else.

I was reading a Nancy Drew book, so I went to the small porch off Grandma's bedroom. Next to my tree at home, this was my favorite place to read. It was shaded by an oak and away from the street.

After a while, I heard voices. Grandma and Miss Dallie were looking at Grandma's flowers.

"Your garden is a sight to behold," Miss Dallie chirped.

"Thank you. Mrs. Lindstrom's boy, Eddie, does it just like I tell him."

"Can we sit a while?" Miss Dallie asked. "My feet are really complaining today."

"You take the swing, Dallie. I like this chair."

Grandma was being polite because there was no way anyone could sit in the swing with Miss Dallie. It creaked as she moved back and forth.

"Sarah, have you heard about Lorene Dobbins?"

I was on the verge of going back to the kitchen but decided to listen for just a minute.

"Well, what do you mean," asked Grandma.

"She made all those trips to Houston, saying she was visiting her college friends, but it seems she was visiting that young man who was here last summer. Now they don't know where she is."

"Oh, my goodness."

"Goodness has nothing to do with it," Miss Dallie harrumphed. "Odella, she works for the Dobbinses, told my Betts that Miss Lorene and her folks had a terrible falling out and two days ago she packed her suitcase and left. No telling where she is." Miss Dallie sounded pleased as punch.

"Do they think she's gone to find that young man?" Grandma asked.

"Odella says she hopes so. He seemed like a real nice sort. But the Dobbinses are so set on their one and only child, they forbade her to keep in touch with him after he left."

"That's never a good idea," Grandma said, clucking her tongue.

They talked a little more about how young people didn't seem to have the same morals their parents did. I went back to the kitchen. Miss Dallie left from the yard, so I didn't tell her goodbye. I didn't mention Miss Lorene to Mama. She'd have gotten on me for eavesdropping.

February 1, 1943

Aunt Evy wrote a letter telling us about Grandma's passing. Getting calls through is harder all the time and she thought it might be easier for Mama.

Marcus read the letter to Mama and me, pausing when Mama needed a rest. I managed not to cry and upset Mama more, but it was hard. I have copied the letter.

Dear Laney, Annie and Marcus,

This will not be easy to read, but I realize you want to know about the last days we spent with your beloved mother and grandmother.

As we mentioned, she became weak and unable to leave her bed just before Christmas. There was pain and Dr. Bailey did his best to keep her comfortable, but it also robbed her of alertness and interest in everyday events as was her usual way. During this time, we discovered Dr. Bailey had been treating her failing heart for several years and she swore him to secrecy. "Just tell them I'm getting old," she insisted.

Mrs. Lindstrom has been our strength throughout this time. She always called when Miss Sarah was awake and able to visit. It was amazing to see how she could perk up for us. She never spoke of pain, dying or anything other than day-to-day concerns and events. She was truly amazing. She talked of you all and how glad she would be when you came home with the baby, never questioning that she would be here to hold it.

Laney, your mother loved all of us with an accepting heart. We are thankful she went in her sleep, looking years younger and faintly smiling. She is truly in a better place.

Everyone in Duddley turned out for the funeral. The church couldn't hold them. Pastor Winslow knew Miss Sarah well and his eulogy brought tears and laughter. He reminded us of her full and useful life, love of family and devotion to friends. We were fortunate that the weather turned off clear, cool, but no chilling breeze. Calm and lovely like Miss Sarah.

Riley and I are grateful for having had her in our lives. He is at the cemetery this morning planting a garden of Miss Sarah's favorite plants in the family plot. Tomorrow, her dates will be inscribed on the stone she shares with Mr. Dickey.

The letters and cards are still coming as the word spreads. I plan to place them in an album so the family can easily pass it around and see each piece. Afterward, I will mail it to you.

Everyone sends love and good wishes. We are happy that you, Laney, and the baby are healthy as you approach that wonderful day. Take good care of all yourselves.

Love, Evy

February 8, 1943

I received a letter from my daddy today. I hadn't heard from him since before Christmas and tried not to worry because he has told us that being in the Pacific aboard ship makes mail uncertain. It was his Christmas letter and I cried thinking of him so far away from his family in San Antonio.

Virginia and the boys spent the holidays with her parents and our grandmother McMillen. I am glad for them, but it didn't make up for Daddy's absence. Though I've never met my brothers or Virginia, I feel a growing closeness as we exchange letters, pictures and cards. I always share Daddy's letters with Mama because though he never writes directly to her, he always asks about her, the baby and Marcus, sending his love and best wishes.

I hope with all my heart we can become a family once this war is over. We'll be a different kind of family, but one that loves, respects and has fun together. When I wrote this to Buddy, he said Uncle Riley and Aunt Evy treat him like a son and he looked forward to being part of the larger family. My heart skipped several beats.

The war news is some better. Our navy fought fierce battles at Guadalcanal. American troops are slowly pushing the Japanese out of New Guinea and other islands. Marcus and I listen to the news on the radio after Mama goes to bed. I don't like listening, but with Daddy in the thick of it, how can I not? Please God, keep him safe.

February 17, 1943

Yesterday when I came home from school, Josh was with Mama. I waited until he came downstairs. Even though he's a lot nicer than he was at first, he's still prickly when it comes to talking with me about Mama. Before I could ask, he spoke.

"Mrs. Roberts called to tell me your mother had fallen. It seems she got up without calling for assistance." He frowned. I was scared and didn't know what to say. He continued. "I've warned her that a fall can cause her to lose the baby as well as seriously injure herself. Today she was lucky." He paused again.

"Thank goodness," I whispered. My heart was beating a mile a minute. I felt like it was my fault because I'd never mentioned her getting up alone to Marcus. Bertie thought she could keep a close eye on her.

"When does Marcus get home?" Dr. Berlinn asked.

"Around six," I said. It was almost four.

"I'll come back this evening at eight. We have to talk." He smiled a half smile. "All of us."

"Is there something I can do?"

"Yes, go upstairs and stay with your mother. I've given her a mild sedative, but if she wakes up, I want someone there. Do not let her get up and walk without support. Call Mrs. Roberts to help you." He shook his head. "I don't want to frighten any of you, but her condition is more precarious the nearer we come to her due date. Lying in bed saps her strength and interferes with her sense of balance. On the other hand, normal activity threatens the success of her delivering. A fall could end everything. Try to make her understand."

He gathered his things and walked toward the door.

"Take care of your mother."

Before I could speak, he opened the door and was gone. I ran upstairs. Bertie sat next to the bed. Mama opened her eyes when I came in, smiled wanly and drifted off to sleep. Bertie got up and led me away from the bed.

"I'm so sorry," she whispered. "I thought she was asleep, so I went down to start dinner like I always do when I heard the noise." She paused and daubed her eyes with a handkerchief.

"It's not your fault, Bertie." I put my arms around her. "Mama has been feeling better and she thinks she can go back to her usual ways. You know how she is."

"I should have made sure she was asleep."

"She's good at pretending so we'll think she's okay and doesn't need all this attention." I was irritated with Mama. I put away my things and brought a school assignment to work on. Bertie, still upset, went downstairs to fix dinner. Mama's breathing settled into a deep, regular rhythm so I knew she was resting well. Bertie brought me some cookies and milk.

I had just finished my assignment when Marcus walked in. He was earlier than usual.

"Josh called and says he'll be here to talk with us. He told me what happened." He spoke quietly. "How's your mother?"

"She's resting."

Mama opened her eyes and smiled when she saw Marcus. She reached out her arms for his embrace. She noticed me and smiled.

"Hi, honey. I didn't hear you come in."

"You've had a good nap," I said.

"Josh and his pills." She laughed.

"He tells me you had a fall this afternoon," Marcus said.

"Oh, I just missed a step and fell against the bed. I slid rather than fell."

I didn't mention that Bertie heard the noise from downstairs.

"You're supposed to ring the bell when you need to get up." Marcus spoke softly, but firmly.

"It's only a few steps to the bathroom and Bertie has enough to do without running up and down those stairs all day long." Mama's voice rose in defiance.

"Josh is coming over this evening and we'll talk about this," Marcus said in his calm voice.

I slipped out of the room because I don't like to hear them disagree nor do I think I should listen to conversations that don't include me. My eavesdropping days are pretty much over.

February 16, 1943

Bertie was able to find two older ladies in her neighborhood who are retired nurse's aides. June Lacey and Mary Towne are experienced in private nursing and work part time. One comes before Marcus leaves and stays until noon when the other comes and stays until he returns. I offered to stay with Mama when I got home from school, but Marcus overruled me. He said I needed time to do homework, practice piano and visit with Mama. June and Mary will arrange their own schedules. Marcus requires that one of them be with Mama at all times. On weekends, we take care of her. Ethel has offered to help as well.

June and Mary started yesterday. Mama said she liked them and thought they would do fine, but she was against it. Marcus wouldn't budge. It was either June and Mary or a nursing home for expectant mothers Josh recommended.

A letter from Buddy came today. Billy Wilkerson, who joined the marines last year when he finished high school, was killed in the battle for Guadalcanal. He and Buddy played together on the baseball team. I am sad thinking about Billy's family and Buddy wanting to go into the navy. Oh, please, God, let this war end soon.

February 22, 1943

Today was a holiday. Ethel picked me up at eleven and we went over to her apartment in Arlington for lunch and to work on my story for *The Student Voice*. The one-room studio has an adjoining kitchen, dressing room and bath. A bow window looks out on a courtyard.

"I love your apartment," I said.

"It's small, but I'm here so little, it's all I need."

Tuna fish sandwiches were delicious with carrot sticks, potato chips and a glass of milk. We visited a little while and then tackled my story. Ethel is a wonderful teacher. There were things to correct, but she never makes me feel dumb. When we finished, I had learned many new things and wanted to write even more.

Ethel made hot cocoa and sliced some pound cake. We sat at the table.

"Annie, I have something to share with you, and I need your help."

I was surprised, but answered, "Yes, ma'am," because I would do anything she asked.

"I'm sure you've noticed Josh and I spend a lot of time together."

I nodded, because my mouth was full of cake.

"Well," she paused and smiled. "We're getting married."

"Married. That's wonderful." The thought had occurred to me, but I figured Josh was too wrapped up in his career as well as being shy. I'd never seen him look at Ethel in any special way or take her hand like Mama and Marcus. I could tell Ethel thought he was special, but she tried to hide her feelings. "When's the wedding?"

"That's what I want to talk with you about. Your Mama's delivery date is mid-April and Josh needs to plan around that. Since she is doing so well, we have decided on Saturday, March 27 which gives us about a month to plan."

"That's not much time," I said, remembering the weddings for Mama and Marcus and my aunt and uncle.

"It's going to be a simple affair," Ethel said. "We'll have a civil ceremony and small reception for our families and a few friends."

"No church?" I asked before I realized I'd asked one of my forward questions Mama always got on me about. Ethel smiled.

"Josh is Jewish and I'm Christian. To avoid family discussion or clashes, we thought it best to have a friend of Josh's, a judge, perform the ceremony." She paused and smiled. "I hope you will stand with me."

I wondered how Josh liked this idea, but didn't ask because I didn't care. Ethel, whom I adore, wanted me and that's all that mattered.

It concerns me that Mama won't be able to go. She doesn't complain, but I know she is tired of being cooped up. Ethel realizes this too because when she took me home, she didn't let on we'd decided anything.

"Laney, I would like to have Annie stand with me. How do you feel about it?"

Mama was happy for me. Ethel told her about the wedding and reception, asking Mama's opinion on details. Mama made Ethel promise to bring her a piece of the cake.

"I'm going to see if Josh will let you have a glass of champagne too." Ethel gave Mama a long hug.

Ethel will wear a cream-colored linen suit with a pale blue blouse. We looked through my closet and found the new yellow pique dress

I planned to wear for Easter. Mama noticed I was slimmer and said it improved the way the dress hung. I can hardly wait for March 27.

Ethel stayed until Marcus came home, so she could tell him the news. He smiled and hugged Ethel, chuckling, "I wondered how long it was going to take you two. All my best wishes."

This has been a wonderful day.

March 7, 1943

The wedding plans are progressing with a few bumps. Very few family members will be able to come. Ethel's family in Houston is unable to get train tickets. Josh's mother and father will come from Boston.

Mama asked Ethel how many guests were attending.

"At last count it was twenty." Ethel paused. "We're having difficulty finding a place for the reception."

"We moved the ceremony from afternoon to late morning," Josh said. "I hoped to get a room at the Southern House. I've just talked with them and they're not certain they can accommodate us."

"I have an idea," Mama said. She waited until all eyes were on her. "Why not have your reception at Maison Claiborne?" Mama grinned as she faked a French accent.

No one said anything for a few minutes. We all looked at Josh. A smile spread across his face.

"And what do you have in mind, Madame Claiborne." Josh mimicked Mama's French accent.

I couldn't believe he was getting into Mama's mood. Maybe he does have a sense of humor.

"I didn't complain when you informed me there was no way I could go to your wedding. Now it seems that fate has taken a hand and wants to bring the wedding, at least the reception, to me. What do you think of that?" I hadn't seen Mama so cheerful in a long time.

Our house isn't large, but it could easily accommodate twenty guests. Without any argument, they began planning. Mama promised not to get involved in any preparations and to let us wait on her during the reception.

"Otherwise, Madame Claiborne," Josh said in his French accent, "I shall carry you myself up zee stairs and lock zee door." Josh bent over Mama, kissed her on the cheek and whispered in her ear. She chuckled and kissed his cheek.

March 28, 1943

The wedding and reception were a success. I wondered how the older Berlinns felt about a civil ceremony, but apparently, religion was not an issue with Josh and his parents. They'd met Ethel once before, but you'd have thought they'd known and loved her forever. Josh has two brothers and Mrs. Berlinn told everyone how blessed she was to have a daughter, at last. Ethel said she felt as though she had family with her, after all.

Mama looked beautiful and was good as promised. A large group of people hasn't always been her favorite thing, but being cooped up must have made her appreciate society a little more. When she tired, she asked Marcus to take her upstairs. Josh checked to make sure she was all right. Marcus stayed with her.

The caterer's clean-up team took care of the mess, which really wasn't bad. Ethel and Josh went upstairs to tell Mama goodbye. They were spending the weekend at the Willard Hotel. They've decided to go on their honeymoon when the war is over. That's what our soldiers, sailors and their new wives have to do.

I had a wonderful time. I'm especially glad Mama was able to enjoy herself. Just a few more weeks and I will have a brother or sister. Can life be better?

April 13, 1943

I can't believe how much has happened in these last two weeks. I will begin at the beginning.

On Tuesday, March 30, I came home from school in one of the worst rainstorms I've ever seen. Bertie was with Mama because June and Mary were both sick with spring flu. This day I came home early because Bertie had a doctor's appointment downtown at three o'clock.

I made coffee for Mama and me to have with cookies. We visited a bit and Mama seemed to doze. I was engrossed in my homework when Mama's cry startled me.

"It's the baby, Annie," Mama gasped. "It's coming."

"Oh, Lordy," was my idiot response.

"Call an ambulance and Dr. Berlinn's office. Hurry," Mama cried out in pain.

The telephone was downstairs and I didn't want to leave her, but a louder scream sent me flying.

When I picked up the phone, there was no dial tone. I banged on the cradle, but got nothing. We'd had some outages lately during thunderstorms, but there hadn't been any lightning all afternoon, though the rain came down in sheets. I shook the base of the telephone and the hand piece, but it was dead as a doornail. I rushed upstairs to Mama.

"The phone's out of order. What should I do?"

Before she could speak, Mama screamed, her body convulsed. I rushed over and began rubbing her arms and hands. After what seemed like forever, she relaxed. She closed her eyes and I couldn't tell if she was breathing. I listened to her heart to be sure she was alive.

"Mama, what are we going to do?" I whispered as much to myself as to her.

"Looks like we're going to have ourselves a baby." She managed a weak smile and closed her eyes again.

When Bertie, June and Mary talked about delivering babies, they hadn't made me leave the room, but now my mind was blank.

"Mama?" She opened her eyes and smiled. "Shouldn't I be doing something to get ready?"

"You're right, honey." As she began to instruct me, I remembered some of those conversations. I went down to the kitchen to get water boiling, found a clean stack of cotton cloths Bertie kept in the pantry and took all the towels out of the linen closet. I tried the phone, but it was still out. Mama screamed again and I hurried upstairs. I found alcohol and scissors in the bathroom.

Mama was lying still. "How close are the pains?" I asked.

"I don't know honey. Maybe you should start timing them?" She grimaced and said, "Write it down so we can be sure." I got a pencil and tablet from my room.

Though I was more frightened than I'd ever been in my life, I knew not to let Mama see. I wiped perspiration from her face. She gripped the spindles of the headboard until her muscles contracted like lengths of rope pulled tight. The next scream was sharper and longer.

I kept track of the pains and they got closer, then further, then closer. Mama tried not to scream, but I told her to let it out. Watching the pain twist her face and contort her body was worse than the sound of her voice. I found some lotion and rubbed her feet, legs, hands and arms in between the pains. Mama smiled and told me how much she loved me.

After one long, excruciating pain, I heard the front door slam.

"It's me, Bertie."

A rain-soaked Bertie came through the door and gasped when she saw Mama.

"Oh, Lordy. Is that baby coming?"

She took off her raincoat and went over to Mama. She took her pulse, felt her forehead and gently massaged Mama's stomach. I told her what had happened and everything I did to get ready.

"Well, Missy, looks like you and I are going to help your mama birth a baby." She looked at me, smiled and held out her arms for a hug. She must have seen how bad I needed that. "As far as I can tell, your mama is doing fine and we just have to wait 'til that little one is ready."

Bertie explained how she hadn't been able to get a bus and had walked back in the driving rain. "I've seen lots of storms, but this is a doozy. I'm not surprised the telephone went out. I saw some big trees lying across the lines. Sparks flying. Lucky we still got electricity."

It seemed like forever, with the pains getting harder and closer. Bertie knew when the time had come and she told Mama to push. After Mama gave a particularly hard push, I found myself holding a bloody, yelling little person. I remembered to protect the head and we made sure the cord wasn't wrapped around the neck.

"He's a boy," I crowed. Mama breathed a heavy sigh and Bertie's chuckle sounded like happy clucking.

"Mrs. Claiborne, your baby is perfect," Bertie said, and began taking care of the cord. He was a mess but everything was there. I bathed, diapered, dressed him in a warm flannel gown we'd made and wrapped him in a receiving blanket. When Mama was ready, I laid him in her arms.

It was after seven o'clock by the time we heard Marcus come through the kitchen. He must have thought it strange to see no dinner on the stove, because he bounded up the stairs and literally burst into the room.

"Laney?" He saw what had happened and worry lines creased his face. "Are you all right?" He hurried to the bed and Mama held the baby out to him.

"Meet your son." Though she was tired, her smile was beautiful. Tears slipped down our cheeks, including Marcus. He sat on the bed cradling Mama in one arm and the baby in the other.

"Have you decided on his name?" I asked. We'd talked about names, but with his coming early, I wondered if they'd decided.

"Yes," Marcus said. "As a matter of fact we chose names for a boy and a girl last night." Marcus chuckled.

"He's Jefferson Roscoe Claiborne," Mama said, reaching out to hug me.

"Jefferson is popular in the Claiborne family," Marcus said. "It's my middle name. Roscoe is the name of someone we love very much."

"I want to call him Jeff," Mama said.

I'm pleased to have him named for me.

The telephone was working again and Marcus called Josh who came over as soon as he managed all the detours caused by the storm. He said Mama came through better than he expected, especially since she was early. He told Mama to rest and not go up and down the stairs. He would check on her and the baby the next day. He told Marcus to bring her to his office in three days so he could examine her and the baby more completely.

I have to admit I was scared to death while Jeff was coming, but now I understand what a miracle is.

Bertie warmed up the soup she'd made earlier and we had dinner upstairs with Mama. Jeff slept in the cradle that had been in Marcus' family for generations. Marcus brought it from South Carolina, cleaning and refinishing it in the garage. He'd completed it two weeks ago.

We went to bed around eleven. Mama was tired and Jeff slept fitfully. She had put him to her breast, but he didn't nurse long. I didn't feel tired, but when my head hit the pillow, I was sound asleep.

Josh came the next day and was happy to see Mama continuing to do well. He congratulated Bertie who told him she couldn't have done it without me. He turned toward me, smiled as though seeing me for the first time.

"Congratulations to you too," he said, taking my hands and holding them for a long moment. "Perhaps you have a calling." I was astounded. He wasn't being sarcastic.

April 20, 1943

What a difference a three-week-old baby makes. There's always something going on concerning the care of the smallest member of the family. I wish I weren't in school so much of the day.

I'm torn when I leave in the morning. Jeff cries a lot and everyone says I have the best touch for soothing him when his colic is bad. Because Mama isn't able to breast feed, I give him his bottle, cuddle him and rock him to sleep. Sometimes we rock long after he's asleep. The diapers aren't great, but I take my turn. It's amazing how spit-up doesn't smell so bad after a while.

Mama is recovering, but doesn't have much stamina. She isn't able to walk to the bathroom without help. Josh says she lost strength because of prolonged bed rest. He has prescribed a regimen of getting up and walking around the room every hour and vitamin B shots once a week. Dr. Berlinn thinks she may have lost more blood than we realized.

I wrote to Buddy, telling him about Jeff. Even though he cries with the colic and there are the dirty diapers and spitting up, I told Buddy it's worth the smiles, coos and that little hand grasping my finger. I described how I hold Jeff on my shoulder to get up the bubbles, and rub his back when he pulls up his legs and snuggles. I wonder how Buddy feels about babies.

Jeff helps take my mind off how much I miss Buddy even though we write two or three times a week. He is working with Dr. Ford a lot now and plans to go to veterinarian school. I hope this war is over before he goes into the navy. Otherwise, it could be ten years or more before he can finish school. I will graduate the year after he does and if the war is still on, I may join the WAAC. Ethel has an interesting job working on the director's staff. She wants to take me over to her new office in the Pentagon as soon as she is settled. She says if the war is still on when I graduate, she will help me through the application process. I haven't told her about Buddy and me.

April 27, 1943

We've settled into a routine with Jeff and though we're busy, it's organized. Bertie cooks and takes care of the house, including the laundry and grocery shopping. June and Mary help Mama with Jeff. She wants to do everything, but she gets tired easily. Jeff is thriving. Some days it seems he has grown while I was at school. I find it hard to do my homework when I hear him. Mama and Marcus say I'd have him spoiled rotten if they weren't around. Maybe so, but I think spoiling makes him happy.

As we get ready for the end of school, activities are reaching a crescendo. I am on the committee to plan the May Cotillion. I don't know why I was chosen. I had to look in past yearbooks to see exactly what a cotillion is. I hope I can do a good job and not embarrass myself.

Yesterday some of the older girls were talking about their dates. Now, that's a problem. I hope Anita can help me. I don't know one boy in Washington D.C.

I am excited about getting a place on *The Student Voice* staff next year. After my two pieces on women in history, Mr. Sterns, the faculty advisor, asked me to be one of the story editors. Anita warned me that Rhoda Evans, the senior who will be the chief editor, is a witch. She's a great writer, but everyone watches their P's and Q's working with her.

I'm concerned about Mama. She isn't regaining strength. Josh is going to put her through some tests this next week. She tries so hard to take care of Jeff, but by the afternoon, she is exhausted and has to sleep. June and Mary are very good about trying to let her do for Jeff, but they also watch Mama carefully. They talked with Marcus and he called Josh.

We had a letter from Aunt Evy the other day. They are busy too. Leatrice had another baby and is only able to work one day a week. Aunt Evy does the rest. She mentioned Buddy working with Dr. Ford and they think this is right for him. They have hired my cousin, Travis, to fill some of Buddy's time. I raised my eyebrows at that, but I'm sure Uncle Riley is able to keep him in line.

I talked to Anita about the cotillion the other day. She is my closest friend and I can talk to her. The other girls are nice enough, but I don't feel at ease with them the way I do with Anita. They seem to think Texas is still part of the Wild West and several have mentioned my Texas twang, so I've been working on it. I've noticed Ethel doesn't have the accent and I asked her about it.

"First of all, you don't have a twang like some Texans," she said. "Second, don't let it bother you. Some of the southern accents I hear are syrupy enough to attract bees. You speak clearly and unaffectedly. That's what's important." I've thought about it, but I'm trying to speak without any accent like people on the radio and in the movies.

Anita says most of the other girls come from wealthy families and have known one another since they were born. It's not easy to break in is how she put it. Anita's father is on the D.C. police force, one of the commanders under the chief. The other day she told me how she became a student at Norwynn.

"I wouldn't be going to Norwynn if it weren't for something that happened to my father about ten years ago. He was a patrol officer in a precinct where most of the residences were mansions. One evening he walked through the neighborhood, checking as he always did when he heard screaming from one of the large houses. My father saw two men coming through the gate. One had a large bundle in his arms. Father tackled him and knocked him unconscious. The other man ran to a parked car and fled. It turned out they were kidnapping a small boy, the only child of this family. They planned to ask for ransom. The family was so grateful to my father, they insisted on rewarding him with a large sum of money. It was enough that my two brothers and I have been able to attend the best schools in D.C. They promised to send us to college if we wanted to go."

"That's an amazing story," I said. "Are your brothers in college?"

"My older brother, Elbert, finished at Georgetown last year. He's a second lieutenant in the army at Ft. Benning, Georgia. Jess was at Georgetown, but dropped out to enlist in the navy. He's in a pilot training program in Pensacola, Florida and will finish in another year. He'll be an ensign and probably assigned to an aircraft carrier in the Pacific." She paused for a moment and I knew she was thinking of her brothers. "I try not to worry, but we haven't heard from Elbert in two weeks, so we think he may be on his way out of the country."

We talked about dates for the cotillion. She had asked a cousin to go with her, and she thought he might have a friend for me. Anita said she would insist her cousin find someone who wasn't a total zero.

"Beggars can't be choosers," I said. We laughed.

I wrote to Buddy and told him about my "date." We'd agreed a while ago that we would go out with others when it was a special occasion.

April 21, 1943

I am so busy I can hardly see straight. The cotillion is taking a lot of time. Judith Ross is the senior chairman and she's a perfectionist. The sign, *CLASS of 1943,* which will hang over the stage where the orchestra plays, has been redone three times. First, it didn't sparkle enough. Second, the curve was slightly off. Third, the "L" in "class" was taller, but Judith thought it looked better so all the other letters had to be redone. It's two weeks off and I can't wait for it to be over.

It's always good to get home and spend time with Jeff. June and Mary have changed his formula and the colic is getting better. He's a cheerful little boy when he feels good. I think he knows me, but they laugh and say he knows anybody who pays him attention. We'll see.

Marcus came home earlier today. He and Mama spent time together upstairs as always. I was downstairs with Jeff when they called me.

"Annie, your mother and I received word from Josh today about the tests." Marcus wasn't smiling, so I braced myself for some bad news. "Josh gave me a long and detailed explanation which I'm not able to repeat. Suffice it to say, it's a miracle your mother was able to carry Jeff as close to term as she did." He paused. "The other part is your mother will have surgery as soon as she's regained some strength." Marcus stopped when he heard me gasp. I was certain the next word out of his mouth would be cancer. A girl at school lost her mother who'd had a baby followed by surgery for cancer. Josh's report frightened me.

"Annie, I know this is hard for you, but we promised not to keep you in the dark. Would you like to talk to Josh?"

"Is it cancer?" I whispered. My heart raced and my mouth and throat were so dry I couldn't speak.

"Oh, sweetheart," Mama reached for me to come sit on the bed next to her. She put her arms around me and squeezed gently. "It's not cancer. I'm going to be all right. Some of my insides are a mess and I will feel better without them." She chuckled and kissed me on the cheek. I breathed a sigh of relief, but the pit of my stomach continued to twist and turn.

Chapter 20

Journal, August 1943

August 12, 1943

April 30, 1943 is engraved on my heart forever. As I walked home from school, the sunshine, trees and shrubs with their fresh leaves and bright blossoms filled me with a sense of new beginnings. As always, I went upstairs to see if Mama was awake. Bertie called from the kitchen where she was preparing dinner. June had taken Jeff out in his carriage.

As soon as I saw Mama, I knew she would never again open her eyes or smile at me. Her chest was still. I touched her cold, motionless hand.

My heart pounded and my throat felt dry and tight. I looked at my beautiful mother, serene, peaceful in another world. I kissed her forehead, cheeks and pale lips. She wasn't there, but something made me think I might be able to bring her back—if I were quiet, if I waited, if I prayed hard enough—she might open her eyes. I don't know how long I sat next to Mama, holding her hand, before Bertie came into the room. I began to sob.

The next days are blurry and events are scrambled, but one incident is etched in my memory. June brought Jeff, asking if I wanted to give him his bottle, something I always loved doing. Instead, I turned and ran upstairs to my room. I slammed the door. Thoughts jumbled through my mind. I didn't try to muffle my crying. He was the reason Mama was gone. Those thoughts didn't become words, but I was ashamed, certain everyone knew, as though I'd spoken.

Soon Marcus knocked on the door. We cried, we talked, we cried, we talked. We still do, but that evening he brought me back from a terrible place. That was the beginning of my accepting Mama's death, learning to live with the knowledge I would never hear her voice. In the days following, in spite of his own pain, Marcus continued to comfort me. I helped care for my little brother, healing in his laughter, his cooing, and my love for him.

We brought Mama back to Duddley and laid her beside Grandma Dickey. I go every day and talk to her. My tears are more than enough to water the flowers.

Marcus went back to Washington D.C. three weeks after the funeral. Ethel went with him. Marcus is part of a classified project and had no choice. He came back for a week in June and again in July. Day after tomorrow he is coming to get Jeff. I must decide whether I will go back with them.

Jeff and I have been with Aunt Evy and Uncle Riley all this time and I couldn't have lived through those tearful days without their love. Jeff is thriving in Aunt Evy's care. I find comfort in feeding him and rocking him to sleep. I am so sorry he will never know our mother.

Writing about Mama is hard, but Ethel and Aunt Evy have asked me to take up my writing again. They believe it will help me to go on, as Mama would have wanted. They love me and they're right. I will never be the same without Mama, but I must try to be her daughter, the one she hoped I'd be.

August 15, 1943

Marcus arrived in Houston yesterday. The agency he works for provided a private plane. When I asked, he grinned.

"Oh, they think I know some things they need and they want to keep me safe." He chuckled. "I hope they don't find out different. It beats those crowded trains."

Last night we discussed whether I should stay in Duddley or return to Washington and finish at Norwynn. Marcus, as always, listens and lets me have my say.

"If I stay in Duddley, I will miss you and Jeff terribly, but if I go, I will be leaving Mama." I didn't mention seeing Buddy every day if I stayed, though I'm sure Marcus has thought of that. We talked about how a diploma from Norwynn will enable me to go to just about any school I chose. "Norwynn has changed my life and I will miss my friends and teachers. Living in a city like D.C. offers more opportunities." I was torn.

"I know this isn't easy for you," Marcus said. "If it were possible, I'd make our home in Duddley, Texas. That's what I plan to do when this war is over. In the meantime, I must stay in Washington and finish my job. I've made a commitment."

"Yes, I understand." Marcus loves me and this is hard for him too.

"The thought of leaving you here is more painful than I would have imagined. You are my daughter. But this is your home, your family, where you remember happy times with your mother." He paused. "Riley and I stopped by the cemetery yesterday. I felt her presence." He sighed. "You do too, don't you?"

"Yes." Airy kisses on my cheek remind me of her love.

We sat in silence for a few minutes. Marcus took my hands.

"Annie, there are two reasons I must take Jeff with me." He looked away for a moment, then turned and smiled. "It's important that he knows I am his father; not some nice man who comes every once in a while, makes a fuss over him, then leaves. Our servicemen have to do that every day. Some will never come home to their children. For those who do return it will take time to close the gap. We don't know how long this war will last. I'm older and there could be no closing the gap for me and Jeff."

"Oh, Marcus." I never think about him being older, but I understood.

"The other reason is selfish. I can't face living without Jeff, my son. I want to come home to him every day. I want to hear his laughter, wipe away his tears. I want to watch him grow; hear him say, 'Daddy.'"

Though Aunt Evy and Uncle Riley asked me to consider staying, they didn't insist. If I stay, I will miss caring for my brother, seeing him grow and hearing him laugh. I want him to know I'm his sister.

What should I do, Mama?

August 18, 1943

After morning chores, Buddy and I took a picnic lunch to my favorite spot on the river that meanders through Uncle Riley's place. The shallow water ran noisily over the rocky bottom, splashing against the boulders lying on the edge. I always hear a melody made by the water playing with loose rocks.

The willow tree was green and full, completely still in the hot sun. Many times this summer Buddy and I sat here. He listened as I talked about Mama and cried. He held my hand, dried my tears. He let me rant and rave, never saying I had to be strong, brave, that time heals. I was tired of hearing those empty words.

"I'm really trying to get over it. To be the girl Mama wants me to be."

"You won't ever get over it, Annie," Buddy said. "We learn to get through it. A little bit one day, more the next day and less another." His daddy has been gone almost a year. I will remember those words.

I shared my dilemma over leaving Duddley.

"It isn't easy, Annie, but be sure you make the decision that's right for you. Think about your life."

I told him leaving Duddley felt as though I would be leaving Mama. I told him about the airy kisses. He lifted my chin so that I looked into his eyes.

"You know where your mama is? Right this minute?" He touched my cheek. "She's wherever you are. Those airy kisses? They'll follow you forever." He paused. "You know how my daddy lets me know he's around?" I shook my head. "I feel warmness on my right ear where he used to give me a playful pinch to say he loved me."

Buddy put his arm around my shoulders and we sat for some time before he spoke.

"Marcus is right about finishing at Norwynn. You're intelligent, and with a good education you'll be able to follow your dream." We didn't say anything for a while.

"I also want to stay here because it might be our last time together for a long time," I said. Maybe forever, I thought, since he planned to sign up for the navy when he graduated next spring.

"Annie, don't make your decision on our being together." He smiled. "If you stay here, it will be wonderful seeing you every day, but after that you'll be here without me." He didn't add, "Maybe forever."

On the way home, he apologized for "preaching" and said he would be with me, regardless of what I decided.

This evening before supper, Marcus and I took a walk around the dairy so we could talk without interruption. He waited for me to speak.

"I've made up my mind," I said, reaching for his hand. "I want to go back with you and Jeff. I want to finish at Norwynn."

Marcus squeezed my hand. "You have no idea how happy I am. It's not easy for you, and I will do everything possible to make your decision the right one."

Marcus suggested I talk with Uncle Riley and Aunt Evy after supper. They weren't surprised, nor did they let their disappointment overshadow their good wishes. They realize the advantage of my going to a better school. They're glad I'll be there for Marcus and Jeff.

When Buddy finished evening chores, he invited me to go out to the barn to see the new calf he'd pulled several days ago. She was healthy and feeding hungrily. Her mother looked pleased with herself.

"You really like this kind of work?" I asked.

"I sure do. Dr. Ford is very good about letting me do a lot of stuff, but he's always there in case I need help. I hope this war doesn't last too long, so I can go to school and be a real veterinarian."

We watched the animals, thinking our own thoughts, until Buddy took my arm and walked me to the back of the barn, where we couldn't be seen from the front stalls.

"Annie, I've wanted to tell you something." He cleared his throat. "I guess you know how I feel about you?" He swallowed hard. His face flushed.

My heart pounded and I could feel my face turning red. I waited.

"Annie, I love you. I always will." He spoke in a whisper, as if telling me a secret. He pulled my willing body slowly into his arms. My head rested on his chest and I heard his heart pounding.

"I love you, Buddy. I always will." My voice was sure. I brushed back the lock of hair that always slipped over his forehead.

We kissed, softly, uncertainly at first, then deliberately. When we parted, he held me in one arm while he reached into his shirt pocket, retrieving a blue velvet jeweler's box.

"To remind you who loves you," he said.

My hands shook as I opened the box and gasped at the gold heart-shaped locket. RA was inscribed with flourishes.

"It's beautiful, Buddy. I'll wear it forever." I gave him a quick kiss and hug. He took the locket and opened it. It held our faces clipped from recent snapshots. Before I could think of what to say, he closed the locket, placed the chain around my neck and fastened it. He kissed my neck where the chain closed.

Chapter 21

Journal, September 1943–November 1943

September 5, 1943

We've been back a little more than two weeks. It feels like home, but different without Mama, though in a way she's here. Marcus and I have talked about feeling her presence, her love for us. I've felt some airy kisses too. Marcus hasn't mentioned anything like that. I'm almost afraid to talk about the kisses for fear they will go away.

We flew back in the special airplane, stopping for several hours in Oak Ridge, Tennessee. Marcus had to see someone with whom he works. Most of the trip, Jeff either slept or cooed and laughed, but he was tired by the time we reached National Airport. Marcus says I'm good with Jeff.

Bertie had everything ready for our homecoming. June and Mary have settled into their schedules and it's working well. Marcus goes to work earlier and is home by five.

Ethel and Josh are busy moving into a house in Arlington. They were glad to leave apartment living even though it means longer commutes. They have a standing invitation for Sunday dinner with us, and Josh always checks to make sure Jeff is healthy and progressing on schedule.

Jeff is sitting up and seems to notice everything and everyone. I love hearing him laugh. It's more like a cackle. June and Mary make sure he's clean, fed and happy. He's probably spoiled, but we've decided he's thriving on it.

School starts day after tomorrow. I look forward to being an editor on *The Student Voice*. Ethel says it will make me look at writing in an entirely different way.

I miss you Mama.

September 12, 1943

Being a junior at Norwynn is different. The younger students are deferential and the teachers are more demanding. Seniors are friendlier and show some respect, especially if you work on *The Student Voice*. Rhoda Evans, the student editor, is different from what I expected. She's definite in her ideas, but asks for input and listens. I intend to learn and work as hard as I can.

It's good to be with Anita again. She caught me up on what I missed at Norwynn. The Spring Cotillion was a success. Her cousin couldn't take her because he's serious about a girl who didn't like the idea. He asked a friend, John Delaneo, to take Anita and they had a wonderful evening. They are just good friends, according to Anita. Maybe I'll tell her all about Buddy one of these days.

Marcus and I spend time together after we put Jeff to bed. This evening I told Marcus about my job on *The Student Voice* and he surprised me.

"Annie, have you thought of writing about you and your mama—your life together?"

I didn't answer right away. "Actually I wrote some before …"

"I'm glad to hear that because your stories will be a good way for Jeff to know about his mother when he's older. No one can tell the story except you."

The thought had crossed my mind, but I pushed it aside, thinking it would be too painful.

"I realize it will be difficult," Marcus said. "But if you go slowly and take a break when it hurts, I think you can do it. You're an insightful writer and your love for your mother will come through. I believe that."

September 19, 1943

I spend as much time with Jeff as possible. Today was sunny with a hint of fall, so I took him for a long walk in his stroller. I propped him up because he loves to look at everything. He's beginning to point and make comments in his own language. People we meet along the way love to see him smile and hear him laugh. That cackle gets them every time.

School is going well. I have six classes. Mrs. Lee teaches American history. Tiny and homely is the only way to describe her, but she's funny and loves to teach a subject she knows well. Miss Kahn teaches algebra and we learn or else. Miss Johnson has all the science classes, and this year I'm in her biology class. I will have her for chemistry next year. Mrs. Botts combines biography with literature. Mr. Sterns teaches creative writing for juniors and seniors as well as supervising *The Student Voice*. He's a bit dramatic for my taste, but I like the way he criticizes without making you feel like a dummy.

We're busy on the first issue of *The Student Voice* or *The Voice* as everyone is calling it. I will be the junior copy editor. A senior editor does the real editing. We edit every story that comes in and return it to the writer, whether or not it is published. Rhoda and Mr. Sterns decide what goes into *The Voice*.

We had a letter from Aunt Evy saying all is well. They miss us and we miss them, but we are all where we belong. I'm glad to see Marcus and Jeff every day and to be at Norwynn.

Buddy and I write several times a week and nearly always on the same day. I wonder if there is something to mental telepathy. He's working hard because he wants good grades when he applies for college, whenever that will be. He still plans to sign up for the navy when he graduates instead of waiting to be drafted. I keep hoping the war will be over by then, but it doesn't seem likely. Even though the tide has turned in our favor, the Japanese show no signs of surrendering. The Germans are fighting as hard as ever, refusing to surrender unconditionally. Marcus says we have the resources to win, but it will take time and many lives.

I haven't heard from Daddy since July. He was on a ship, staying busy. He frequently comments on how well the young crewmen handle their difficult and demanding jobs, how brave they are and how they look out for one another. He says they are mature beyond their years. He never complains or lets on how he feels, but I can tell he hurts when those young men hurt.

Daddy wrote me a letter after Mama died which I keep in my bedside table and read every night before I go to sleep. It seems like he's here, helping me get to sleep and wake up in the morning feeling at peace. What will I do if he doesn't come back?

September 26, 1943

I've given up piano lessons. I don't have time to practice. Marcus says I'm learning one of life's important lessons: making choices, not doing some things at all so that I can do other things well. I love the piano and learning to play has taught me more than music, but I will never be a concert pianist and teaching doesn't appeal to me. Writing is my passion and I hope to do it well enough that people will want to read what I've put to paper. A hard choice, but that's it.

This past week, *The Voice* received fifty-six submissions. Since this is my first time, the two senior editors gave me twelve stories and divided the remainder. They've been very good about answering my questions and making suggestions. Rhoda and Mr. Sterns choose no more than a dozen stories for each issue. Mr. Sterns sees this as a learning process, not a competition. I'm impressed with the writing, which is proof of Mr. Sterns' teaching ability.

Jeff had his six-month check-up this past week. Marcus took him to a pediatrician Josh recommended. A tooth is showing and the doctor gave Marcus information on how to deal with painful teething. I hope Jeff has an easy time. We had a good walk this afternoon. He fell asleep on the way home and didn't awaken when Marcus put him in his crib.

Buddy is planning to come for Thanksgiving. Marcus suggested he come at least a week before the holiday and stay for a week after.

This should make it easier for him to get tickets. I hope it works out. It seems like a year since I saw him.

October 3, 1943

After we finished editing the stories last Tuesday, Mr. Sterns and Rhoda selected ten for the fall issue. Mr. Sterns meets with the staff, reviewing each story submitted, pointing out why he made certain edits, where we had done well and where we needed to be more careful. I am learning to be a writer.

Ethel and Josh came for the afternoon. Ethel and I cooked a New England boiled dinner, the first time for either of us. It took most of the afternoon, but it was fun being in the kitchen. Josh, from Massachusetts, thoroughly enjoyed it. Marcus was polite, but I could tell it wasn't a favorite with him, so I guess we won't see it often.

I had a letter from Daddy last Friday. His ship was damaged in a battle, but they made it back to a safe port. He was treated for minor burns on his arms and hands in a hospital, but says he is fully recovered and waiting to be assigned to another ship. I try not to worry about him, but when I listen to the news or see pictures in newspapers and magazines, it scares me.

I think about Buddy going into the navy. Marcus is very understanding. We discuss the events we read about and follow the news on a wall map in his office. Though Marcus and I don't share prayers, I am comforted when we sit quietly, each with our own thoughts. I know Mama is there too.

Buddy will be here for Thanksgiving. I can't wait to see him. Marcus is going to ask if I can get time off while Buddy is here. We want him to see as many sights as possible. It'll be good because we haven't seen much of Washington's monuments and museums—too busy living. I hope we get to Mount Vernon.

I wish you were going to be here, Mama.

October 10, 1943

Jeff is doing well. Teething makes him cranky, but Bertie rubs his gums with a mixture the doctor gave Marcus. Rocking helps too.

Marcus works long hours and is called in on weekends. He looks so tired some days. I worry about him, but he is still his calm, caring self and I think work takes his mind off Mama. I've wondered how he bears losing two wives he loved so much.

Some days I miss Mama as though she left us yesterday. I know she's watching over me, but it's not the same as being able to touch her, talk to her. I try not to let Marcus see my sadness, but he guesses. When he works late, I keep his dinner warm and have dessert with him. He says he appreciates my company. If he's not too tired, we play scrabble or cribbage.

October 17, 1943

I am so tired. I hope I can remember everything I want to write. Marcus went out of town on a business trip for a week. Bertie stayed around the clock, and Ethel was on call. Marcus telephoned every evening.

Bertie and I noticed how Jeff looked for Marcus at the time his daddy ordinarily came home. Friday afternoon he was fussy and it took a while for him to go to sleep. He's teething, but his behavior was unusual. Marcus got home just as Jeff was waking up from his afternoon nap. Bertie said his eyes got big; he laughed his funny cackle and reached out his arms. When Marcus picked him up, he snuggled against his daddy's neck and hummed. He does that when you hold him tight. Sometimes it almost sounds like purring. Bertie said Marcus was laughing and crying at the same time.

Last week all of my classes had midterm exams. I think I did okay, but it was hard. *The Voice* came back from the printer and we distributed it on Thursday. Mr. Sterns recognized the staff at Friday's student body meeting. He complimented the authors, whose work was printed, encouraging everyone to submit material for the next issue. I have to admit I love seeing my name as staff, even if I am the lowest one on the totem pole.

Yesterday, Anita and her mother came by and picked me up to go shopping downtown. It was fun because they know where to shop and find nice things in spite of the shortages. I needed a new overcoat for the coming winter. When I tried on my old one, the sleeves were too short and it wasn't long enough. Bertie measured me and I've grown two inches since last winter. Now I'm Mama's height, five feet three. I wonder if I'll grow much more. Buddy's almost six feet tall so I can grow a few more inches, but I don't want to be as tall as my husband. There, I've written it—my husband. I hope he's thinking the same.

I wonder what you think, Mama.

October 24, 1943

Fall is here, more beautiful than last year. I can't get over the many colors. Pink and red are my favorites. The yellow and orange create striking contrasts. Frisky air makes me walk faster.

Miss Johnson planned a field trip for this coming Thursday. We're going to Rock Creek Park to observe the flora and fauna. We've studied the plants and animals common to this area. She says Rock Creek Park is a good place because so much of it is in its natural state. She's not making it easy. Not only do we have to identify what we see, we must fully describe it and note anything that seems unusual. She says we'll be surprised because Mother Nature loves variety.

Anita is having a Halloween party at her house on Saturday. I haven't been to a party since I moved here, so it should be fun. Besides her girlfriends, she invited her cousin and some of his friends who go to public school. Mrs. Mason called Marcus to tell him she and Anita's father would be at home directing traffic and they would like me to stay overnight. They will bring me home the next day on their way to church. I am looking forward to going, but I wish Buddy were here.

Aunt Evy's letter came yesterday. Uncle Riley is recovering from an encounter with his prize bull, Rodrigo. My uncle's back was turned and though he heard the charging animal, it wasn't soon enough to get out of the way. It happened in the far pasture, but he was able to climb into his truck and drive home. He has some cracked ribs and many bad bruises. Dr. Bailey was surprised he wasn't hurt worse, but it will take a while for his ribs to mend. Aunt

Evy says Ben is able to take over more of the heavy work—Buddy, Jimmy and Travis, are putting in more time too. Aunt Evy says Uncle Riley went down to the pasture a few days later and shot Rodrigo. My uncle said it wasn't the first time the bull tried to gore him, but it would be the last. Aunt Evy says they'll be having beef this winter, even though it may be a little tough. Uncle Riley was fond of that old bull.

October 30, 1943

Mama has been gone six months. It's hard to believe I can hurt so deeply without coming apart.

Jeff is seven months old today. I am always amazed at how happy he is most of the time. Those teeth are giving him some trouble, but he smiles and shows them off. It's as though he knows how cute he looks.

Anita's party was a success. There were eight boys and eight girls. Bertie helped me dress as a witch. She loaned me a big black hat and we dyed an old sheet black. A few tucks here and there and we had a witch's billowing gown. A broomstick and some black Dentyne gum on a front tooth made me look like the real thing.

We bobbed for apples, played pin the tail on the black cat and square danced. The Masons have a large house with a cellar underneath, which they finished off as a recreation room. There is a pool table on the far side and room for dancing. The Masons popped corn, served candied apples, pumpkin tarts and fruit punch.

I met John Delaneo, the boy who took Anita to the cotillion. He's very good looking and I can tell he likes her. Anita's cousin, Mike Mason, was very nice to me and I found him easy to talk with. He said he would like to take me to a movie, but I told him I'm not allowed to go on dates. He's seventeen, Buddy's age, and good-looking too, with red curly hair and blue eyes. He laughs a lot and likes to sing along with the music. I thought it strange that Mike would suggest a date since he'd told Anita he was serious about a girl.

I'm counting the days, nineteen, until Buddy is here. We've arranged Marcus' office so that Buddy can sleep on a rollaway bed.

This next week we'll be editing stories for *The Voice*. There were fifty submissions and this time I have fifteen to edit. I like editing and I know I'll write better for it, if I ever have the time. I'm learning how to phrase my critiques to encourage instead of discourage.

November 7, 1943

Jeff is becoming more active and tries to crawl when we put a quilt on the floor. He's jabbering more all the time. It's fascinating to watch a child grow. I'm glad Marcus decided not to leave him with Aunt Evy and Uncle Riley. He'd have been loved and cared for, but I don't think Marcus would be doing as well. His grief is unrelenting, but Jeff makes him laugh and forget the pain for a little while. Jeff affects me the same way.

Marcus and I plan to show Buddy as much of D.C. as possible. I hope the weather is good. We're going to take the train to Baltimore and then to the Naval Academy in Annapolis, since Buddy is going into the navy. Marcus thinks he can get Buddy an appointment to the Naval Academy, if he's interested. "I'm hoping your idea appeals to Buddy. If he got an appointment, it would keep him out of combat for another four years. Surely, this war will be over by then."

"You're protective and I don't blame you. This war is taking a terrible toll on our country. We're losing too many of our best and brightest. I'll do what I can."

My teachers have agreed to give me time off while Buddy is here. I will have assignments to complete and tests will be awaiting my return.

I received a letter from Daddy last week. He's working long hours and misses us. He tries to be cheerful, but there's an undertone saying he's tired and homesick like the young sailors he cares for.

November 14, 1943

Buddy leaves Houston tomorrow morning and will be here at six o'clock Thursday evening. Bertie, June and Mary tease me about my boyfriend. I don't try to explain how he is really the best friend I've ever had, and I've missed talking with him more than they would believe. I know our boy-girl relationship is stronger, but our friendship is what matters. Sometimes I try to imagine what our life together would be like. We haven't talked about managing two different careers. I don't know whether he has thought about it or not.

It's time to put Jeff to bed. If he's fussy, Marcus lets me rock him to sleep. Marcus is a loving father to both of us. He tries to make up for Mama not being here.

We miss you, Mama.

Chapter 22

Buddy

November 29, 1943

Our visit ended too soon. Marcus called a cab for Buddy this morning. He suggested I stay home from school. The last ten days were incredible and I need time to pull myself together. Perhaps recording Buddy's visit will help, though there's an ache around my heart and I miss him more than ever.

—

Buddy's train was late, which isn't unusual these days, and we didn't get home until after midnight. June stayed over to care for Jeff.

A crowded train didn't allow for much rest, so Buddy slept most of Friday. On Saturday, we drove to Mount Vernon. Though the air was crisp, sunshine ruled the day and we had a great time. I love the drive along the Potomac even with bare trees.

George Washington's home is beautiful and I wondered how he, a tall man, managed to sleep in that short bed. A guide explained not all the furniture was original, but of the period. The quietness and solemnity at the tomb gave me goose bumps. I will never forget the view from the front veranda to the Potomac. Buddy and I tried to imagine what it must have been like to live there all those years ago.

Ethel and Josh spent Sunday with us. Bertie insisted on cooking dinner. Afterward, Josh drove us to Rock Creek Park. Buddy enjoyed the zoo. Josh was interested in Buddy's plan to be a veterinarian, trying to persuade him to be a medical doctor.

"With people, you know where it hurts and how bad," he said.

"Yes, and you hear about it when you can't fix it," Buddy replied, grinning.

Marcus got tickets to Annapolis for Monday, returning on Wednesday. We stayed two nights in a hotel in downtown Baltimore, a bit expensive I thought, but Marcus said he was lucky to get it. We went to the Naval Academy on Tuesday. The campus is spectacular with old buildings, beautiful grounds and ships along the waterfront.

When Marcus first suggested that Buddy apply to the Naval Academy, he demurred, saying the war would be over before he graduated. Marcus pointed out that Buddy would get a first rate education, ensuring his acceptance to any veterinary school, and it was possible the war would go on for a long time because there were no signs of surrender in spite of the Allies' increasing successes.

Buddy agreed to talk with someone in the administration office. When they came out, Buddy had a bulging folder and Marcus looked pleased. I breathed a sigh of relief. Buddy said he didn't think he had much chance.

Ethel and Josh invited us for Thanksgiving at their new home. Buddy and I went over early so I could help Ethel with dinner. Josh took Buddy with him to the hospital where he checked on his patients. I think he was still trying to change Buddy's mind. They picked up Marcus and Jeff on the way back.

Jeff is almost eight months old and crawling everywhere. I was pleased to see Buddy get on the floor and play with him. Jeff knows a good thing when he sees it and had a wonderful time. When Jeff cackled, Buddy imitated him, making Jeff laugh more. When I started to give Jeff his bottle, Buddy asked to try. Jeff went to sleep in his arms and didn't awaken when Buddy put him down in the portable crib Ethel keeps for him.

Dinner was chicken instead of turkey, which is almost impossible to find. With our Southern touch, everything was perfect. I noticed that Ethel and Josh smiled at one another often, their hands briefly touching. I hope Buddy and I will be like that someday.

We spent Friday at Arlington cemetery. The Tomb of the Unknown Soldier is unique. The precision of the guards and their appearance reflect respect and honor for all those buried there. Two soldiers are always on duty. Walking through the cemetery, we heard the rifle fire and a mournful bugle playing taps. I wondered if the tribute honored a recent casualty, or someone who'd served and survived an earlier war. Nearby, the Lee Mansion is another beautiful house with an interesting history. I have a lot of reading to do.

The next Saturday, we visited the Lincoln Memorial, the Jefferson Memorial, the Washington Monument, and the National Museum of American History. We agreed that Buddy would have to come back so we can spend more time at the history museum.

We spent Sunday afternoon at The Smithsonian. Again, there was too much to see.

"I'll put this on my list for that return visit," Buddy said when we left after four hours.

"This is my second visit and I'll have to come back with you," I said. As we spoke, I wondered if we were fooling ourselves about there being another visit. If Buddy signed up for the navy after graduation, there might not be another visit. I didn't spoil our time by saying these things.

Monday we met Marcus at the Pentagon. What a marvel. It's the largest office building in the world and almost another city with shops and restaurants. Buses run all the time to let people off and pick them up at a terminal inside the building. We had lunch in a formal dining room reserved for field grade military officers and ranking government officials. Marcus had never mentioned his official status. I learned what the number of stars on a general officer's uniform meant.

Marcus was off for the afternoon and took us to the capitol. Congress was not in session, but it was impressive to visit the Senate and the House of Representatives. Beneath the rotunda, the area was filled with statues of presidents and famous statesmen. Buddy and I agreed his next visit should coincide with Congress in session.

That was the last of our sightseeing and we returned home for a quiet dinner. Buddy would leave the next day. Jeff was in good spirits and Buddy had a last romp with him. When it was bedtime,

Jeff clung to Buddy, as though he knew he would be leaving. Buddy gave him his bottle, rocked him and put him to bed.

Afterward, Marcus visited a bit and then excused himself, leaving Buddy and me alone. We put slow music on the record player and danced a while, not saying anything. After all the elation and laughter of the last days, I was at the other end of my emotions. Buddy didn't say anything, but he held me tight and rested his chin on my head. After a while, we sat together on the sofa, holding hands, still not able to talk. Finally, he began.

"Annie, you'll never know how much I've loved being with you. Getting on that train tomorrow will be the hardest thing I've ever done."

"Letting you go will be the hardest thing I've ever done." I swallowed hard, not wanting to spend our last evening in tears.

"I wish you could come to Duddley for Christmas." He looked at me and smiled.

"I wish so too, but Marcus isn't able to take time off and I can't travel alone."

"Will you be able to come for my graduation in May?"

"Ethel and I are talking about it. She wants to see her graduating students—you all were in her first high school class. She also wants to visit her cousins in Houston. Since she's in the army, she may be able to get us a roomette on the train."

"That would be great." Buddy grinned. "Have you thought about spending the summer until I sign up for the navy or go to Annapolis?"

"Yes, but I haven't mentioned it to Marcus. I don't think he'll mind, but we have to talk it over."

We sat for some moments until I broke the silence.

"Buddy, there's something I've wondered about." I paused.

"What's that?"

"When you become a veterinarian, where do you plan to work?"

"Well, I'm hoping it'll be Duddley, but that depends on Dr. Ford. Right now, he says he's glad he has me because his practice has grown and he can't find another vet to work with him because of the war. The only reason he's not in the service is that he has no sight in his left eye; a horse kicked him when he was a kid. By the time I get my degree, he may already have someone. In that case, I'll have to look around, but I'll stay as close to Duddley as I can."

"Why ever for?"

He looked at me for a moment, as if he hadn't heard right. He grinned and squeezed my hand.

"Because that's where you'll be."

I smiled. Buddy had no idea what my dreams and aspirations were. He knew I liked to write and always had my nose in a book, but I hadn't talked about my plans to be a writer.

"Buddy, I don't want to live in Duddley." I said.

He looked puzzled. "Why not, Annie? I thought you wanted to spend the rest of your life where you grew up, where you and your Mama lived. Not in that little house, but near your family."

"Doing what?"

"Being my wife for one thing," he paused with surprise on his face, but continued. "I want to spend my life with you. I want to come home to you every day." He paused for breath. "If not in Duddley, then anywhere you want to be is where I want to be. There are horses and cows everywhere." He leaned over and kissed me lightly. When he started to pull away, I held him closer, our lips together. I don't know how long we kissed, but my heart was pounding when we finally parted.

We sat there not saying anything until he spoke.

"I love you Annie. Will you marry me—someday?"

"Yes."

It took a while to get to sleep with everything that was running through my head.

Chapter 23

Journal, November 1943–December 1943

November 30, 1943

I was glad to get back to school today, where there wasn't time to think. I handed in my assignments and was relieved I'd missed only one math test. When asked about my visitor from Texas, I referred to Buddy as my friend. Everyone assumed it was a girl. Anita had some difficulty keeping a straight face.

Mama has been gone seven months and it hurts like always. I wonder what she would say about Buddy and me. Obviously, I wasn't thinking about her when I kissed Buddy long and hard. Even now, I'm glad I did and look forward to more. I've loved Buddy since the day he knocked Emile Corse down and bloodied his nose, grinning up at me, and telling me to run home.

I'm sure Mama would have something to say about me promising to marry Buddy someday. I'm almost sixteen with another year of high school and four of college. I know our love will last through whatever comes.

We didn't discuss careers that last evening. It didn't seem like the right time to tell him my plans in the middle of his proposal. At least I know he doesn't want to spend his life in Duddley just to join Dr. Ford's practice. We'll find a way.

December 5, 1943

Buddy called to say he arrived in Houston safe and sound. Uncle Riley met his train, and Aunt Evy had a wonderful dinner waiting for him. We had only three minutes, but it was good to hear his voice. I've written four letters already and I can't wait to hear from him.

Mike Mason called inviting me to a Christmas dance at his school. He apologized for not calling earlier, but said he knew I had out-of-town company. He explained that we'd double date with Anita and John. I thanked him for his invitation and said I'd have to talk with Marcus.

"That's great. I understand." He must have expected a refusal.

I talked with Anita who knew he was going to ask me.

"Mike's a good guy," she said. "I think you'll have fun."

"What about his girlfriend—the one who didn't want him taking you to the cotillion?"

"They broke up about a month ago, right after my Halloween party."

Later, I talked to Marcus.

"Do you miss going to school dances and movies with friends?"

"Sort of. But it's okay."

"What kind of young man is Mike?"

I said he was nice looking, easy to talk to and polite. I didn't mention my refusal when he'd asked me to go to the movies with him at Anita's Halloween party.

"Would you like to go?"

I didn't say anything for a moment. "I love to dance."

"You're concerned about Buddy?"

I nodded and related our conversation the night before Buddy returned to Duddley.

"I can understand your dilemma, but remember you and Buddy are young and have quite a few years before you can make a life together." I started to speak, but he put his finger to my lips and continued. "I'm not belittling your feelings for one another or your plans for your future. However, you and Buddy need to enjoy being young and that includes the social side of these teen years. I can't imagine Buddy not wanting you to go to a dance with your friends. He knows how much you like to dance." Marcus chuckled. "You two have been friends all these years. You trust one another. Do you know how wonderful that is?" I nodded. "Mike sounds like a good fellow and he is Anita's cousin, which counts for something. I can't tell you what to do, Annie. You think about it and do what your head, as well as your heart, tells you." He put his arms around me and kissed the top of my head.

When I called him, Mike thanked me over and over. I look forward to being with other kids, dancing and having fun. I wrote Buddy a letter.

Uncle Riley recovered from his encounter with Rodrigo. He went to an auction and bought a young bull he named Simon. Aunt Evy says he thought a less dramatic name might help.

December 12, 1943

Christmas is almost here and ordinarily I'd be making or buying presents. Marcus and I talked about it and decided we won't exchange gifts, but will donate to The American Red Cross. There will be toys under the tree for Jeff and money gifts for Bertie, June and Mary. Ethel and Josh said their gifts will go to the USO.

Christmas cards are difficult this year. Our family and friends know about Mama, but Marcus and I couldn't bear omitting her name. We decided to sign as "Marcus Claiborne and Family."

Ethel and I went to lunch at a place on Connecticut Avenue that she'd heard about. It was a treat since we haven't done it in a long time. Ethel is like my aunt since Mama's been gone. She's easy to talk to and always gives me her honest opinion. I told her that Buddy and I were getting serious.

"I'm not at all surprised," she said. "Your feelings for one another were obvious at Thanksgiving."

"Really?" I could feel my cheeks reddening.

"Even Josh noticed."

I decided to wait for another time to tell her about our promise, my concern about Buddy going into the navy. I don't know how to talk about it. I told her about my hesitation in going to the dance with Mike, but she assured me Buddy would not be hurt.

"You have an unusual relationship. A trust."

"That's what Marcus said."

"You were good friends throughout school. I remember when Mr. Longmire was accused of murdering Mrs. Hooper, and Buddy was staying out of sight with your uncle, you were his courier for assignments and books from the library. When we were in Duddley last May for your mother, Buddy was there for you. One thing: make sure Mike knows about Buddy."

"Oh, he does. I mentioned Buddy when I called to accept his invitation. When Mike asked if I liked to dance, I exaggerated a bit about how much Buddy and I danced in Duddley. I'm sure Mike got the message."

"That should take care of it," Ethel said.

I hope my letter won't make Buddy think I care less. I thought about calling, but decided that would make it seem more important than it is. Marcus agreed. I told Buddy he should always feel free to go out with his friends and not miss school events because of me. Every once in a while, I wish I hadn't accepted Mike's invitation.

I wish you were here, Mama.

December 20, 1943

I have mixed emotions about the dance. The music was great. Mike is a good dancer and he didn't mind my dancing with others, though he cut in quite a bit. We sat out some, but the din discouraged conversation. One boy, who asked me to dance several times, was very good at the jitterbug. I love it, but have to concentrate. Some girls from Norwynn were there. They seemed surprised to see Anita and me.

After the dance was over, Mike dropped Anita and John off first. On the way to my house, Mike talked about his plans to enlist in the marines when he graduates next May. I thought this was a good time to say my good friend, Buddy, planned to go into the navy. Mike didn't comment and soon we were at my house.

When the car stopped, I waited for Mike to get out and open my door. Instead, he turned and pulled me toward him. I didn't want to hurt his feelings, but I didn't want him to kiss me. I started talking.

"Thanks for a great evening. I really enjoyed myself." I tried to move out of his arms, but he was too strong.

"The evening isn't over until you thank me like you mean it." His lips brushed mine, as I turned my head. I was scared, but angry too.

"Mike Mason. Take your hands off of me." He held me tighter.

"Let go!" I pulled with all my strength.

He released me suddenly and I fell against the door.

"Okay, Miss Prim and Proper." He laughed softly and turned to get out. I was furious and ready to scream my head off if he touched me. He followed me to the door and waited as I inserted the key.

"I'm sorry, Roscoe Ann. I didn't mean to frighten you" He gave me a quick hug, walked to his car and waved as he got in.

Marcus said goodnight from his room and I was glad he didn't come out to talk.

The next day when Marcus asked about the party, I could truthfully say the party was great. I didn't want to tell him about Mike. I don't know whether I will mention it to Anita. Monday when I got home from school, Bertie was excited because someone had sent me a beautiful Christmas arrangement.

"That's going to look wonderful on your Christmas table," she said. Then she grinned. "Who's your admirer, Roscoe Ann?"

I read silently, "Sincerest good wishes for a Merry Christmas from someone who admires you and hopes you will give him another chance." No signature.

"Oh, it's that boy who took me to the party. He says Merry Christmas to all of us." I tucked the card inside my jacket pocket. I sent a brief thank you note.

December 23, 1943

Yesterday we heard from Daddy. We were worried because his last letter was dated October 1. He is in a hospital in San Diego, recovering from burns and a minor spinal injury. After his ship was torpedoed and sank, he hung on to floating debris more than twenty-four hours. He said his recovery is going well and he will be able to resume his duties, but not on a ship. Virginia wrote the letter, saying the boys are with her sister in San Antonio and doing well. Marcus was able to contact him and said he sounds like himself and he wants me to stop worrying. Marcus laughed. "He knows you well after such a short acquaintance."

I also had a letter from Buddy. He was glad I was going to the dance with friends. He assured me he hadn't missed anything he really wanted to go to. I feel better, but after Mike's pass, I don't know if I want to go out again.

Today Marcus took the afternoon off and we drove out to the Maryland countryside to look for a tree. We put it off as long as possible, but it was easier than I expected. We remembered how Mama always looked for the perfect tree, so we tried to find one we thought she'd like. Decorating was fun with Jeff cackling, babbling and trying to get into the middle of everything. June held him and let him pick the ornaments. We omitted lights because of the war. We bought evergreen garlands to drape over the doorways and the stairway railing. A wreath of greens, cones and holly went out on the front door. Bertie served spiced apple cider with sugar cookies. I played some carols and Jeff babbled along. It was different without Mama.

Mike called to wish me a merry Christmas. He asked about the family, and sent his greetings, just as though nothing had happened. I wanted to hang up but decided if he was going to act as though nothing special had occurred, so would I. He asked if we were having Christmas at home. His family was getting together at his grandparents who live in Fairfax. His negative comments about his cousins, and the number of people who would be there, made it sound like he was fishing for an invitation. I ignored his hints and said we were having a small family get-together since it was our first Christmas without Mama. He asked me to go ice skating the day after Christmas. I told him I didn't know how to ice skate and wasn't interested in learning. He paused, and then said, "I understand—maybe another time. Merry Christmas, Roscoe Ann." It was impossible to tell if he was angry, disappointed or didn't really care. He hung up before I could reply.

I told Marcus about it later and how Mike tried to kiss me. He said I'd done the right thing and not to let him get under my skin.

"You've behaved with good sense and dignity. You've also learned an important lesson about men." He patted me on the shoulder.

December 25, 1943

Christmas morning with Jeff was special. He didn't know which toy to play with. First, it was the jack-in-the box, then the wind-up car with a little man who popped up and down. The spinning top made him cackle happily. Aunt Evy and Uncle Riley sent him a cow that mooed when wound up. Bertie, Mary and June gave him a carousel that played a tune as it went around. He wanted to take the animals off. I gave him storybooks. After a while, he tired and was ready for a nap. He hugged the stuffed puppy Marcus gave him until he fell asleep.

I was surprised when Marcus gave me a small box, wrapped in silver paper with red ribbon.

"Marcus? We said no presents."

"It's from your mother and me."

My hands shook, but I managed to open it. A ring, the one Marcus gave Mama when they were engaged, nestled in the velvet. Mama's birthstone, a blue sapphire, was surrounded by small diamonds. The sapphire had been in Marcus' family and he added the diamonds for Mama.

"She would want you to have this now, to remind you how much she loves you. How much I love you." Tears glistened in his eyes. I put my arms around him and he bowed so I could kiss him on the cheek. I didn't cry, though my heart felt as though it would burst. Marcus slipped the ring on my right hand. It fit perfectly.

Ethel and Josh arrived shortly with David. Ethel called last evening to say Josh's nephew had come unannounced. They knew we wouldn't mind, but they wanted to let us know there would be another at the table.

Ethel brought a standing rib roast and we served it with mashed potatoes, carrots and peas, sliced cucumber and onion salad and my Parker House rolls. Ethel made her fruitcake back in October and I looked forward to it, but we decided to save the cake for later with eggnog. Jeff, whom we'd fed earlier, sat in his new high chair and chewed a small bone Ethel fixed for him. He used those new teeth as though he'd done it many times. He babbled and cackled throughout the conversation. Afterward I gave him a bottle and took him upstairs for his afternoon nap.

When Josh introduced him, I was sure David would rather have been somewhere else, but he smiled, didn't say two words during dinner. About Buddy's height, he's probably the handsomest boy I've ever seen. His black hair is crew cut and thick black lashes ring brown eyes. He has a strong nose and full lips that would be perfect except for a tightness that looks like he might be gritting his teeth. As the afternoon passed, it was hard to tell if he was bored or lost in thought. When Marcus or Josh spoke to him, it was "Yes sir, no sir," with very little conversation. I wondered if that was because he goes to a military academy.

While the adults talked, I sat on the window seat, watching small swirls of snow spin away and disappear. About six inches fell the night before, and though the sun was bright, there was no melting. David read the newspaper.

After a while, I became aware of someone sitting down on the seat beside me and was surprised to see David. He smiled and pointed outside.

"How about a walk? It's close in here," he whispered. "Fresh air will do us good."

My answer surprised me. "That sounds great. I'll get my coat and hat." I interrupted the adults and told them we were going for a walk.

"It's cold out there. Dress warm," Ethel said.

I put on another sweater, my heaviest coat, gloves and a woolen hat. My knee-high boots are fur lined and warm. David was dressed for the weather too. I wondered how he looked in his academy uniform.

He held my arm as we walked down the cleared sidewalk that still had icy spots. He began talking after we crossed the street and I forgot all about his looks.

"Thanks for getting me out of there. What a bunch of fuddy-duddies."

I didn't know what to say.

After we rounded the corner, he took out a silver cigarette case, snapped it open and offered it. "Would you like one?"

"No. I don't smoke." I couldn't keep the irritation out of my voice. Fuddy-duddies? Cigarettes?

He lit up with a matching silver lighter, exhaling a large puff. "How old are you?" he asked.

"I'll be sixteen in March." Idiot, I told myself. Are you trying to impress him?

"You look younger."

I looked up at him, trying to think of something to put him in his place. He was smirking. I decided, why bother.

When we came to a street that hadn't been cleared, he took my elbow and made sure I didn't lose my step in the slush. It was icy in spots. I moved away from him as soon as we reached the curb. We walked in silence.

"You don't have much to say, do you?" he chuckled softly.

"How old are you?" I snapped.

"I'll be eighteen on March 15."

I thought he was being smart and narrowed my eyes when I looked up at him.

"No, it's the truth. The Ides of March. My folks said they should have known then."

"Known what?" What was he getting at?

"It was a bad day for Caesar and for my parents. Except, I'm still here."

The pain in his voice was real and I dared not look at him. A few minutes later, he tapped my arm and I was dumbstruck when I saw the silver flask. He unscrewed the top and offered it to me, a question on his face. I shook my head and he muttered something I couldn't understand. Just as he raised the flask to his lips, a car approached—too close to the curb. I thought it was going to hit him. Without thinking, I pushed him away from the curb and the flask fell to the ground, its contents running out on the slush. David burst out with a string of swear words. I turned around, headed for home. He ran after me, grabbed my arm, stopping me in my tracks. I was scared and he must have seen it in my face.

"I'm sorry, Roscoe Ann." He let go of my arm. "I'm not going to hurt you." He sounded like he meant it. "Sorry about my language. It wasn't aimed at you."

"It's okay," I said. "Let's go home."

He bowed his head and took a deep breath. "What are you going to tell them?"

I didn't answer right away. "I'm not going to tell them anything—unless you keep acting like an idiot." I'd never been around anyone like David.

He exhaled in relief, and then spoke. "If I have to go back to that house and listen to more of that sh ... sorry. I'll go out of my head. Honest." He put the flask back in his pocket and looked at me with the saddest eyes I'd ever seen. "Why don't we go downtown? See a movie? Anything but sit in that house."

If we went downtown for a movie, it would be dark before we returned. I didn't want to do something that would worry Marcus.

"I understand, David, but we can't just go off like that. Marcus would worry. Ethel and Josh too." I don't know why, but I was beginning to feel sorry for him.

"We'll take a cab and call them from the theater."

"A cab? Downtown?" I couldn't imagine spending all that money to go somewhere that wasn't an emergency. He read my mind.

"Money's no problem. My folks have plenty and pay me to stay out of their hair."

I realized I was out of my league with David, but I was no longer afraid of him.

"Look, David, We haven't come far. Let's go back and call a cab from my house. It'll be better if we do it that way."

Without a word, he tucked my arm in his and we retraced our steps.

"Do I have to go in?" he asked as we neared the house.

"Don't you think it'll look strange if you don't?" I could see Marcus dragging him inside.

When we reached the house, David came in, but lingered near the front door.

"Sounds like a good idea," Marcus said. "Don't you think so?" He turned to Ethel and Josh, who nodded, but looked surprised and uncertain. "More fun than sitting around with a bunch of fuddy-duddies." Marcus pulled out his wallet. "I'll get the cab."

"That's okay, Mr. Claiborne," David said. "I can take care of things."

Marcus paused, looked at David, and grinned.

"Of course you can take care of things. You'll have to forgive an old fellow like me. Roscoe Ann's your date, but she's my daughter." Everyone laughed. Except me. Date? I didn't say a word, but it took all my self-control. Now I am wondering just how offhand Marcus' remarks were. Could it have been his way of saying he was concerned about his daughter and he wanted David to know it?

We had to wait for the cab, but David and I walked up and down the sidewalk, enjoying the sun.

"It's nice to be on a date," he said. "I broke up with a girl last summer. She didn't like my drinking either." He took my hand and held it as we walked. I decided this was the right time.

"I'm dating a boy in Texas."

"That doesn't sound very serious. You up here. Him there?"

I took the plunge and said, "We plan to marry someday."

"I don't see a ring, except the one on your right hand."

"He can't afford one yet. This was my mother's."

"Sounds like a new way to brush off a guy."

"I never thought of that, but it might be a good idea."

Thank goodness the taxi pulled up.

On the way downtown, David told me about the military academy he attends. He doesn't like it and wants to drop out and enlist, but his folks won't let him. He will go to college when he graduates. His dad's connections in Washington will keep him from being drafted. I let that go because obviously it wasn't David's idea. I talked about Duddley; to my surprise, he was especially interested in Uncle Riley's dairy.

The cab driver suggested we see "A Guy Named Joe." I love Van Johnson. For the record, David was a perfect gentleman.

It was dark and cold when we got home. We enjoyed a light supper and I was happy to see David contribute to the conversation. He'd never had fruitcake before and Ethel beamed when he asked for a second piece. They'd saved some eggnog, plain.

We were standing behind the adults as they were leaving. "Thank you Ann, I had a great time." David took my left hand, raised it as though to kiss it, but instead stared at my empty third finger, shook his head and whispered. "Who knows?" No one noticed. I didn't correct him when he called me Ann. I liked it.

December 30, 1943

My relationship with David has improved. He came over the next day and we went for a long walk. I asked him if he left his flask and cigarettes at home. He grimaced and nodded.

"I'm not against drinking," I said. "I drink wine at home on certain occasions. Last year I had my first spiked eggnog. Marcus says all God's gifts are meant to be enjoyed in moderation."

"That's reasonable whether there's a God or not."

I decided not to get sidetracked onto that subject.

"What concerns me is you carry it around with you. Why?" I asked

"I don't want to shock you, but I've been drinking since I was twelve."

"I don't want to shock you, but I think that's awful."

"I have it under control. You'd never have guessed if I hadn't offered you a drink, would you?"

"I don't look for things like that."

287

"Well, you don't have to worry about me. I can handle it."

"Maybe so, but please leave your flask and cigarettes at home when you visit."

He stopped, grinned and pulled out his empty pockets.

David's a reader and we like many of the same books. He wants to write for a newspaper or magazine someday. He plans to write a book. Says it's already coming together in his head.

"The trouble is, my dad wants me to go into his business. Money is the most important thing in his life. I'm an oddball because I don't want to be like him."

I told him his father would be very proud of him when he saw his son's name in magazines and newspapers. When David won the Pulitzer Prize for his first book, there would be money too. David smirked and I punched him on the shoulder. He picked up a handful of snow and lobbed it. I returned the favor and soon we were laughing and brushing snow off our clothes.

The next afternoon we played gin rummy with Ethel and Josh. When the telephone rang, Ethel answered, spoke a few words and called David.

"It's your mother."

He grimaced and moved unenthusiastically from the table. The telephone was in the hallway and he stood as far from the living room door as possible. We couldn't have listened if we'd wanted to.

Ethel served mugs of hot-spiced cider and holiday cookies. I've become a devotee of hot cider, something I never had in Duddley. Josh gathered the cards into a stack.

"I doubt that he'll be in the mood for games." He nodded toward the hallway.

"I thought they planned to be here the day after Christmas," Ethel said. I assumed she meant his parents. David never talked about them.

"They send their best wishes for the new year," David said as he entered the room. He was trying to control his anger. Ethel offered him a mug of cider, but he didn't see it. He turned back into the hall and before Josh could reach him, David slammed the front door. We heard him clatter down the front steps. I ran to the window and saw him running across the snow-covered lawn. He paused at the sidewalk, as though deciding which way to go.

When we talked about his drinking yesterday, he showed me a driver's license that had the wrong birth date. He'd paid someone to make it so he could buy drinks in a bar.

"Can't they see you're not twenty-one?" I was astounded.

"They don't take a good look. If you can pay, you can play." He smirked and I wanted to hit him.

After David stormed out of the apartment, Ethel and Josh went looking for him. I came home. I told Marcus about the incident, but not about Christmas day or the driver's license. I knew he would be disappointed in me and upset with Josh.

I'm trying to figure out why I feel the way I do about David. I haven't fallen for him, but I care what happens to him. I'm angry with his parents who don't seem to mind what he does or what becomes of him.

Mama, I wish you could tell me what to do. It's been eight months.

December 31, 1943

This has been quite a year. Marcus and I had dinner tonight; just the two of us, after Jeff was asleep. We talked about our joy in Jeff's arrival, our continuing sorrow at losing Mama.

"I'm so glad you decided to come live with Jeff and me," Marcus said.

"Yes, I am too. I miss Buddy, Aunt Evy and Uncle Riley, but this is where I belong. You and Jeff are my family."

Ethel called later, apologizing for David's behavior. I assured her it hadn't upset me, and I hoped David was all right.

"David has problems," she said, and told me what happened.

They were suspicious about David's drinking from the beginning, but hadn't been able to catch him. They didn't like it, but he had his parents' permission to smoke. Before they brought him to our house, Josh told David he'd better be on his best behavior or else. David swore he wouldn't get out of line. Josh mentioned his concerns to Marcus, but they decided to give him a chance. He seemed sincere, they knew I wouldn't put up with any shenanigans and would blow the whistle. Well, I didn't come through on that one.

Ethel said they found him in a tavern, lying on the floor, out cold. David came in drunk and the bartender spotted the phony card. When he refused to serve him, David became belligerent. Everyone in the tavern insisted he'd slipped and hit his head. He wasn't hurt bad, but Josh took him to the emergency room. After they tended his injury, Josh had him admitted to the unit for alcoholics and let him spend the night. Josh brought him home this evening. His parents are flying in tomorrow.

"Josh thinks David belongs in a treatment center for alcoholics. He told Josh he's been drinking since he was twelve. Can you imagine?" Ethel said.

"I'm glad his parents are coming," I said.

"David said to tell you he's sorry." She paused. "Josh wants to know if he drank when he was with you."

"No," I said, without adding it was because I'd accidentally knocked it out of his hand. "Please tell David I will remember our time together and to take care of himself."

"I'll tell him. That may help more than anything right now." She paused. "I'm sorry, but with all this, I have to cancel our plans for tomorrow. Thanks for understanding. I'll be in touch." We'd planned to have New Year's Day at their house.

I have a lot to think about. Mama?

Chapter 24

Journal, January 1944–February 1944

January 1, 1944

Marcus, Jeff and I spent New Year's Day like any other day. Ethel came over to visit. Josh and David had gone to pick up his parents at the airport. She gave me an envelope.

"From David," she said. I walked over to the window before opening it.

Dear Ann,

Can you ever forgive me? I can't forgive myself for being so insensitive and stupid. I hope I haven't spoiled your holiday. Please try to forgive me. The time I spent with you was very special and I won't ever forget. Thank you too, for not giving me away to Josh. That helps me want to straighten out. I promise I will try hard.

Sincerely, David.

Marcus gave me a questioning look.

"David's apologized for his behavior. He asks me to forgive him."

"I think he's truly sorry," Ethel said, "but Josh says he's been a problem to his parents since he could talk." She smiled. "Though I don't think talking is his problem."

I didn't say anything, but I think his parents are a problem as well. They don't spend time together or seem to be concerned about what he does. David doesn't respect them or care whether he sees them or not. I'm glad we're not that kind of family.

Buddy called and we had a brief visit. We're looking forward to his graduation. I didn't mention David.

January 3, 1944

Ethel came over for lunch yesterday. Josh was at the hospital. David and his parents were spending time together.

"I'm sorry our holiday turned out this way," she said. "I'm hoping David and his parents will begin to listen to one another." She shook her head. "There's a lot of work to be done."

"I hope so too." I paused. "David's intelligent. I know he could do better."

"You're right, and after last night I am more hopeful."

Ethel told me how his parents, Bill and Carol, announced they had come to straighten him out, "once and for all." While David and his parents talked in the living room, Ethel and Josh sat in the kitchen. It got louder and angrier. When David came out into the hall and grabbed his jacket, heading for the front door, Josh tried to stop him. David lost his balance and they fell to the floor. No one was hurt. Josh decided he and Ethel would join the conversation, and set some ground rules: no yelling, no leaving the room.

"They talked about everything that had ever been wrong between Bill and Josh, Bill and Carol, David and his parents, as well as the differences they'd had with the four grandparents. I know that family inside and out." She chuckled softly.

When Josh recommended putting David into treatment for alcoholism, Bill refused.

"He couldn't imagine a son of his being an alcoholic," Ethel said. "I think he was ashamed. He kept insisting, 'He's just a kid.' Carol was in tears. David clammed up. Then Josh dropped a bomb. 'I don't think David belongs in that military school.' The silence was deafening. 'Since you and Carol don't have the time to make a home for your son, I want David to come live with us.'"

"Did you know Josh was going to say that?" I asked.

"No, I was as surprised as everyone else, but I stood up to get their attention and said, 'Absolutely.' Carol sobbed louder. Bill was silent."

"What about David?"

"He looked like he'd been struck by lightning. Josh asked what he thought about it and he said he felt like a piece of damaged furniture being traded off. Josh said he was right to feel that way, but he was just the piece we needed to complete our new home."

"Amazing," I said. My amazement was mostly with Josh.

"David didn't say anything in front of his parents, but when they left the room he gave Josh a bear hug, thanked us and promised to do his best. He knows he needs help."

Ethel went on to say David realizes his parents love him in their way, but it doesn't include spending time with him and listening to him. Ethel and Josh gritted their teeth when Bill or Carol cut David off in mid-sentence to talk about something else. Every time David went out the door, Bill shoved money at him and made remarks about how much he cost.

"How long will they be here?"

"They leave day after tomorrow. Bill needs to get back to Florida for a government contract he's bidding on." Ethel shook her head. "To be honest, I'm looking forward to it."

"I bet David is too." I couldn't help it.

"I believe he has mixed feelings. Children love their parents in the worst of circumstances. David knows his folks want what they think is best for him. They have a difficult time communicating." She smiled at her understatement.

"What about school?"

"Josh is going to see if Mathew J. Carson will accept him. David's school record isn't good, but fortunately a couple of Josh's patients are on the board."

Mathew J. Carson is a prestigious boys' school in Arlington. I was surprised Josh would use his position like that, but it's the name of the game in Washington: politics, prestige and a good school for your child. I wonder if Marcus had to play to get me into Norwynn.

January 9, 1944

David seems to be settling in with Josh and Ethel. He called me after his parents left. He apologized again for his behavior. I said it was all in the past, and the future is what's important. I thanked him for his note. He's having some difficulty adjusting at school. Says it's not friendly. I told him to smile more. He has a wonderful smile. He didn't say anything about coming over which suits me fine. I don't want to get too chummy and have him get the idea I can forget Buddy.

We've begun editing for *The Voice*. I haven't written anything I think is worth submitting. There are some good writers at Norwynn. I need to work harder.

Buddy's studying diligently because he needs good grades when he applies for college. I was hoping he'd get an appointment to Annapolis, but Marcus says his papers didn't make the deadline. I'm hoping this war will be over before he graduates. Marcus says that won't happen even though the Allies are doing better on both fronts.

Some days Jeff seems to take a growth leap during the time I'm in school. He's crawling everywhere and pulling up on things. The cackle turns into crowing when he manages to stay upright for several minutes. I have an idea he will be walking soon because when he's standing, he waves one arm until I take it. When he let's go with the other hand, I take it as well and we walk until his chubby legs give out.

We miss you, Mama.

January 16, 1944

I was worried about Marcus. He worked long hours, leaving the house at five and coming home at five so he could spend time with Jeff and me. Sometimes they called him in on Saturday and Sunday. He looked tired most of the time. When he began to lose weight with none to spare, Josh insisted he come in for a physical.

There's nothing seriously wrong except he's working too hard. Josh prescribed that he cut back on his hours and eat regular nutritious meals three times a day. Otherwise, Josh threatened to go to the Pentagon and tell his agency they were killing him. I don't think he could get in, but it made Marcus listen. He isn't working twelve hours a day and weekends. Bertie is cooking up a storm. Ethel reminded him he needed to take care of himself for Jeff and me.

David calls about once a week. I've become his listening friend. He studies long hours trying to get off probation. His grades at the military school were not good. He sees a psychologist who works with teen alcoholics.

I've learned some disturbing things since moving to a big city. I know some of the boys in Duddley sneaked their daddies' beer or moonshine, but I never heard of alcoholism in kids. At Norwynn a couple of girls had to leave because they are going to have babies. Their boyfriends are away in the war. I heard Bertie and Mary talking about married women dating servicemen while their husbands are away. War wounds people, in uniform and out.

Anita asked me to spend a weekend at her house. I thought it sounded great until she mentioned inviting John and Mike over for dinner on Saturday evening. I asked why she wanted to invite them.

"My folks aren't happy about my going out on dates with John— even double dates. 'Things happen,' they say. This is the only way we can see one another."

"Why do you need me? Can't you invite just him to dinner?"

"They say it will look like John and I are going steady and have their blessing." She paused. "I know your heart belongs to Buddy and so does Mike."

"What else will we do besides have dinner?" I didn't want to be with Mike.

"My folks have agreed we can go downstairs and play games. We got Monopoly for Christmas. We can put on music and dance too. Knowing my mother, she'll find excuses to see if we're having fun." Anita made a face. That surprised me because I thought she and her mother were on good terms. I wonder if Mama and I would have come to this.

Mrs. Mason called Marcus and they will pick me up Friday. Marcus is invited to Sunday dinner and will bring me home. I still have some misgivings, but we'll see.

January 23, 1944

David called twice this last week. He's beginning to like school and is working hard to bring up his grades, as well as writing for the school newspaper. His English teacher is a poet who published a collection last year. David said he had to write a poem for a class assignment and the teacher liked it. He's decided to write more. I asked to see them.

David surprised me, saying he might want to be a doctor. Being around Josh and Ethel is affecting him sooner than I expected. His sessions with the psychologist must be helping. He doesn't sound like the same person.

Marcus is looking better. Bertie is a wonderful cook and we're all eating healthy. Bertie has become like a member of the family and I said as much to her the other day. She gave me a hug, and then held me away, laughing. "That would be nice, but you're the wrong color." We hugged again, laughing. I never knew colored people in Duddley the way I know Bertie, Mary and June. I thought it was the norm for Negroes to be poor and not too smart, but I'm learning the truth about that. I see Negroes working at the Pentagon and in stores. They dress well and drive nice cars. I never saw that in Duddley or Houston. I'm going to ask Marcus about this.

Jeff's jabber is turning into words. He calls Marcus "Da" and I'm "Wan." We think he's the smartest little boy there ever was. It makes me sad that he doesn't have a reason to say "Mama."

January 30, 1944

Friday after school, I went to Anita's. I loved sitting around their family table for dinner. Anita's two older sisters were there with their babies. Their husbands are away in the war as are her two older brothers. Her youngest brother is in junior high. There was conversation going in several directions and constant laughter. They made me feel at home. I remembered how much fun we had when everyone gathered at Grandma Dickey's.

On Saturday, Mrs. Mason took us downtown to shop. She always knows where the sales are. I was annoyed when Anita cut her mother off in mid-sentence several times, or turned up her nose when her mother suggested buying things that I thought looked nice. I wondered what had gotten into her. This different Anita puzzled me.

Even though I tried to persuade Anita to keep it a girl get-together, she invited John and Mike for Saturday dinner with games and dancing afterward. She also got the idea we should invite another friend, Nan. She insisted I call David. I hadn't told her about David's problems, just that he was going to live with Ethel and David until his parents resettled. I don't remember how that came about, but she pounced on it.

"He needs to get out and make friends," she said. "Nan's good company and doesn't have a boyfriend."

Mrs. Mason fixed hamburgers, French fries and apple pie. I wondered how she's managed to find so much Coca-Cola. She knows what boys like. Downstairs, David, Nan, Mike and I set out the Monopoly game, but Anita wanted to dance with John. Soon they had their arms wrapped about each other in the darkest corner of the room, hardly moving at all. We ignored them, but I was uncomfortable. Even Mike seemed ill at ease. David and Nan hit it off right away and didn't seem to notice. Anita heard her mother coming and reached over to turn on a lamp. They moved quickly to the table. It looked like they were joining in the game. That's how it went all evening and I couldn't wait until it was time for the guests to leave.

"Wasn't it a wonderful party?" Anita enthused, as we were getting ready for bed.

"Not particularly."

She stopped in mid-whirl, a surprised look on her face. "Did Mike get out of line? I warned him."

"Mike was a perfect gentleman, but it felt like we were there so you and John could neck."

"What did Mike say?" she snapped.

"I told you he was a gentleman, but he looked miserable and I think he was as glad as I when the party was over."

"Really, Roscoe Ann. You're a stick in the mud. Is that how you treat Buddy?" Her remarks stung.

We climbed into our beds without another word. The next day Marcus came for dinner and I got through it, but on the way home, he asked me what was wrong. I told him everything. A slight smile crossed his lips, but his voice was serious.

"I'm sorry you had to be part of that, but you were right to tell her how you felt. Anita's a good girl, but when love comes along it's hard to be a teen." That's all he said, but I heard the unspoken comment: I'm glad you and Buddy are different.

I thought about the evening in the barn and the last night of Buddy's Thanksgiving visit. Circumstances hadn't required deception. Maybe I wasn't so different.

I love you, Mama.

February 16, 1944

David called and asked me to go to a Valentine's Day party at his school. He asked for Mike's telephone number so he could invite him as my date. David wants to take Nan, but Josh and Ethel said that they'd give their permission only if it was a double date.

Mike has called a couple of times since Anita's party, but I haven't accepted any of his invitations. Now, I felt like I'm asking him on a date so we can chaperone David and Nan.

I talked to Marcus about it. He thought it was a good idea.

"You need to socialize with your friends," he said. "You'll make a good chaperone." He chuckled.

The party was fun with good music and good dancers. Mike was very polite and didn't say or do anything to aggravate me. He asked about Buddy and said to give him his good wishes when I wrote next. Why do I feel that he's insincere?

I've written to Buddy about my social life, but I haven't told him about Anita's behavior or Mike's good wishes. I don't know how to put that in a letter. I miss Buddy in so many ways, especially our conversations. He always helps me sort out things.

Sometimes I wonder if I should have stayed in Duddley, but when I watch Marcus with Jeff I know I belong with them. Watching Jeff grow and change is wonderful. He pulls up on everything he can reach. When he lets go to take a step, he lands hard on his bottom, but laughs and gets up to try again. He's working hard to talk. Marcus is now "Da Dee" and I'm "Wan Nee." When Marcus reads to him, he nestles against his daddy and seems to understand every word. When I read to him, he points to the pictures and I tell him the names of the animals and objects. He babbles something that sounds like he is trying to repeat what I say.

Marcus is following Josh's regimen as well as he can, but there are days when he's exhausted. I can't help but worry even though Marcus tells me, "You and Jeff are my anchor. When I come home, you bring me back to the real world and show me how good it is to be family."

The Voice will be out next week. I submitted an essay about the frustrations and limitations of being a woman in a man's world. It wasn't accepted. Mr. Sterns' comment was, "Your views are valid to some extent, but you may look at things differently when you are older and experienced." He commented favorably on my technical skills as a writer.

February 25, 1944

Norwynn had its quarterly training day for staff and faculty today. Ethel invited me to go to the Pentagon. She was on vacation, but something came up and she went in to take care of it.

She introduced me to the people she works with and I met the WAAC Director, Oveta Culp Hobby, a small woman who is very pretty and smiles a lot. We went to lunch with two of Ethel's friends. It was fascinating to hear them talk about their experiences. They, including Ethel, hope that one day women will be assigned to more of the jobs relegated only to men.

"Do you mean going into battle? Carrying a gun?" I asked.

They smiled and said that would be up to my generation.

After lunch, we went out to the courtyard, a contrast to the large, noisy building surrounding us. We sat on one of the benches and basked in the unusual sunshine. I asked Ethel what it was like to be in the army.

She said her job as an assistant to Director Hobby consisted of working on special projects. Depending on the issue, she accompanied Mrs. Hobby to meetings and sessions of Congress. "It sounds interesting and exciting," I said.

Ethel laughed. "It's both those things, and requires a sense of humor."

I asked if she thought I'd make a good auxiliary. Of course, she said, "Yes," but warned it wasn't easy. Women with a high school diploma went to basic training that was physically and mentally challenging. After that, depending on work experience, auxiliaries started at the bottom rank-wise and did what they were told.

"We all take orders, including Director Hobby, but it is a less stringent life if you become an officer."

"How do you do that?" I asked.

"Women with college degrees and work experience are being commissioned without going through basic training. They take an

Officers' Candidate Training course. They've also set up a training course for women in the ranks, who have skilled work experience, to attain a commission." She paused and looked at me. "Are you interested?"

"I might be. If the war is still on when I graduate next year, Buddy will probably be out on a ship somewhere. I can always go to college when the war is over."

"Talk to Marcus," she said. "I have some material you can read too."

I wish you were here, Mama.

Chapter 25

Journal, March 1944–May 1944

March 15, 1944

Ethel and I are planning our trip to Duddley. She was able to get a roomette all the way to Houston and back, which will make the trip easier. We will leave on May 13, a Saturday, arrive in Houston May 16. Graduation is May 20. Ethel will spend the rest of her time in Houston visiting relatives and friends. I will stay with Uncle Riley and Aunt Evy until I meet Ethel at the depot for our return trip on June 10. I wish I could stay longer, but Ethel has to get back and I can't travel alone. Buddy will sign up for the navy after he graduates, but they don't usually leave right away. I would like to stay until he goes, but there is no way.

Ethel, Josh and David were here for dinner last Sunday. David still has a problem listening to adult conversation. After dinner was over, I suggested he and I go for a walk. Jeff was down for his nap; otherwise, we'd have taken him in his stroller. He loves to be outdoors, pointing and gabbling.

We walked without talking for a bit. David's question surprised me.

"How serious are you and Buddy? I know it's none of my business, but Mike wanted me to ask you. I guess he wants to make you forget Buddy. He says he doesn't see how you can be serious about someone who's far away and will be even farther away once he goes into the navy."

"Mike is nice, but I don't think he knows much about friendship and trust."

David looked puzzled. "What do you mean?"

"Buddy and I have been friends since first grade when he beat up a boy who was going to hurt me. We've always said what was on our minds and never told another soul. If I had a problem, Buddy helped me think things through. Yes, it's harder now that we don't see one another every day, but at the same time our trust and friendship has grown stronger." I decided to trust David. "Buddy is the person with whom I want to spend the rest of my life."

David stopped walking, reached out to stop me. "I hope I find someone like you." He paused. "I'll tell Mike I asked you, but I don't think he'll understand your answer."

We walked a long way that afternoon, talking about everything. I have a new friend I can trust, though not in the same way as Buddy.

March 30, 1944

We observed Jeff's first birthday with a small cake and candle after dinner. Bertie, June and Mary celebrated with us, singing "Happy Birthday," and helping him blow out the candle. We had gifts for him and I think he enjoyed tearing off the wrappings as much as the contents. He took his first step alone today. Life will be different when he is walking.

Mama, your little boy lights up our lives.

April 2, 1944

Last evening Josh and Ethel came for dinner. David had dinner with Nan's family. After a while, I asked to be excused. I write Buddy almost every day and Daddy once a week. Soon I heard the phone ring and Marcus said it was for me. Mrs. Mason spoke.

"Is Anita with you?" Her usual calm voice shook. When I said, "No," she continued. "Roscoe Ann, she's gone and we don't know where." She began to sob. I was stunned.

"Mrs. Mason, I don't have any idea where she is. When did she leave?"

Anita's father took the phone and told me she had been in her room all afternoon, angry with him and her mother. When Mrs. Mason went to get her for dinner, she was gone. A note on her desk said she was with John and not to come looking for them. A call to John's parents revealed that he'd left his Saturday part-time job early, but hadn't come home. I motioned for Marcus. He talked with the Masons, telling them we'd let them know if Anita contacted me.

I didn't get much sleep that night. We called the next morning, but there was no answer.

After breakfast, Marcus and I drove over to the Masons. They were returning from Mass. There was no word from Anita. The Delaneos came while we were there. Mrs. Delaneo's eyes were red and puffy and her husband wore a deep frown.

"We think they may have gone to Maryland, planning to marry this coming week," Mr. Mason told us. "John just turned eighteen and they'll lie about Anita." We didn't stay long. Marcus says they knew something was going on, but didn't guess they would go this far.

No one at Norwynn said anything. No one questioned me about her absence. I learned later that the faculty knew.

April 9, 1944

Marcus and I went over to see the Masons yesterday afternoon. John and Anita came in while we were there. They were married. The Masons were so relieved they didn't chastise the couple, but Anita's mother couldn't stop crying. John's father wasn't so calm and promised his son a "good talking to." Marcus and I didn't linger.

Later Anita called to apologize to Marcus and me. From her tone of voice, I think her folks made her call. She hasn't said anything else and I think I've lost a good friend. She won't be allowed to return to Norwynn, which is a blow to her family. Miss Featherstone, the principal, says it is school policy and no exceptions have ever been made. John is leaving for the army in three weeks and Anita will live with her parents. Mr. Mason has been talking with Marcus, which is why I know as much as I do.

I didn't understand why John signed up for the army before his graduation that is just six weeks away. Marcus told me that John and Anita are expecting a baby and they decided if they were married, he would be able to support her by signing up. Marcus thinks they will still need help from their parents. A new private doesn't make much money. "They've chosen a hard row to hoe," he said.

John is taking his exams early and will receive a diploma before he leaves. I wonder if Anita would have been treated differently if she'd been in a public school. She has another year to graduation. I hope she'll find a way to finish and go on to college. She wanted to be a teacher.

I've written to Buddy and will be interested to see what he thinks.

April 15, 1944

I received a letter from Mike Mason. I can't decide whether to answer or not. I almost didn't ask Marcus to read it because he is so tired in the evening and he likes to be with Jeff. Sometimes we visit, but lately he's had work to do for the next day.

After dinner, he asked me if I was okay.

"Yes, I'm fine."

"You seem preoccupied. I hope you're not worrying about Anita."

"No. I don't see her since she's not in school. John's leaving next week and I haven't wanted to take any time away from their last days together." I paused. "But I do have something on my mind."

"Let's hear it."

I excused myself to go upstairs and returned with Mike's letter. When Marcus finished reading, he looked at me, smiling. "I didn't think he was capable of such eloquence." He handed me the letter.

"I hadn't thought of it like that," I said. "It's seems presumptuous. He knows Buddy and I have a special relationship. Why would I be interested in him? He's okay, but not special. He knows it too. I've made it plain. He asked David to ask me how serious Buddy and I are."

"Is that so? Sounds like he doesn't take no for an answer." Marcus chuckled.

"It isn't funny." I hadn't expected this reaction.

"No, it isn't. I'm just reminded of another young man some thirty plus years ago. He set eyes on this beautiful young woman who was engaged to the town's most eligible catch. Cupid's arrow hit the mark. This young man sent her flowers, composed poetry for her and took every opportunity to impress her."

"Was that you?"

"None other." He chuckled some more. "I was sure she was meant for me."

"What happened?"

"She wrote a short note asking me to leave her alone. Then she married the other guy and lived happily ever after."

"Oh, Marcus. I can't believe you'd do something like that."

"Love makes people do some mighty foolish things. Look at your friend Anita."

"Are you saying I should write Mike a short note and tell him to leave me alone?"

"What do you want to do?"

I said I'd think about it. I've written Mike a letter, not a short note. That's not my nature. I said I appreciate his high opinion of me, but it hasn't changed my deep and abiding feelings for Buddy. Nothing can change that. I wished him well and asked him not to contact me again. Please.

Mama, I miss you more every day.

April 23, 1944

The Voice, our last for the year, came out today. We did four issues this year and Mr. Sterns said it exceeded his expectations in every way. I learned about editing and look forward to next year.

I had a letter from Buddy commenting on Anita and John. He thinks they will have a difficult time but understands how they must feel. Says he thinks about how tough it will be for us when he's away in the navy. Education is important for both of us and we have to think about our future when the war is over. Our hopes and plans must wait. It won't be easy.

The war is being hard fought by both sides. There is heavy bombing over Europe. Russia liberated the Crimea. Our forces in the Pacific are fighting to regain islands from the Japanese who have also launched offensives in India against the British and in China. It is a world war. The Allies have made some headway, but it looks like it could go on for a long time. I will be so glad to see Buddy next month. I miss him terribly and try not to dwell on his being in danger soon.

Anita called. John left last week and she cries when she's not throwing up. Being pregnant is an unpleasant experience—her words. She says her mother has assured her it will stop after a while and then she can look forward to being a mother. I get the feeling she's not convinced. Anita asked about Norwynn. She misses her classes. I tried to be encouraging about going back after her baby is born. She says Norwynn is out. They don't enroll married women. John's parents are blaming Anita for the situation—her words again.

Marcus invited Ethel and Josh to spend April 30 with us. They continue to be our strength.

Mama will be in our hearts.

April 30, 1944

We had a wonderful day with Ethel and Josh. David decided to come too. It was a day like last year, sunny, warm and everything starting to bud and bloom. We decided to pack a picnic and go up to Great Falls, a park on the Virginia side of the river, north of McLean. There were a few people already there, but we found a table near the river where we could see the water tumbling over large rocks.

I can't explain what happened, but there was a feeling of peace and calm as we ate our lunch, talked about Mama, and our life without her. Marcus recalled his coming to Duddley and meeting Mama and me.

"She was lovely, unpretentious, and mother of a little girl just like her." He paused. "But she didn't think much of me the first time we met."

"I remember that," I said and we laughed.

"Your mother was a remarkable woman and no one was more surprised than I when she said she loved me." Marcus smiled.

David and I went out on the rocks to sit and watch the water. It was noisy and misty, so we didn't try to talk. I was surprised he had come along. Usually he spent most of his time with Nan. On our way back he spoke.

"Nan and I broke up."

"I'm sorry to hear that." I paused. "May I ask what happened?"

"I thought everything was going good. We had fun together and we talked about everything. Yesterday, when I called, her father answered. He told me Nan wasn't going out with me anymore and not to call again.

"Oh, David. What in the world?"

"I don't know. I was wondering if you can find out what I did."

"I think you'd know if you did something, but I'll call. I look on you as a big brother and am concerned for you."

He smiled. "You know what a jerk I am. Being with Nan has made me want to do better. I haven't had anything to drink since I started going out with her. I'm doing well in school too."

"I'll see what I can find out."

We stayed until the sun began to wane and a chilly breeze sprang up. On the way home, Ethel sang with Jeff who is learning more words and can almost carry a tune.

I know you were there, Mama. My cheeks told me.

May 7, 1944

I called Nan and she said John Delaneo's father told her dad that David was an alcoholic and had been thrown out of a military school. She started crying.

"I can't believe it's true, but Daddy won't listen. He's afraid we'll do what Anita and John did."

I called David and suggested he talk to Josh, who called Mr. Delaneo and Nan's dad. Josh made his case, because Nan and David are back together. Her dad apologized. David thanked me and I reminded him that Josh was the one who straightened it out. I hope he will realize how much Josh and Ethel care for him.

Ethel and I went shopping for our Texas trip to look special for Buddy's graduation. We had to remember how much warmer it will be. Shortages continue because of wartime, but I found a pale green eyelet pique dress with short sleeves and a straight skirt. The top has a sweetheart neckline that will show the locket Buddy gave me.

Epilogue

1952

Buddy graduated at the head of his class May 20, 1944. I listened with a lump in my throat, dabbing away tears, as he gave the valediction. He was six feet tall and good looking in a gentle, masculine way. Aunt Evy tailored one of his dad's suits so that it fit perfectly. He wore the blue and green, Duddley High colors, necktie I gave him. That wayward lock of hair broke from Aunt Evy's efforts and hung over his forehead.

His voice was rich and deep. He was friendly, sincere, and strong—like Marcus. I realized that the boy I'd loved all those years was a man who knew who he was and where he wanted to go—and he loved me.

The next three weeks went by faster than I'd expected. Buddy signed up for the navy but continued working with Uncle Riley because they were busier than ever. He trained Joe Timmons to take his place. Joe's father was a navy Seabee somewhere in the South Pacific.

Dr. Ford looked for someone to help with his practice. So far, the only one interested was Mary Pearson; pretty, tall for her age and the daughter of a farmer. Mary liked working with animals. Her daddy wanted her to quit school and work the farm with him and a brother. She told Buddy she was determined to stay in school, go to college and become a veterinarian. I asked Buddy what he thought.

"She's gone on calls with us a couple of times and helped pull two calves. Mary's strong and learns fast, but she's a girl and I think her dad's been talking to Dr. Ford."

"Being a girl shouldn't matter," I snapped. "Girls are nurses, and a few are doctors in D.C. Nurses are overseas in the war. I think her dad is being selfish."

"You're absolutely right." Buddy grinned. He took my hand and laced our fingers. We were at our favorite spot on the river. We reminisced and talked about things we hadn't written in our letters. He smiled when I told him about Mike Mason.

"I don't know why you're smiling." It aggravated me that he didn't seem to understand how it made me feel.

"I'm just admiring the way you took care of my competition. I can understand him wanting to beat my time, and I'm glad to know you're not looking around." He leaned over and kissed me. "I love you Annie. I always will."

We spent as much time together as possible. It was good seeing friends. We went to the movies and to the drugstore for sodas and ice cream. Most of the time, we walked down by the river or sat rocking on Uncle Riley's front porch. We held hands. I can still feel his touch.

Duddley was much the same in spite of a war that encompassed the globe. We were surprised and encouraged when 155,000 Allied troops landed on the beaches of Normandy in France on June 6, 1944. It was called D-Day. Our losses were heavy, but they broke through the German defenses and pushed inland. The newscasters called it the largest amphibious military operation in history and the beginning of a hard fight. The Germans showed no signs of surrendering even as the tide turned against them. On June 13, Germany launched a V-1 Flying Bomb attack on England. Hitler considered it revenge for the invasion. He thought Germany would win with this weapon.

The war in the Pacific intensified as U.S. forces retook islands the Japanese had captured early in the war. They established bases from which they bombed Japan. The war in China and Burma continued, though the Japanese finally left India.

One evening after we listened to the news, Buddy asked me to go for a walk. We headed to our place on the river. The day had been particularly hot and it was still warm, but a slight breeze picked up and lifted some coolness from the water. We sat for a while, no words. Thinking back, I wonder if silence was our unconscious way of stalling our goodbye.

"Annie, we have to talk about it."

"I know." My heart began to pound and I was afraid I was going to cry.

"I got my notice today. I'm to report to the Great Lakes Naval Station on July 15."

"They didn't waste any time." I didn't want to sound sarcastic, but I did.

"With increased operations by the Allies, there's a need for recruits."

"You mean with so many men being killed." How could I have said such a thing?

"That too. But I intend to come back."

I threw my arms around him; my face buried in his neck. I began to sob. He put his arms around me and held me tight. I don't know how long we sat wrapped in one another, but he waited for me to stop crying before he loosened his arms, tilted my face up to his and kissed me for a long time. The touch of his lips calmed me. I settled into his arms and returned his kiss. We parted for a moment then lay down on the grass side by side. We kissed again. Buddy and I were one. I never wanted to let go. Finally, Buddy took my arms from his neck and sat up.

"We'd better take a breath." His voice was hoarse. "I love you with all my heart, Annie. I don't want to ruin what we have."

I didn't know what to say. I loved him so much I never wanted to stop, but he was right. I sat up and wrenched myself from the lovely place he'd taken me.

Two days later Ethel and I were on the train for Washington D.C. She made sure I didn't let my thoughts get me down.

—

Looking back at that time in my life, I wonder how I got through it. Uncertainty came at me from every direction. I was worried about

Buddy, even though he was not yet in harm's way. My daddy had gone back to sea. Marcus worked long hours. My teachers at Norwynn piled on the homework, assuring us it was for our own good, meaning we would get into good colleges. Mr. Sterns wanted to put out five issues of *The Voice*.

Jeff was the only one who didn't worry me. He walked soon after his first birthday and was always in a hurry. June and Mary earned their salaries taking care of him. When I came home in the afternoon, I took him out, read to him, or played whatever he was in the mood for. He wanted to talk and learned new words every day. His cackle became a cheerful belly laugh. He made me happy, thankful.

Jeff was Daddy's boy and Marcus came home on time unless there was an emergency. Some days we spent the time together, but mostly I went to my room to do homework or write to Buddy.

I didn't let myself think about how it might have been if Mama were still there. The sharp pain was subsiding, but at times, it felt like the day I found her. Marcus once asked if I still felt the airy kisses.

"Yes," I said. "I don't know when to expect them, but they always make my heart beat a little faster. I expect to see her if I turn around. It comforts me to think she's looking out for me."

"I don't feel anything physical," Marcus said, "but I've begun to dream of her more often. I know she loves me and likes the way I'm caring for you and Jeff."

We hugged and went down for supper.

—

I was almost thirteen when the Japanese attacked Pearl Harbor. I knew people died and that our country was in danger. The next year we moved from quiet Duddley to the political center of our nation where I enrolled in a private girls' school and my life changed forever.

Marcus, Mama and I listened to the news and read the newspaper. We talked about what went on in the world, in our country and in our new surroundings.

After Mama was gone, Marcus and I followed the battles on a large wall map in his office. Marcus was especially good at explaining and answering my questions, but I must admit that at first the war was more a matter of shortages and inconveniences. I remember the aggravation of wearing panties that fastened at the waist with a small button. Elastic had gone to war, along with gasoline, car tires, meat, mustard and ketchup. I bought war stamps and saved tinfoil for the war effort.

After Daddy went to the Pacific, I took the war personally. I listened to the radio, waiting to hear news about the Pacific. Even so, it was impossible to know if he came under fire, because the censor would black out the name of his ship if he forgot and mentioned it.

It was during this time that I became closer to his family in San Antonio. Virginia and I corresponded, and though we were never able to get together during the war years, our hearts and minds blended into a loving relationship. These days, I visit them whenever possible, enjoying younger brothers, a caring stepmother and my daddy.

Uncle Riley was a member of the American Legion. When three men from Duddley were killed, he helped the families make arrangements for military ceremonies and get through the red tape that came with the sorrow. He drove families to visit loved ones recovering at Brooke Army Hospital in San Antonio.

One evening during my visit, I heard him talking to Aunt Evy. They were on the back porch, and true to my history, I couldn't help overhearing as I cleaned up the kitchen.

"You know, Evy, I always hoped we'd never have another war. The first one was terrible, more than you can imagine. 'The war to end all wars.' I can hardly bear to think what these boys are going through, nearly three years of hell. When will it end?"

That was the first and only time I heard my uncle talk about war. I began to understand why he was different from my other uncles who'd been too young to go to war, and then too old. He was always reserved, but sometimes I could tell he wasn't in the same place with the rest of us. I know now, that though he came home from the war unscathed physically, his memories haunted him.

—

Buddy reported to Farragut Naval Training Station at Lake Pend Oreille near Bayview, Idaho instead of the one in Michigan. His letters were irregular because of the rigorous schedule. We hoped he would get leave after basic training and come to D.C. Instead, he went to San Diego where he trained to be a radio operator. He enjoyed that and was able to write regularly. When I didn't hear from him for a month, I knew he had gone to sea.

I finally received a letter, and he was excited about being on a large ship doing what he'd been trained for. He was in a responsible position and worked long hours. Living conditions were crowded and noisy, but the food was good. His letters arrived in bunches like Daddy's.

Soon after Buddy reported for duty, Marcus brought a service flag with two blue stars for our front window. Seeing the flags made me sad.

"If you'd rather I didn't put it up, I'll understand." He smiled and took my hands. "I think of it as a way to honor Buddy and your daddy, to express pride and hope to those who see it. This war has taken a terrible toll on our country. Though the outcome looks hopeful, young people are still dying. Putting up two blue stars says we honor all our service men and women each day." He paused. "Think about it, Annie. I'll respect your feelings."

I went to my room, trying not to cry, but I did. I remember wondering how I could look at that flag every day without fearing the blue stars might become gold.

I had trouble getting to sleep, thinking about the little flag. I dreamed of walking down a street where all the houses had service flags. Some had blue stars, some gold. Some flags had more than one blue star, more than one gold star. Some had a blue and a gold star. A warm light and soft music surrounded me. I was at peace. I didn't tell Marcus about my dream, but I asked him to put the flag in our window. It turned out that whenever I came home and saw the flag, it reminded me they were safe.

—

Christmas in 1944 was sparser than ever before. If it hadn't been for Jeff, we'd probably have done without the tree and decorations. He seemed to understand that something special was happening. Teaching him to leave the ornaments alone was never ending. Christmas morning our little boy was overwhelmed for a moment when he saw the toys under the tree. We had looked high and low before finding three train cars that went around a small track. A teddy bear, almost as tall as Jeff, intimidated him at first. When I hugged the bear, he became curious and let me wrap the bear's arms around him. It wasn't love at first touch, but in a couple of days, Teddy went everywhere with Jeff.

We had dinner with Ethel and Josh. Jeff was thrilled to discover gifts to unwrap. We had a good Christmas, though I missed Mama as much as the year before. Being with Ethel and Josh made a difference. They'd become family.

Several days later we learned that David had been wounded. We talked with his parents in Florida. They were devastated, not knowing his condition. Marcus went to the Pentagon and learned that David was expected to live and would be evacuated to the United States. There were no dates or times, but we were relieved he was out of the conflict.

David's parents came, and we were all at Walter Reed Hospital when he arrived. In the battle for Bastogne, he lost his left leg below the knee and suffered serious damage to his torso, arms and head. David received the Silver Star for saving most of his platoon. Two years later he recovered sufficiently to leave the service. After he and Nan married, he enrolled in pre-med at Georgetown University in D.C. He's at Johns Hopkins now for his residency in orthopedics. Eventually, he and Josh will practice together. The last I heard, David was a teetotaler.

Jeff was two on March 30, 1945. We took him to the Museum of Natural History, the section with animals and fish. He couldn't see enough, fast enough. Marcus bought several books with pictures of what we'd seen. Looking at the pictures and insisting that one of us read the names to him was one of his favorite pastimes.

Jeff played with the train nearly every day. One evening Marcus came home with more cars and track. We put it in the living room, removing the coffee table. Marcus and Jeff spent many hours on the floor. Eventually, Marcus renovated the basement where they set up a long track. It's still a favorite pastime and they've begun constructing scenery and buildings along the track.

Jeff is a third grader now and more curious than ever. He looks like Marcus. He is quiet and thoughtful. His gentle smile reminds us Mama is part of him too.

—

The teachers at Norwynn made sure we'd graduate with a good education. Soon after the senior year started, we began looking at colleges and universities. We'd done some of this in our junior year, but now it was time to decide. The teaching staff mentored graduating students through the process of choosing a college or university, unless their family had ties to a particular institution that assured their acceptance.

Mr. Sterns was my advisor. He wasn't surprised when I told him I wanted to major in English with a minor in journalism.

"I can see you doing well as a teacher of English or a journalist," he said. "However, I believe your chances of advancing are better if you focus on English. To teach, you will also need education credits."

"I don't plan on being a teacher," I said. "Writing for a newspaper or a magazine is what I plan to do. I realize it's hard, but it's what I've always wanted."

"That's a difficult field for anyone, but more so for women," Mr. Sterns said. "Those who succeed, sacrifice much of their personal lives. You are a lady, Roscoe Ann. I don't see you putting aside your personal values to achieve in a field that is rampant with egoists, people who stop at nothing to achieve their ends. They will run over you unless you become one of them and learn to survive in a dog-eat-dog world."

I was astounded. Where had Mr. Sterns been before he came to Norwynn? Had he been run over? Had someone snatched away his dream? I knew he had a poor opinion of women who ventured into what was considered a man's world, but this was another dimension of his antipathy.

I was touched by the fact that Mr. Sterns seemed genuinely concerned about me. He went on to say he had always been impressed by my intelligence and writing. With my gifts, as he called them, he suggested I consider working toward becoming a university professor of English. He also mentioned government, particularly the State Department.

"He seems to have your welfare at heart," Marcus said. "Some of what he says about journalism is true of any field where women are in the minority. I don't know that being a college professor is any easier. Government work can be tedious and advancement isn't always guaranteed. I think you should work with Mr. Sterns, and look at as many career fields as possible that will allow you to write. Once you're in college, journalism classes will give you some idea of what working as a journalist will be like. You might want to apply for a spot on the school newspaper or the yearbook. The world is changing, Annie. I see women doing all kinds of work and they're doing it well. Many will return to their former lives after the war is over, but others will stay and compete. With your intelligence and common sense, I know you can do anything you want to."

Georgetown University was my choice because I could live at home. I majored in journalism with a minor in French.

—

My senior year at Norwynn was busy, but I managed to write Buddy nearly every day. Before I fell asleep at night, my thoughts were with him, though I never dreamed about us.

Fighting was deadly in the Pacific. It took many American lives to recapture the islands. The Japanese didn't surrender readily and most of them died fighting. We knew there was a build-up for a final invasion of Japan. After the war, we learned that everyone on the Japanese home islands, youngest to the oldest, was instructed and prepared to fight to the end.

At first when Buddy's letters came in bunches, I tried reading one each day, but it didn't work. I read all of them every day until the next ones came. Buddy and I played a game. We included a paragraph or so that pretended to be written after the war was over. He'd write about saving a calf and I'd tell him about an interview I'd done. We built a house. It was silly, but it kept our minds off our fears. I sent jokes and stories I hoped would make him laugh. We were more in love with every letter.

Working on *The Voice* took my mind somewhere else. I submitted two stories during my senior year. One was about Marcus uncovering the truth of Mrs. Hooper's murder. The other was about Mama and me before I started school. Mr. Sterns liked them and did no editing.

—

Anita had a little girl in December of 1944. She called and asked me to come over. We weren't close after she left Norwynn and it seemed strange to see her as a mother, but she was happy with a healthy baby. John was in England, safe from the raging battles. He'd been wounded earlier, but recovered and was assigned to a hospital as a medic. After the war, John went to the police academy and became an officer on the D.C. force. They have three children. We exchange Christmas cards.

Mike Mason, Anita's cousin, trained to be a pilot somewhere in Florida. He missed the war, but made the navy his career. I've wondered how his life turned out.

Recently I had a letter from Aunt Evy telling me about the Spencers. It seems Mr. Spencer, my first piano teacher, was called back to duty as a special agent, which explained the family's sudden departure. He worked with the French Resistance in France, was captured by the Germans and executed. Frankie joined the marines in 1944. He returned in 1946 and took vows as a Catholic seminarian.

—

On the second anniversary of Mama's death, April 30, 1945, Marcus, Jeff and I took a picnic lunch to Great Falls. Jeff was fascinated, watching the water rush over the large rocks. He didn't understand why he couldn't jump into the small pools along the bank that looked like a fun outdoor bath.

We had the place almost to ourselves. After lunch, we walked up the river a ways. Marcus carried Jeff because there were many rocky and uneven places. On the way home, we talked about Norwynn. I mentioned my work on *The Voice*.

"Have you thought anymore about writing stories for Jeff?" Marcus asked.

"As a matter of fact, I have. One will be in the last issue of *The Voice.*"

"That's wonderful. It will mean a great deal to him one day. You and your mother had a special relationship and you have a gift for making those memories come to life. I can't tell you how glad I am to know you've found time to do that."

—

The war continued with the Germans and Japanese losing ground, but showing no signs of surrendering. On April 12, 1945, President Roosevelt died suddenly at his retreat in Warm Springs, Georgia. He was the only president I'd known and it frightened me that this strong man, who always reassured us, was gone. Who would lead our country during this terrible time?

Marcus came home early that day and we sat at the kitchen table, drinking lemonade. He assured me that though we'd lost a great leader, it shouldn't make a difference in the war. Our Constitution provides for the vice-president to take over and it wasn't likely he would change major decisions already made. The military would continue to carry out plans to defeat the German and Japanese forces. I asked him about the new president, Harry Truman.

Marcus took a few moments before he answered. "Some people are concerned, but I think he's got both feet on the ground and is a lot smarter than he's given credit for. Vice-presidents have a problem demonstrating their abilities, especially in the shadow of a dynamic person like Mr. Roosevelt. Fortunately, with our form of government, it isn't just the President who makes decisions."

I thought about the Roosevelt family, remembering how we grieved for Mama. Besides his wife, there were five adult children, grandchildren and his little dog, Fala.

Less than a month later, the war was over in Europe, but the fighting continued in the Pacific and Far East. I was thankful the waiting was over for families whose loved ones would be coming home, but many of us continued to wait. I worried more than ever. Daddy sensed my fear and his letters were cheerful and encouraging. Buddy played down being in danger. I had no idea where they were. Each time I looked at the service flag hanging in the front window, I prayed for Buddy and Daddy. I didn't have the sure belief and deep faith of my daddy, but I believed in a higher power and gave thanks that the stars on our flag were still blue.

—

I suppose I will never know why, but the day after the first atomic bomb fell on Hiroshima, Marcus came home in the afternoon looking like he did the day we buried Mama. His face was gray, his shoulders stooped. He apologized, said he didn't want to be disturbed, and went up to his bedroom. Bertie and I were confused and worried, but we did as he asked. Mary took Jeff out when he awoke from his nap. At dinnertime, I went upstairs with a tray and knocked on Marcus' door. He opened it, looking exhausted. He took the tray and set it on the dresser.

"Come in, Annie." He hugged me for several minutes, saying, "I need some time. I'll be all right. Tell the others." He let go of me, and I looked into his eyes. I'd never seen such sadness. I reached for him and he kissed the top of my head. "I'll be all right."

The next day he was better, but after the second bomb was dropped, he never went to his office again. Marcus and Jeff continue to live in D.C.

—

The last three letters I received from Buddy arrived May 16, 1945. He hinted that the fighting was nearby, but said he was out of danger. We learned later that he was in the battle for Okinawa on a cruiser attacked by Japanese Kamikazes. The ship was destroyed. Many of the crew were rescued, but Buddy was listed as missing in action.

Marcus spent hours, but was unable to get any further information on Buddy. He tried to console me, saying it was possible Buddy was picked up, but there was a problem with the paperwork. Daddy wrote that often servicemen turned up safe and sound after being reported missing. Buddy is still missing.

I don't know how I got through my graduation from Norwynn, or four years at Georgetown, but I knew if I didn't, I would be admitting Buddy was gone forever. I didn't believe it. I'm convinced Buddy is waiting for me to find him.

—

After six months of intense job hunting, I almost gave up following my dream. Mr. Sterns was right. Women were not welcome in journalism. Even though my first name got their attention, "Ann" put them off and I received a boilerplate rejection. A few editors gave me interviews just to see if I was male or female.

Marcus rescued me. I lived in New York, but had my old room at his home in D.C., visiting him and Jeff as often as possible. I told him that I was seriously thinking of giving up on being a news writer.

"Use your initials. That might help with the people who shy away from female bylines. It sounds stronger."

When Marcus suggested I use my initials, I decided to use my legal name. R.A. McMillan finally got me in the door of an editor who hired me. His publisher, who never considered women for a writing position, didn't notice until several of my stories caught his eye. He shrugged and that was that.

Tomorrow I'm off to Okinawa as part of a team. Writers and photographers will gather information on Okinawa's recovery following the war. A special issue, commemorating the end of World War II in the Pacific, will come out in August.

We'll be in Okinawa three weeks to do the story. I will remain and find Buddy.